GUARDED
by death

H.L. SWAN

Hey, Dad!

The Angel of Death has been abroad throughout the land; you may almost hear the beating of his wings.

-    John Bright

Prologue

Pierce

The black of night surrounded me as I sat atop a towering mountain overlooking the dark waters off the coast of Brazil. A moment of quiet before the pull took over my body to collect.

I'm the shadow that lurks in the darkness, the damned. Doomed to walk eternity on earth, tucked away from humanity.

It had become routine, a reflex I had collected after I became the Angel of Death, the collector, the reaper... whatever you **want** to call it. A routine that took me mere moments, a year's worth of work in minutes. Some people would love the abilities that come along with this the strength, the speed, and most of all the wings.

I've always enjoyed nighttime the most, that's when I feel most human. Kneeling on these jagged rocks in the pitch black of night with the bright stars above. It makes everyone see things how I see them, in black and white.

The waves crashed violently against the jagged rocks below, but they couldn't muffle the blast from my tattered wings as they stretched on either side of me. I took off to do my duties and it was at that moment, on my last stop that I noticed something wasn't right.

I make myself invisible while I'm collecting, a body will be on the ground and I just fly over and bring their soul to the crossroads. I sensed a soul about to be collected in a bar, so I went in expecting it to be like any other night.

But fuck, was I wrong.

It was my last stop of the night, and I had plans to grab a drink once my work was completed. I walked into the crowded club; the strobe lights dancing with my eyes across the room as I searched for the soul.

And at that moment was when I saw color for the first time in centuries, that was when I saw *her*.

The light surrounding her was almost blinding in the dark, bustling room. She was dancing with her friend and who I'm guessing was her boyfriend. I immediately didn't trust him, the light surrounding him was dark and vile, nothing compared to the pure white surrounding the girl.

She adorned her small frame with a bright red dress. I didn't realize at the time what color it was since it

2

had been so long, but I will never forget that dress. I couldn't remove my eyes from her, I had to take in the beauty.

I snapped out of my trance, realizing this was the girl whose soul I was supposed to collect, but it couldn't be. It wasn't her time.

Something else was in the room, another force manifesting around us. The energy shifted in the space, no one noticed, of course, but it was thick throughout the air. I looked for the cause and that's when I lost sight of her. A strange feeling coursed through my veins, was it panic? Yes.

The realization hit me quickly, a demon is here, and it wants her. They go after pure souls and they can see her light. The boyfriend.

I was thankful and terrified when I felt the pull to her. He had her at the back of the building and was sucking her life away, I could feel it. The connection was intact, and I could feel her fear.

In a rage I stormed through and found them, he had her pinned to a wall. The situation confused me, because a moment ago the boyfriend was human, so how was he sucking the life from her?

When I pinned him against the back door, his obsidian eyes caused no argument to the truth. The boyfriend was in fact, a demon.

"You can't have her!" I snapped in an unfamiliar, primal voice. Confused by the mix of emotions I was feeling. His eyes panned to me, and the natural blue of his irises seeped back in.

I turned to the girl, thankful to see her okay.

Such light should never exist in my world, only eternal darkness.

If only I had left her alone... she wouldn't have gone through so much.

But I won't deny the truth, I'm a selfish bastard.

One

Birthday
Scarlett

T he whipping sound of my heavy
comforter flying off my body wakes me
from a deep sleep. With narrowed eyes I
look around my bedroom, it's too bright in here.

Colorful confetti floats around me, landing on top
of my plush white comforter. I can tell by the golden
anklet next to my face who is jumping on the bed, my
best friend Liv. "Get up! It's your birthday. Time to
celebrate!" she yells too loudly in the quiet room, but I
can't contain my smile.

I peek over to my nightstand and check the time.
"Who let you in at nine a.m.?" I sit up, stretching my arms
out wide.

Liv places her hand over her heart as if I've physically hurt her, which makes me laugh. "Your mom, she was happy to see me. Unlike you!" She pushes out her bottom lip, pouting.

"Just go back to sleep with me. Two more hours and I'll be happy to see you, I promise." I lay my head back down on the pillow, struggling to pull her down with me.

With a laugh, she peels herself from my grip. "Are you excited about tonight?" Of course, she's ignoring my offer for more sleep and jumping to our plans for later. "I can't wait to use these fake ID's! I think mine looks somewhat like me. Your new name is Katie." She slides the North Carolina ID into my hand with a huge grin on her face.

I groan. "Do we have to go? Can't we just go to the beach and then come home and binge watch horror movies? I'm sure my mom wouldn't be opposed to ordering pizza." I give her a hopeful look, but she isn't budging.

"You only turn eighteen once, Scar. You need to experience life more, do something reckless for once." She winks, and I know protesting further is a pointless endeavor.

I playfully roll my eyes at her. "I'm only eighteen. I can buy a lottery ticket if you want?" I snicker. "Going to a club and pretending to be of drinking age when I don't even like alcohol is your kind of fun, Liv."

Her response is a simple shrug of her shoulders.

I love Liv but we are polar opposites, yin and

6

yang.

Even so, I wouldn't change a thing about her. Except for maybe the fact that she is here, over-celebrating my birthday so bright and early. It could have something to do with my birthday falling on the first official day of summer break. Our last real summer break, to be exact. The first time being actual adults before we ship off to UNC. I snicker to myself.

"What's so funny?" She jumps up and frowns, planting her hands on her hips.

"Nothing at all. Thank you for the confetti, Liv. You're helping me clean it up later." I laugh at the sudden panic in her eyes.

Her hair blankets her face when she shakes her head. "Not a chance. Come downstairs. Your mom is making pancakes!" she squeals. I reach for her, but she bolts out of the room, making her way downstairs in a rushed sprint.

I hop out of bed and stumble to the bathroom. Not taking much time on my appearance since I know we're about to head to the beach. Any make up I put on would melt off and my hair will be a puffy mess if I don't throw it into a bun. After placing a white bikini under my oversized T-Shirt, I bounce down to the kitchen.

The sweet scent of blueberries and homemade pancake batter hits my nose, making my stomach growl. Mom is carefully ladling a thick mixture onto a hot griddle. When she sees me, her face instantly lights up.

"Happy Birthday Scarlett! Blueberry or just a regular pancake, sweetheart?" she asks, a wide grin taking over her face.

I rub my eyes, trying to hide from the morning light pouring into the kitchen. "Blueberry, for sure." I tell her. Shuffling towards the delicious smell, I sit down on the wooden bar stool at the island.

I give her my best sleepy grin, but the gesture does nothing to calm the guilt that's seeping into me. She is trustworthy so the fact that I know I'm about to lie about what we're doing tonight makes my stomach turn. That's going to be Liv's job.

I'm eighteen now, but I still know my mom wouldn't approve of me going to a club, and I live under her roof for a few more months.

Mom dances around the kitchen, an unfamiliar pep in her step that makes me tilt my head. "Feel any older? I can't believe my baby girl is all grown up now." Her tone is laced with sadness, so I give her a bright smile.

I shrug, wondering if I do feel more mature. "I guess? I just feel tired." I glare over at Liv's smiling face, suddenly wishing I was a morning person so I could be bright-eyed like her so early in the morning.

Mom wipes her floured hands on her apron. "So, what do you want for your birthday?" She asks. I look down at the damaged phone in my hands, wincing at the large crack down the center.

I wiggle it in the air. "Maybe a new screen?" I ask.

"You and phones." She laughs but I feel guilty. I hate making my mom pay for things like this, once I get my check from Pop's she won't have to help me so much.

I know she doesn't mind, and Dad left a huge insurance policy behind which helps us tremendously, but still. If I would have been more careful and not dropped it when that guy ran into me on the street, this wouldn't even be a conversation and I could be asking for a new radio in my car.

She pulls a neatly wrapped rectangular box out of a nearby drawer. "What is this?" I ask, reaching my hands out. She nods for me to open it and I pull apart the pink bow on top that's been done perfectly, my mom is a stickler for wrapping gifts with finesse.

"I figured you were going to ask for a new screen, but I decided to just get you a newer phone!" she beams. I run around and wrap her in a tight hug. "Careful or you're going to get flour all over you!" she laughs in my hair.

"Thank you, Mom, really I love it!" I sit back down in my seat, admiring the shiny new iPhone.

She looks between me and Liv. "So, what are you ladies doing today?" she asks. I quickly glare over at Liv for moral support... okay maybe not for moral support, more for her ability to lie.

"Probably go to the beach and do a little shopping at the boardwalk!" Liv says excitedly. This is true, the daytime plans aren't a lie, but I still feel bad for lying at all.

Mom nods her head, taking a sip of juice. "What about tonight? Coming back here for a movie marathon?" She knows me so well.

I grin nervously, about to blow our cover. "Umm,

9

we're actually staying at my place." Liv sounds hopeful. My mother's face doesn't show that same emotion.

She pours a tall glass of orange juice and slides it across the table to me. I take a long sip; thankful I haven't brushed my teeth yet.

I nearly crack under her watchful gaze. She tilts her head, trying to read us. I know what she's thinking, our house is Liv's home away from home. We rarely ever stay at Liv's house; her parents aren't really involved in her life. They go on extended vacations and leave her behind. This week is no exception, but we aren't going to talk about that.

Liv leans back in her chair, not a single shred of worry lining her face "My parents are going to cook and we're just going to have a chill night," Liv realizes her mistake when my mom's face lights up.

"Should I come? I can bring a dish." She asks.

"Eh, thanks Ms. Wells but-" Liv stumbles.

"Hey, don't you have that date tonight? Brock or...?" I finally interrupt. I'm confident now, although I can't remember the name of the guy my mom's been dating for a few weeks.

"Brian." She corrects with a warm smile. "Honey, I can cancel if you want." She takes a bite of her pancake.

I shake my head. "No Mom enjoy your date! Besides, it's only Thursday. We can always have a family dinner this weekend." As the words come out, my mother's wrongful trust in me makes her perk right up.

She nods, dusting out her apron. "Okay then, that should be fun girls. I hope you have a great time!"

"Just make sure you tell me everything about your date tomorrow." I wink, and it makes her blush.

Changing the subject, Mom focuses her attention on Liv. "Don't forget to take your medicine, sweetheart." She reminds her.

"Got it, thanks!" Liv replies as she pulls a bottle of iron pills from her bag. Downing a couple with a glass of juice. She constantly forgets to take them and one time she zoned out, causing my mom to call her parents. So now Liv's mom – Becca - asked us to always remind her.

A small puff of black smoke rises in the air. "What's that smell?" Liv wrinkles her nose. Mom darts for the stove cursing under her breath as the burnt scent seeps through the kitchen. We can't help but laugh as she tosses the smoking pancake in the trash.

After breakfast, I brush my teeth and grab my overnight and beach bag before heading out the door.

We slide into my Altima, cranking the radio to full blast. Enjoying the perfect summer breeze that's flowing through the open windows. Summer is perfect here, warm weather and clear skies. Not to mention the short drive down to the beach. The perks of growing up on the coast in North Carolina. We pull into the parking lot and, luckily, we find a spot. The beach is crowded today, like usual.

I fluff a blanket onto the warm sand and place my favorite book next to me. Seeing the familiar, happy faces of our classmates enjoying their newfound freedom is a great feeling. Music is playing and the waves are rolling in. As I rub suntan oil onto my skin, one of my longest friends -Zack- walks over to us. He's a good guy, and I've always liked him as a friend. Although, I think he wants more than that.

"Hey Liv, Hey Scarlett," Zack says my full name of course, and he flashes a flirty smile.

"Hey, Zack!" Liv and I say in unison.

He shakes the blond hair from his face. "Do you two want to go down to the drive-in tonight? They're playing Jaws for summer break; Max is coming too." He sits next to me on the blanket.

I go to speak, but Liv beats me to it. "Thanks, but we're going out tonight, girl's night for Scar's birthday!" she sings, pointing in my direction.

He rubs a large hand over his face. "Happy Birthday Scarlett! I meant to text you this morning. I like you being an older woman." He laughs, slinging his arm around me.

"Haha, Zack." I playfully punch him in the stomach.

After catching up for a moment he stands up. "Well, you two have fun tonight. I'll see you later." He waves bye and turns to walk off. Before he gets too far, his eyes pan back to me. His smile is charming as he runs a hand through his salt drenched hair, "I know you're busy tonight but maybe on Saturday, we could do something? I'm having a thing at my place for all of us graduates since my parents will be in the city for the weekend," he suggests.

"I'm working at Pop's until 7 tomorrow, come by! I'll let you know about the party then." I say happily, I always have a good time with him.

I lay down on the blanket as Zack finally joins his friends. It doesn't get passed me when he sneaks glances my way every once in a while.

"I don't know why you don't just give that poor boy a chance," Liv says, gesturing her pink nails towards Zack.

I can't help but laugh. "You know how I am with him; I wouldn't want to jeopardize our friendship. We've been friends since we were seven, why don't you date him?" I ask quizzically.

"Because he doesn't look at me like that." Her eyes trail from mine to where Zack is standing. I look over at him, taking in his longing expression as he quickly darts his eyes back to the friends in front of him.

I let out a dramatic sigh and roll over to grab my book. I read for what feels like hours while I enjoy the warm sun tanning my back. My stomach growls, and I look over at Liv who is staring in Zack's direction, completely lost in a daze.

From my peripheral vision I note a dark figure staring in my direction. An unusual sting of fear washes over me as my eyes pan to the tall silhouette, who seems to vanish into the breeze.

Too much sun and not enough food, I tell myself. I'm paranoid for no reason. No one is watching you Scar, chill. "Hey, do you want to go to your house? I'm starving," I beg Liv with a playful pout.

"Yes! Let me go wash off this oil in the ocean, wanna come wi-" Before she can finish her sentence, I'm darting to beat her there. The water is cool against my hot skin as I throw myself into the ocean. Liv is yelling 'cheater' behind me as she runs into the waves. We splash each other for a while, laughing and enjoying the lazy summer day before we head to her house to hang out until it's time to get ready to go.

My fingers are crossed that tonight goes well.

Two

Thirsty Thursday

The early part of the night was spent in a cloud of hairspray and perfume as we tried on dresses and skirts. Liv ended up in a black mini dress with matte black stilettos, ankle breaker heels on.

I, without having any say, wore a tight red dress, as short as Liv's. I opted for wedges, though. Liv knew I would be stumbling all night in stilettos, so she didn't complain.

The warm summer breeze flows through the car as we drive to the city. The further we go the darker the roads get; the GPS is taking us to an unfamiliar spot.

"What happened to the big club downtown?" I

look over at Liv in a confused state.

She bats her lashes innocently. "Well, I heard they make sure to check ID's there ever since some kid got so drunk, he threw up on a cop, and I didn't want to risk them getting cut up, so The Luxe it is." She shrugs.

Great, now I'm hoping the fakes won't get past the bouncers and we'll have to go home. I'm not opposed to fun, but all this makes me a little nervous.

And while I'm scared of the unknown, I can admit I am a little excited about my first trip to a nightclub. Although, now I know we're going to a place that doesn't check ID's so my nerves work back up and my excitement dwindles. If they don't care enough to check, how good could this bar be?

My idea of a good night is the opposite of Liv's, she loves dancing and bouncing to the rhythm of the music. I, on the other hand, don't dance. Music, I do love. I'll take a good concert over a club any day. I guess that's why I am so nervous about tonight, it's out of my comfort zone.

That can be a good thing though, right? I try to remind myself that this won't be the end of the world.

We park a block away from the club and trot over to the old brick building with neon beer signs plastered across the front. I shouldn't be surprised when the muscled bouncers let us in, without checking anything.

Walking into the dimly lit club I become acutely aware of the eyes that are focused on my best friend. She's a beauty no doubt, with her long blonde locks cascading down her back and legs that make her taller than half the guys here.

A striking contrast to my petite height and frame. Most of the guys here probably couldn't see me through the crowd, and for that I am thankful. I'm in no mood for flirty conversations tonight. A fun girls night is all I want. Hopefully, Liv and her charm are off for the night.

The music is lively, inviting me to tap my feet. I'm hoping I can get over my shyness to enjoy the night. I see Liv over by the bar dangling her parents debit card between her manicured fingers. A mischievous grin adorns her face when I walk closer. "Mai Tai or Pina Colada?" She asks.

"Liv, you know I don't drink; besides I'm driving." I remind her with a bashful smile. She then points up to the 'Thirsty Thursday' sign and winks.

She dances with her shoulders. "I just want you to loosen up a bit, schools over and we're going to college in a few months! It's your birthday, it's time to celebrate. Plus, one drink won't hurt after we've been here for hours. I'll even order some wings!" she grins, knowing my weakness is food.

I feel a small tap on my shoulder. "Hello, ladies." A semi-deep voice says from behind me. Turning around I note two guys standing in front of us.

"Hi," Liv says with a striking smile as she eyes the blonde one. "I'm Liv, and this is Scar."

She's such a flirt. I smile at the boys. The other one, with cropped brown hair and bright blue eyes, reaches his hand out to me.

"I'm Logan and this is Carter, nice to meet y'all."

He says with a bit of a southern drawl. Good looking, too. He's wearing a nice button-up and has dark jeans on. I shake his hand.

The blonde one, Carter, says, "Did I hear the word birthday a minute ago?"

They look between us until I raise my hand bashfully. "How old?" Carter asks.

"Eig... Twenty-One." I shout the second part a little louder than necessary. Liv quickly glances at me and starts snickering.

"Let me get you, two ladies, a drink," Logan offers.

I shake my head, sending them a smile. "I'm okay, thank you though." I reply.

"I'll have a Pina Colada!" Liv charms with a sweet grin.

"Coke?" Logan offers and I nod in relief.

At least they aren't badgering me to have a drink like Liv. I get why she wants me to loosen up, but she just doesn't get my method of relaxing.

I watch with amusement as Logan tries to juggle four drinks in his hands, pushing his way through the crowd surrounding the bar. He hands me my drink and I thank him. Quickly, I gulp down half of my coke. Extremely thankful for the sugar-induced pick me up.

My mind is starting to ease as the conversation begins to flow. I find out Logan is a senior at UNC, and he tells me all about the campus. I am much more comfortable now. They both seem polite and nice, so when they ask if we want to dance, I surprisingly really want to.

Liv grabs my hand as we scramble to the middle of the dance floor. Bass rumbles the floors and the music courses through me, giving me chills.

The guys sway with us to the exciting rhythm of the tunes. The lights around the dance floor are brilliant, dancing to the beat of the music.

After about a half-hour the whirling movements get to me. "I feel a bit dizzy," I mutter quietly. Liv doesn't hear me, but Logan does, thankfully.

"Do you wanna go outside for some fresh air?" he offers, and I quickly oblige. He grabs my hand and escorts me through the massive crowd. My body feels heavy as we make our way through the swarm of people.

Logan holds my arm and leads us through the thrumming crowd, I can barely make out where the front door is. The blips of strobe lights do nothing for me to see what direction we're going.

I become uncomfortable when my gaze peels from my unsteady feet to the dark hallway we're heading towards.

"Hey, Logan, why don't we go out the front?" I ask, feeling like the room is spinning a bit. The loud music stomps through my body like a stampede of horses, I wait for his reply, but he doesn't give one.

After gently pulling from his grip doesn't work, I attempt to yank myself away. He turns around, making me gasp as I take in his face. I barely recognize the boy I was dancing with two minutes ago. He looks... terrifying.

His innocent blue eyes are now a deep ominous

black, even the whites of them are covered in complete darkness. He looks like something from a horror movie. I flinch from his grasp, but he holds tighter, still pulling us towards the back door.

I frantically search my surroundings for an escape, darting my gaze around the narrow hallway. The further we descend into the darkness, the more I deflate. We make a slight turn, and the bright lights from the crowded dancefloor seep deep into the hallway. Morphing into an ominous beeping of faded light that cast terrifying shadows against Logan's sharp features.

I pull away again, but the gesture doesn't faze Logan who seems to keep an iron like hold onto my wrist. Panic courses through me at the realization of how strong he is. I scream with all my might, which angers him even more.

Logan's striking black eyes hold my gaze as he pins me against a cold, paint-chipped wall. As if he's sucking away all of my energy with his eyes, I begin to feel weak.

Using my wedges as a weapon, I kick him in the shin. To my dismay, it doesn't affect him in the slightest. He is a force that cannot be stopped, and I feel like I'm going to pass out.

Three

Where are my keys?

A sinister smile stretches across Logan's pale face as his large hand wraps around my throat lifting me, my feet dangling off the ground. I instinctively bring both my hands to his and begin to try and pry his fingers off of me.

My eyes flutter and begin to roll into the back of my head the longer I'm dangling in his grip. In a swift motion, I collapse to the ground choking for air. A violent gasp escapes my lips, followed by harsh coughs from the pressure being lifted from my neck.

I feel a primal urge to stop holding my throat, and to run. It's like it's being screamed to me. I look up, my brain focusing on the distant voice. That's when I see Logan flying across the hallway, slamming into the wall across from me.

My tired eyes travel upward, settling on a massive frame standing in front of me. He has to be well over six-foot-tall, black hair, and broad shoulders. A shiver rakes through my body, his presence... it's so... familiar. I try to stand but fail, and stumble. Eventually, I catch my footing, using the wall as an anchor.

I hear a low growl rise from the black-haired guy's chest. Logan rears his hand back to punch him, but the tall stranger catches it midair, his other hand pushing me gently back as I try a futile attempt to flee to the back door.

In a blur, Logan violently crashes into the back door that I was about to bolt for. It blows open from the force of his tumbling body.

I tell my feet to head towards the distant music, but they won't move. The room is spinning, or am I?

Logan lifts his head and blood cascades from a cut above his eyebrow. He looks straight into my eyes, a sinister smile creeps up on his terrifying face, and I cringe.

Furiously, the mysterious stranger takes two long strides and picks him up by his collar, pinning him to the metal door frame.

"You can't have her," he seethes.

Logan trains his obsidian eyes on me, but the other man isn't having it. He catches Logan's jaw in his hand, turning him away from me. "Don't look at her," he orders.

The brave stranger releases his grip on my attacker's chin. Logan looks down and shakes his head vigorously, similar to a convulsion. When his gaze pans back up, the demonic black is gone and replaced with a calm, ocean blue.

"Where am I?" Logan whimpers. The stranger pins him harder. "Woah, look I don't know what's happening. I was just dancing with her." He gestures my way, his brows furrowed. "The next thing I know I'm being thrown into a door. What's your problem dude?" He releases his hold on the now frightened Logan.

The strange hero turns away from him with a loud sigh and walks towards me. I'm speechless, he's so intimidating. His massive figure is moving towards me, but he has the most sympathetic look swirling in his eyes.

His gaze roams over my body, checking to see if I've been hurt. "Are you okay?" he asks.

"I guess?" I stated that as a question, unable to put a full sentence together. I'm so dizzy I can barely stand straight. I stumble a bit before he holds me steady with strong, secure arms.

The only thing I can think of comes from my lips, "What's your name?" I wonder, having a need to know who saved me.

He bends down so I can hear him over the faded music. "Pierce." He tells me, his voice soft like velvet. When he pulls back, his smoldering gaze is locked on mine, making it hard for me to speak.

"I'm Scarlett," I stammer, beginning to spin again. "Where's Liv?" I ask in my delirious daze.

"The blonde you were with?" He asks, holding my arm steady.

How does he know who I'm with? "I don't feel okay; I need to find her." My voice is quiet as he grabs my hand, it's nice. Not like the way Logan had pulled me through the hallway against my will, this is a gentle touch. Although I don't know him, I feel safe. He saved me from whatever just happened. I still can't wrap my head around the evil eyes Logan had.

We make it back to the music and I scan the crowd with dizzy eyes. "There she is!" I shout, pointing towards the bobbing blonde in the mash of moving bodies.

"I'm going to get her and get you two out of here," he says in my ear. "Do not let go of my hand, do you hear me?" His kind eyes even out his authoritative tone.

Once we reach Liv, he nudges her arm "Hey, Liv, right?" He scans behind her as he speaks.

"Hey there, who are you?" she slurs, leaning against Carter sluggishly.

He shows her my hand in his and in a serious tone he speaks. "Neither of you are safe, let's go." She glares at me and I'm sure my face is pale from the way I feel. Instantly, she looks worried; she sees that I'm shaking. I'm worried about her though; she doesn't look too good.

"Scar, do you need help?" she leans towards me now, tripping a little as she eyes Pierce. I try to talk over the thrumming music. Pierce keeps a firm grip on my hand.

"This is Pierce, he helped me. I can't explain right

24

now. We need to get outside." Through all of my dizziness, I know I need to get as far away from Logan as I can, which means Liv needs to get away from his friend.

She pushes her body off of Carter and he tries to pull her back to him, wrapping his arm around her waist. "Where are you goin', sweetheart? We just started havin' fun." Carter says.

Pierce's violent glare is set on Carter, who instantly let's go of Liv's arm when he realizes. She waddles over to me and we lean on each other to not fall. Her arm is through mine and on my other side I am still holding Pierce's hand. Afraid that if I let go the weight of the world will make me come crashing down.

Pierce pushes the large metal doors open and I step out, feeling a massive sense of relief. I'm still dizzy, and I can't see clearly, but I feel a little better. I drop his hand and run my fingers through my hair.

Glancing over at him, I study his worried features. "Thank you." I say, unable to hide the tremble in my tone.

"It's no problem, I could tell the guy was a creep," he shrugs his shoulders, but I don't miss the way he's looking at me.

"What happened? Did Logan do something to you?" Liv demands.

I shake my head, trying to piece together what just happened. "I don't know Liv; he was trying to bring me outside because I started to feel weird. But he was leading me to the back door. When I tried to leave, he looked at me and his eyes, they turned-"

Pierce abruptly cuts me off. "He drugged you, I'm guessing both of you," he states in a dark tone, a crease forms between his thick black eyebrows.

I turn towards him, completely stunned by his words. "What do you mean drugged? Why are we just standing here, we need to call the cops!" I shout. I start to trot my way back into the club and instantly lose my balance. Pierce holds me, steadies me.

He shakes his head. "He's not going to be a problem anymore, you two need to get home," he states.

I can barely think but I find a sense of calm as I look into Pierce's bright green eyes, a stark contrast to the midnight black of Logan's moments ago. My body trembles, remembering how scared I was. "But his eyes, I saw them!"

"Scarlett, I think the drugs are messing with your head. The guy was just a creep. He was trying to hook up with you," he says, his fist clenching at his sides.

If whatever we were given is making me hallucinate shouldn't I be getting medical help? I mean, what did he even give us?

It feels like someone put bricks on my chest. "Do we need to go to the hospital?" I cry, looking to Liv in desperation.

"No, you will both be fine. A good night's sleep is what you need." His tone is calm and strong, reassuring us. I don't know him, but I trust him, maybe that's stupid of me but why would he go through all of this trouble to save us if he wasn't a nice guy?

Directing his words towards Liv but keeping his

eyes on me he says, "Are you okay, Liv?" She doesn't respond. I look towards her and she's just staring into the darkness in front of her.

My hands dive into my purse. "I want to go home, where are the keys?" I practically scream. I just want to escape. I begin rummaging through the contents of my overcrowded bag when a warm hand grabs my wrist gently.

A small chuckle escapes his full lips. "Yes, where are your keys? I'm driving you both home."

Four

Mom is going to kill us

A small gasp escapes my lips as I wake, the sun blasts an unwelcome pouring of light in through the window, making my room unbearably bright. *My room?* Stretching my arms out wide, I attempt to collect my thoughts.

"Umm, Scar. What happened last night?" Liv whispers; breaking the silence.

I grip my pounding head. "We were at the club. I don't remember much... everything is kind of a blur," I gulp. A moment of silence spreads between us, giving me a moment to think. The pieces start to manifest, along with my rising heartbeat. "I remember being dragged through a hallway and the brown-haired guy... Logan! His eyes turned black!" I keep my voice low, but a shriek escapes me as I remember more, "but Pierce..." My hand hovers over my parted lips and suddenly the realization hits me. "We were drugged last night."

She tilts her head, studying me. "His eyes turned black?"

"I'm sure of it. Well, I think I am. We were drugged though so that may have been a part of it. I was so scared, Liv, if it wasn't for the Pierce guy, I don't know what would have happened to us." I can feel tears welling in my eyes.

Frown lines appear on her tired face. "Oh, Scar I'm so sorry, you didn't want to go last night, and I forced it on you. I ruined your birthday. I remember you were so scared." She sighs, slumping over in defeat.

I shake my head. "No, not at all. You were trying to make it fun for me. This is in no way your fault. We're safe and that's all that matters." This is true, we are safe. But how did we get here?

"Pierce... he was the tall one, right? He was holding your hand." she nudges my arm, sending me a small smile. "Woah, Scar! What happened?" she stammers, grabbing below the purple bruise that lays on my arm.

I touch the sore spot, gulping. "The Logan guy, he grabbed me pretty hard."

Remembering the events that unfolded last night it's hard to forget the beautiful, angelic face that saved me from a monster. The way his jet-black hair curled at the ends right above his thick brows. How his height towered over everyone around him, how he looked at me with deep concern through his emerald eyes. Even though I was nothing more than a stranger, he helped us. I am grateful he got us to safety, and I want to thank him, but how?

"He took us here last night," I state, still collecting my thoughts. "I remember giving him my keys."

"Why did he take us here and not my house?" she asks.

I shake my head. "I'm not entirely sure, maybe we were just out of it and told him to bring us here? I don't remember anything after he grabbed my keys," I shrug.

Looking to my nightstand, a mixture of guilt and worry washes over me. There are two glasses of water, still cold with ice, and headache medicine sitting on my bedside table.

"Great! Mom's going to kill me, we probably stumbled through making all kinds of noise late at night. She was still sweet enough to leave this for the both of us," I groan, gesturing to the water. My voice is not at a whisper anymore. She knows what happened and she is going to be disappointed. I hope she knows I didn't drive last night but she would be equally concerned about a stranger getting us here.

"Time to face the music." I groan.

"Better to get it over with now," she says as she shrugs out of the bed. We both down the waters; I've never been so thirsty before.

"Don't forget your medicine," I remind her,

waiting as she takes two of her iron pills.

We creeped downstairs after changing, I made sure to put a hoodie on over my clothes so I can hide the bruise. Now we are just waiting for the screaming match that is about to begin.

My mom is not strict by any means, she'll be more disappointed that I lied. I'm eighteen and it's not like she can ground me but it's the respect factor. There was trust in our relationship and I broke it.

I enter the kitchen and notice that it's oddly quiet, the stove clock reads half past nine. Early enough for me, but my mom's an early riser. "She must have gone to the store," I suggest to Liv who is rummaging through the fridge.

"Eggs?" she suggests while grabbing the carton from the fridge with a gallon of orange juice.

"Please! I'm starving." My stomach growls as I watch her cook. After a few minutes, I hear the loud clanking of metal from the garage door as it pierces through the quiet kitchen making my headache even worse.

We both brace for impact. "We don't know how much she knows so keep quiet. If anything, I want to protect her from finding out we were drugged. I don't want her to think about what could have happened to us last night," I cringe at the thought.

Liv nods, scraping the sides of the pan with a spatula. "Good idea, she'll probably just think we were drunk. Let the details come out as she tells them." she places the scrambled eggs on two plates and jumps onto the barstool beside me. "Besides, your mom is cooler than you think, I hardly believe she's going to flip."

Mom walks through the door that leads to the garage, dangling a pair of black heels in her left hand. Confusion makes her face contort as she looks between us.

"Hey, girls... I didn't think you would come home so early?" She places her keys on the hanger, a deep red blush rising in her cheeks.

An internal cheer rises inside of me. "Hey, Ms. Wells, we got bored at my house, so we decided to come here." Liv and I exchange a quick, 'we might just be saved' glance.

If I wasn't so upset about what happened last night, I would be rolling on the floor with laughter. My mom, my sweet innocent mom is doing the walk of shame, and we are in the clear. We both can't help but fall into a set of giggles as she runs past us to get changed in her room.

Liv dramatically wipes the fake sweat from her forehead and smiles at me. The shower starts running and the sound of a door being closed tells me I'm safe to talk. Then I remember something.

"Wait, if my mom wasn't home last night than who left the water?" I ask curiously.

My thoughts are abruptly cut short when I start to feel nauseous. I quickly run up the stairs and hurl over the toilet. Liv follows and holds my unruly hair from falling into my face. Last night is catching up with me and I have to work at four o'clock. I need more sleep, and luckily Liv agrees and we both doze off.

I fall asleep in moments, my dreams haunted by a black-eyed monster making me weaker as he glares at me with evil eyes. The dreams twist into something more... mysterious. Pierce shows up, making all of the darkness disappear and replaces it with a calm, soothing feeling.

Just as quickly, the peaceful calm is replaced by a loud buzzing in my ears. I swiftly jump up to shut it off so it doesn't wake her up, at least one of us can recover longer.

I hurriedly run a brush through my thick, wavy hair and throw on my ice cream shop uniform. Bright red pants with a red pinstripe shirt, I make sure to throw a long sleeve underneath the button up to hide my bruise.

The outfit is awful but working at 'Pop's Candy Shop' for the past two summers has turned out to be more fun than I expected. The boardwalk is always full of life, I love being there. Plus, you can't beat the view. We're right off the pier, so the huge glass windows give a breathtaking view of the ocean.

Luckily, I find a parking spot close to the docks. After a short walk, I enter through the tall glass doors and it never fails to always bring me back to my childhood. The smell of rich caramel and homemade fudge whirl around me. Every flavor of ice cream you can think of on display. I can still see my family and I sitting happily in the corner booth. I would be sharing a strawberry milkshake with dad as mom watched us with a smile.

Thinking about these things used to make me run but after years without him, I've embraced the memories. I would rather remember all of us being happy, than to think about what happened.

The day went smoothly, it was busy but there were no hiccups. Parents brought their little ones in from a hot day at the beach to cool off with icy treats. The sun is beginning to sink below the clouds, so I'll be getting off soon. I glance at the clock and it reads 6:55.

I toss a rag over my shoulder and begin spraying down the glass display. The bell rings and I realize I forgot to lock it when we closed about five minutes ago. I look at the door and there's no one there. I curiously scan the room and that's when I see him, leaning against the counter and watching me with a crooked grin.

"Pierce," I say softly.

Five

The big pink bear, please

Relief, that I can't fully explain, washes over me. I was beginning to think my semi-unconscious state from the night before had made him up. He came and disappeared so quickly I couldn't be sure what was real last night.

"Hey, beautiful," his smooth voice is deep, taking up all the space in the empty shop. My eyes take in his appearance. Black jeans that are fitted perfectly to him, with a plain black t-shirt that hugs his broad shoulders and muscles. I peel my eyes away and look over at the wall.

"Hi," I say nervously. My stomach is flipping

backward, did he come here to see me? That makes no sense, he doesn't know where I work. "What are you doing here?" I ask curiously as I continue to wipe down the glass.

"Can't a guy get some ice cream?" He shrugs, his voice laced with humor as he slowly walks towards me.

Shit. "Yes! Of course, I'm sorry. We're closed but I can grab you whatever. What would you like?" I rake my fingers through my hair trying to fix it as he looks at the broad selection of ice cream with a thoughtful expression. I must look like a complete mess.

"Surprise me," he smiles. "Make two of them, please."

Ah, there it is. I was foolish to think he would come here to see me. How would he even know where I work? Embarrassment makes my cheeks flush and I frown a little, but why? Why should I care that he's here with someone? I barely know him, it's probably because of what he did for me last night.

He's probably having a romantic boardwalk date, walking along the weathered wood with a girl on his arm as they enjoy their ice cream. I can't help the jealousy that creeps into me, which makes no logical sense. I realize I'm staring off into oblivion and I quickly set my cleaning rag down.

I lift the closed glass back up and grab two waffle cones. "Does she like chocolate?" I say with a little attitude in my voice as I grab the scoop with a little more power than necessary. Not sure why I care.

He grips his chin in thought. "Well I'm not sure,

does she?" He asks, a smirk creeping up his perfect face as he walks over to the door and flips the closed sign facing outward. He turns around and makes his way over to me. Towering over the counter like a giant.

"You want to get ice cream for me?" I blush.

With a nod, he trails the tip of his finger along the countertop. "We need something to snack on when we walk the pier," he laughs. I'm assuming he knew I was a little jealous.

My heart threatens to beat out of my chest. "Did you just happen to show up here, while I was working?" I give him a suspicious look as I scoop out some chocolate chunk from the cold metal pan.

"Well, last night you were freaking out a bit because you had to start your first day at 'Pop's Candy Shop.' You were a bit out of it," he sighs a little.

I stumble, almost dropping the scoop. "Thank you so much for last night, Pierce. I don't remember much about the car ride. I'm not even sure how we made it in the house." I admit, shaking my head.

He seems hesitant to speak, opening his mouth and closing it again. "When you got in your car your friend immediately fell asleep and you were in and out, mumbling things every now and then. As for getting into the house, I carried you both inside, I hope that's okay?" He looks a little bashful which is a funny contrast to his edgy appearance.

I tilt my head. "How did you know where I lived if I was out?" I ask.

"You mentioned something about Liv's parents

being out of town. I got a little nervous about you both being alone, so I asked for your address. I figured at least with your parents' house you would be okay until morning," he says.

"It's just me and my mom but you're lucky she wasn't home; she would have killed me, and you, and Liv." I laugh, throwing my head back dramatically, still reeling about how lucky we got.

He shrugs. "I knew no one was home, there was no car in the driveway, and she wouldn't bother you if she did come home later since you would both be asleep," he says sheepishly. Then, I realized he must have been the one who left us water and medicine. That should bother me, right? That a stranger came into my home, but he was so sweet and took care of us, but there was still ice in it, or maybe there wasn't? My mind is playing tricks on me lately, so I keep my thoughts to myself.

I send him a smile. "Thank you, you didn't have to do all that for us. I hope it was no trouble to go back to your car after dropping mine off," I say, trying to sound appreciative.

"It's no problem. I took a taxi to the club anyway. Are you ready to go? The good rides will be swamped in a bit," he gestures towards the door with a smile.

I can't get rid of the stupid grin on my face. "Yes! Just let me change really quick." I hand the ice cream to him and head to the backroom. I'm thankful I have an extra dress in my bag that was supposed to be used when we were at Liv's, so I can get out of this hideous outfit.

I smooth out my yellow dress and spray a bit of

my perfume in the air, walking through it to make sure it lays on my skin and hair so I smell nice. My white Toms don't exactly match with my dress but it's kind of cute.

I open the doors to walk back in, and Pierce's striking gaze rakes over my body. "Wow, yellow is your color," he smirks. My cheeks burn a little; I think he likes to make me nervous.

I anxiously reach for my ice cream and before I get to it, Pierce quickly grabs my arm. His eyes transition from gazing at me, to glaring angrily at the bruise. "Did I do that last night?" he trails off. I wish I had a cover for my dress, I forgot about the handprint.

I shake my head, taking in the worry lines that crease his forehead. "No, no. It was Logan. You never grabbed my arm." I assure him, blushing from the memory of his hands interlaced with mine.

His stance is rigid, not saying much as we walk outside. As I turn back to the door and put the key through the slot I hear my name being shouted behind us. I look towards the noise and see a group of friends from school. Zack is heading our way. Damnit. I completely forgot I told him to meet me here after work.

As he walks in front of us, I give him a bright smile. "Hey, Zack!" I grin.

He glances over at Pierce with an odd expression. "Hey, Scarlett, you ready?" He asks, his eyes roaming between Pierce and I.

"Hey man, I'm Pierce," he introduces himself, reaching out his hand.

"Nice to meet you." Zack returns his handshake,

then he turns his attention to me. "What do you want for dinner? I'm starving," he grabs his stomach dramatically.

I jump a little as I feel Pierce's arm wrap around my waist, he pulls me close to him. "Actually, me and Scar here are going on a date." I smile when I hear him call me Scar. A date? My heart races a little faster.

Zack looks tense but to be fair I didn't know I was going on any date tonight, but I'll explain that to him later. I'm not complaining though. "I'll text you later Zack, is that cool?" I ask with a nervous smile.

"Yeah, yeah." He waves goodbye and heads back to his friends. I make a shy wave towards the group as we walk away.

We're walking side by side down the long stretch of the pier. Pierce's arm is still around me. Ice creams in hand. The warm summer air melts them faster than we can eat them. I watch as he licks the ice cream that dripped on his fingers, quickly looking away before he notices me staring.

I look around, trying to think of something to talk about but my attention is drawn in front of me to the sinking sun that slowly descends into the ocean.

It's really a romantic sight, and I begin to wonder about Pierce's bold move of throwing his arm around my waist after hearing another guy ask what I wanted for dinner. "How did you know he wasn't my boyfriend?" I ask quizzically.

He shrugs. "I didn't."

I bite my lip to refrain from giggling like an idiot. As we finish our melted cones carnival workers begin to yell for Pierce, challenging him to win their overpriced prizes. He looks over at me, "I was planning on playing to win you something before we left," he laughs and I give him a soft smile.

"You don't have to win me anything," I assure him, but the gesture is sweet.

He moves his hand from my waist to the small of his back as he guides me to the bearded man at the ring toss booth. "It's rigged, they're always rigged," I say quietly as Pierce hands the man cash. An amused laugh escapes Pierce's full lips, accompanied by a boastful glint in his eyes.

The bearded man pockets the money. "Ten bucks gets you five rings. Here you go," he hands the plastic rings to Pierce. "Make one and the pretty lady can choose anything on the small rack here," he gestures to the bottom shelf.

Pierce extends his arm, doing a few fake shots before asking, "How many do I have to make for the that?" He gestures his hand to a large, plush pink bear that hangs from the wooden roof. The worker laughs, "Five rings, perfect game, but you may want to get a bigger set... it's hard to even get one."

Pierce lines up his shot, tossing one after the other. Ting, ting, ting, ting, ting. Perfect game.

He gives the worker a cocky look, "Pick whatever you want Scar," he tells me, his dimpled grin melting me. My fingers land on the large pink bear he spotted.

The man hands it to me, and I look over at pierce. "Thank you!" I squeal, squeezing my oversized bear in the process.

He looks down at me with a half-grin adorning his already perfect face, making him look even more beautiful underneath the colorful carnival lights around us.

Our strides are matched as he slows his pace to keep up with mine. We bypass the faster rides, and I'm thankful. My stomach is already doing flips just from the turn of events my night has taken from him being so close to me.

To my left I see a familiar tent set up, I've passed by it so many times but never gave much thought to having my future read. I walk a little slower to read the sign.

'Mrs. Cleo's Fortunes. $5.'

"You stopped walking." I didn't realize. "Do you want to go inside?"

I ponder this for a moment, I do. I'm curious but will he think it's weird? I'll just go another time, maybe with Liv. "I'm fine," I tell him, I go to walk forward but he gently tugs me back.

His eyes twinkle as I look up at him. "Seriously, I don't mind. Let's go." And with that, we walk through the bead laced doors and into a dimly lit, purple room.

It has your stereotypical decor, a purple crystal ball in the center of a small table, 'ancient' relics from long ago that hold magic, and to finish off the look; a woman with a colorful scarf wrapped around her head is looking at us expectantly. Like she knew we would be coming, of course. I chuckle a little at the sight.

She gestures to the chairs with a serious expression, bowing her head. "Sit."

Six

Take my advice

I have to stifle a laugh as Pierce sits beside me, his lean frame towering over the tiny table. Looking at the fortune teller, I note how her gold hoop earrings shimmer under the deep purple lighting. "What did you two lovers come in for?" she asks, and I blush.

I don't know how to answer that. "We're... we-," Pierce cuts me off, saving me from my embarrassment. Thank heavens for him.

"She'd like a reading," he tells her.

The woman holds out her hand. "Money first."

Pierce reaches for his wallet; I quickly slip the woman the five dollars and he looks at me with a humored yet annoyed expression.

"Give me your hand, young lady," she says, her thick accent taking up the tiny room.

I place my hand in hers and she closes her eyes. Her cold fingertips trace the lines on my palm. "You're destined for greatness," she smiles.

Her head turns to Pierce, but her eyes are still closed. "Now yours," she holds her other hand out to Pierce, he hesitates but I nudge him with my elbow.

The moment he places his large hand in hers she abruptly pulls away. Her eyes fling open and she shoots up from her seat, the sound of her metal chair scratching the floor pierces through the room.

"This one is no good," she looks at me, but she's talking about Pierce.

"Huh?" I ask, tilting my head forward. Pierce gestures to the door as he stands himself.

She turns her gaze to Pierce, the apologetic eyes she used on me have run away, the smoldering expression she looks at him with sends chills down my spine.

"You are smothered in the depths of evil, you will bring nothing but trouble to this girl's life." She steps away from him, her voice trembling, "you will just ruin this poor girl."

Feeling uncomfortable, I make my way to Pierce's side and look to him. "She just wants your money," he fumes, looking down at me; then he turns his attention to her. "Don't scare her," he orders, his voice taking on an edge.

The teller grips the crumpled bills before throwing the money at us. "Take my advice," she says, her attention directed at me.

"She won't be doing that." Pierce informs her.

Why did she say that?

Without another word Pierce interlaces our fingers together, holding me in his large hand in a protective manner as he leads us out of the small purple tent and towards the bright, towering Ferris wheel.

Calm smothers me at his touch. "Well, that was weird," I chuckle.

Raising his dark brows, he shakes his head, "Weird is right."

We stand in line at the Ferris wheel and I look over to the ticket booth. "Did you already get tickets?" I ask, trying to ignore the weird conversation we just had with the woman.

He reaches into his pockets and holds up two tickets between his fingers. "I wanted to be prepared."

I internally swoon. "That's so thoughtful, thank you. You didn't have to do all this for me. You did enough last night."

"You're up!" The attendant yells out over the carnival style music.

My eyes widen as Pierce helps me into the baby blue bucket. It's heavily weathered from the saltwater air rusting it throughout the years. It loudly creaks as we lift up.

Instinctively, I scoot a little closer to Pierce, afraid

of the creaking metal as the wind blows us back and forth.

I clutch the soft bear to my chest in comfort and Pierce chuckles before slinging his arm around me. "You're perfectly safe, I promise. Do heights frighten you?" he speaks with a calming tone.

"Not usually, but this thing is just ancient." I point at the chipped blue paint and the rusted arms that are holding the bucket and he laughs. "The views are worth it though," I admit as my eyes roam the familiar ocean. The sailboats are anchoring for the night and the lights from the pier dance on the darkening waves.

We both admire the views in comfortable silence, and I begin to wonder why he showed up so randomly. I'm not complaining, I'm happy to be by his side. But why was he so interested? He only met me when I was loopy last night, still, I feel a magnetic charge between us and I'm wondering if he feels it too.

Curiosity gets the best of me, "So what made you come here tonight?" I ask nervously.

"You seemed very sweet last night. You kept thanking me and I was interested in knowing more about you." His emerald eyes look over me, making my cheeks heat. The golden light from the setting sun makes his skin glisten.

"I'm glad you came," I tell him, scooting a little closer to his warm body. This is not like me, at all. Flirting with a stranger I don't even know. I push the thoughts back since my interest for this man is outweighing the comfortable bubble that I've placed around myself to never let anyone get too close.

I realize I don't even know where he's from or his age. He looks around my age, but his demeanor seems way more mature. "Do you go to school around here?" I ask. He looks slightly thrown off by my question which only intensifies my curiosity.

Shaking his head with a dimpled grin, he replies, "No."

"Oh," I breathe, not sure what to talk about. He seems like he doesn't want to open up. I nervously tap my fingers on my leg.

"How old are you?" I ask, hoping this is more casual, even though the school question wasn't serious.

"Twenty-One, and you're eighteen? I remember you mentioning it last night." He says.

"Mhmm." I reply quietly as we round the top of the wheel. As if he can sense my fear, he pulls me closer to him.

After exiting the rusted Ferris wheel, I lace my fingers through his. I don't know where that courage came from but when he securely wraps his around mine, I know I made the right decision.

The delicious aroma of fair-style food hits my nose, making my empty stomach groan. "Are you hungry?" he asks, leading us to the colorful booths. I dig into my wallet as we walk up, realizing that my debit card must be at home. I spent my cash on the teller.

A woman with fiery red hair looks between us.

"What can I get for you?" she asks. I look to Pierce, who has his wallet out, ready to pay.

My eyes roam the short menu, trying to find something cheap. "A corndog, please," I say, feeling guilty for not having my card.

Pierce shakes his head, his sharp edges illuminated by the neon signs around us. "Your stomach is growling that loud and you're getting just a corn dog?"

"I'm just a little hungry." The lie doesn't hold when my stomach betrays me.

"We'll have two corn dogs with fries and two cokes, please." He tells her and I thank him bashfully.

Plastic baskets lined with red checkered paper are handed to us and we head for a nearby bench. I didn't realize how hungry I was, this is the first thing I've eaten all day. Before I could even touch the eggs Liv made us, I was hurling over the toilet. I eat quicker than usual, enjoying the food filling my empty stomach.

As we return the trays, I worry in my rush of eating that there's food on my face. I hear Pierce laugh as I attempt to check my reflection in a sliver of steel on the booth. "I'm going to run to the restroom," I say.

He walks with me towards the bathroom and stands at the edge of the pier admiring the water. I steal a moment to observe him, the way his broad shoulders rise and fall as he breathes in the salty air and how his head shakes every so often to move the thick hair from his forehead.

I'm reeling from the turn of events, having never gone on a proper date like this before. I nearly dance into the bathroom like a giddy schoolgirl.

I smile when I take in my reflection. Luckily, no food on my face. Just a happy girl looking back at me with a slight flush in her cheeks. I fix my hair as well as I can and smooth out my yellow dress. I'm happy I decided to throw on some mascara before work, trying to liven up my tired appearance.

I'm so exhausted from the past day and I know I need more sleep, but my body is full of excitement with Pierce right outside. I wonder how long he wants to hang out tonight, I should call my mom and let her know I'll be home late.

Suddenly, the door bursts open, and a man comes charging in.

"Sir, this is the lady's res-" His large hand quickly covers my mouth as he pins me to the wall with so much force it knocks the wind out of me.

I struggle to free myself from his grip, frantically hitting and scratching him. As I look into his eyes a muffled gasp escapes my covered lips. What stares back at me is a familiar pitch black that sends chills down my spine.

Seven

Angels

I scream into the stranger's hand, but my desperate cries for help are smothered by the pressure. I attempt to pull my eyes from his face, but I'm stuck, trapped in his demonic gaze.

He holds me tight against the wall, pinning me harder. I'm feeling weaker every second and my body begins to go limp.

Through my blurred vision, I see Pierce charging towards us. Relief floods me as he rushes to my side, pulling the man away with an iron grip. He violently throws him against the concrete wall, and crumbled rock shatters on the hard ground.

This is nearly identical to last night, except now I

know my hero's name. Why do I need a hero, though? Why is this happening again?

The man's large body slams from wall to wall as Pierce thrashes him around with ease. No matter how much the man is thrown around, his gaze is locked into mine and every time he falls, he gets back up and tries to come towards me as if I'm his target.

I stare in shock wondering how he isn't knocked out yet. With one final blow, Pierce's fist connects with the face of the evil man and he falls to the ground. I gasp when Pierce's glance turns to me, his emerald eyes have transitioned into a deep jade that houses flecks of black.

In a movement so quick I can't believe it's real, Pierce is in front of me wrapping his arms tightly around me. I bury my face into his chest and close my eyes tightly. I feel safe here, but why aren't we running? He is right behind him. We have to get out of here! We will only have a second before the madman pulls him away from my arms.

I frantically start pulling and thrashing from his warm grip. "Pierce! We have to move!" I scream into his chest as he holds me tighter, I feel tears welling in my eyes. My feet slide on the crunchy ground and I start to assess the atmosphere, the sound of waves crashing takes over my thoughts.

My tightly closed eyes open a little to look down at my feet which are now embedded in white sand. I slowly lift my head from Pierce's chest and take in the site around me, completely dumbfounded. The pale white of fluorescent lighting from the bathroom is gone, replaced by silvery moonlight that trails across the ocean.

Tears fall from my eyes. "I'm losing my mind!" I scream at him. Maybe the drugs haven't worn off? He grabs me gently, pulling his body slightly away from me.

"Scar, love, you're shaking." His emerald eyes are checking my body the same way they had the night before. "I'm so, so sorry Scarlett. I didn't know what else to do. I had to get you out of there," he says frantically, running his large hand over his black hair. He looks scared, which is an odd expression compared to his usual cool demeanor.

"What do you mean get me out of there? What's happening to me, I'm going crazy! We were in a bathroom, Pierce! I swear we were!" The sobs strain my ragged voice.

He bows his head, pulling me close. "I'll explain everything, it looks as though I have no choice." He nuzzles his head in my neck, my hair wrapping around us both as it blows with the ocean breeze. "I'm so sorry," he whispers.

He securely holds my shaking hand as we walk side by side down the sand. I can see the lights from the pier at a distance, so I know we aren't far from where I was attacked, which makes me tremble more.

We make our way to a bundle of large rocks that cascade down to the ocean. The waves violently lap on the rough rocks below as we sit down above them on the drier ones. The wind coming from the ocean, along with whatever just happened, makes me shiver. A warm smile crosses his face as he places his jacket over my shoulders.

Although I'm stunned by fear, the sentiment makes me flush.

The thick breeze sends the scent from his jacket to swirl around me. It's intoxicating, the heady aroma of pine and leather hugs me. I inhale deeply, taking in the cool ocean air accompanied by the perfect cologne that is Pierce. It makes me feel warm, and comforted for a brief moment. I concentrate on not crying anymore. I feel like I'm in a dream, confused by what's happened yet oddly at ease knowing who is next to me.

I look to him, he's now in a plain black t-shirt. His intent gaze is directed towards the vast sea in front of us. The glow from the full moon reveals a large intricate tattoo wrapping around his arm from his upper bicep down to his wrist. I stare, mesmerized by the scene taking place on his perfectly sculpted arm.

An angel with dark tattered wings is kneeling on a rock. There's chaos below the sad-looking angel, large black swirls of darkness trace from the rocks down to the fire that roars below. My eyes move over to the scene above and a much different picture is painted. Glorious clouds, detailed so perfectly you can see the bright streaks of light where the sun shines through them. It's a brilliant display of good vs. evil.

I glance back up to his face to see that he is staring at me, sorrow in his eyes as he grabs my hand in his. His voice is low compared to the crashing of water around us. I lean in close to hear him.

"There's no reason to lie to you, it will only put you in more danger if I'm not honest. Besides, you've seen the demons," he states.

"Demons?" I shriek.

"The things that keep coming after you." He gestures to thin air as his face scrunches in disgust. I stare with parted lips, a gasp escaping them.

His expression is haunted. "I'm not sure what you believe as far as religion goes. The world you live in isn't as black and white as you think. There is always a balance that needs to be kept." He hesitates as he lowers his head shaking it back and forth. "I didn't want to tell you any of this, Scar. I'm so sorry." Why does he keep apologizing? He's the one saving me from them.

I ponder what he says for a moment and my gaze shifts to his arm. "Similar to your tattoo? The balance thing?" I ask, and he tilts his head. I trace the tip of my finger on the kneeling angel. "You know, the angel here. He looks sad, like he's stuck in the middle of good and evil. I don't know why he isn't in the sky with the other angels in heaven." I want to say more but the horrified expression on his face makes me stop talking.

His chest rises when he inhales a sharp intake of breath. "That angel doesn't belong in heaven, he doesn't belong anywhere," he sneers.

"I don't understand Pierce, you have to explain more," I plead with him to help ease his hesitation.

He shakes his head. "That's not an angel Scar, well it is, but not in the way that you think. That's the Angel of Death."

I nod, waiting to hear more.

His tone is dark as he points to the angel with

tattered wings. "That angel is me."

I sit in a rigid state, unable to think. Pierce pauses, studying my expression with weary eyes.

"You're what?" I gulp, frantically wrestling with my instincts to run. My mind is telling me to go but my body won't move. I would be dead if it wasn't for him. I don't understand why I'm not more afraid, but I know he won't harm me.

"I know this is a lot, Scar. I'm sorry. I have to tell you mostly everything at once, so it makes sense." He reaches for my hand and a deep groan escapes him when I pull away from his touch. His head collapses into his hands and a long moment of silence passes before he looks up at me, his eyes filled with ancient sorrow.

"I was appointed long ago to maintain the boundary between life and death," he talks quietly, afraid I'll bolt if he raises above a certain decibel. "I was at that bar to collect your soul, Scarlett. No one could see me of course, but I knew something was wrong. Your soul was destined to go somewhere dark but all I could see around you was light. I can tell good from bad in that way, a subtle aura surrounds every person. It's either light or dark, but always subtle," he waits for me to respond, but I can't.

Hesitantly, he continues. "With you Scar, it's so bright, it's almost blinding," he gestures around us, "You're lighting up the rocks around us, and I mean that quite literally." The words are so sweet to my ears that it slightly lightens the thick tension in the air.

I begin to thaw and my eyes trail around us, taking in the darkness. I can see nothing but the faint glow from the moon glistening off the wet rocks and making a trail towards the ocean.

I summon my courage to speak. "I don't understand what that means Pierce, I've got a light around me? I'm good? Yes, I'm a nice person but I don't think I'm something spectacular."

A small chuckle escapes his lips and my heart skips a beat at the sound. "Scarlett, you radiate light. It's not the same as other people, it's very rare. You must have done something extraordinary to be as special as you are, or you're destined to do something great," he looks to me fondly. "The problem is with the light that you radiate… it can attract the wrong kind of monster, the demons," he speaks with grit behind his voice.

I stare back at him with a mixture of horror and curiosity. I need to know more. I inch closer to his face so I can hear him perfectly, ignoring his warm breath as the sweet scent of mint cascades over my cold face. I need to know everything that is happening to me and I need to know everything there is to know about Pierce.

"Why does he want me?" My voice is trembling, confused by the words that are coming out of my mouth.

Pierce lets out a sigh, his chest rising heavily. "I realized the demon had taken over the body of the guy you were with. You see, demons, like the one you've seen, they desire souls that are good, and they will track them down to take them and trap them to an eternity in hell," his voice thunders over the crashing waves as he clenches his fist tightly.

I think about Logan, that must have been so terrifying for him - to have his body taken over by something so evil. My voice is saturated with grief "Poor Logan. It's all my fault that he had to endure all of that."

A deep laugh booms from Pierce's chest, catching me off guard. His eyes lighten when they meet mine. "See Scar, you feel bad for something that could never possibly be your fault. That shows your character. Regardless, demons can only inhabit the bodies of humans that aren't inherently good. The drugs he used were in his pocket already, he would have used them on someone else even if you weren't the target." A frown takes over his face.

"The target?" I shudder, remembering that's exactly how I felt in the bathroom when the man kept coming back to me, even after every violent blow from Pierce.

I never imagined I would refer to myself as a target. I also never imagined I would be sitting with the Angel of Death, so normalcy is out the window at this point.

"The demon... he will jump into whatever body is available to get to you," he tells me. I place my hand over my heart and Pierce flinches. I can tell by the worried way he watches my every movement, that he's scared I'm going to run.

My heart threatens to rip from my chest. Pierce raises his palm, and gently places it over my heart. His voice is calm as he speaks. "Shh, Scar. You have to try

58

and calm down. Your heart is thumping so violently. Do you want to wait a while?" He inquires with wide eyes.

My body relaxes under his calm touch and I open my mouth to speak. "No, I have so many questions," I whisper into the whipping wind as I try to summon a few out of the millions that are floating in my foggy brain. I won't be able to think clearly until I find out more, in truth I don't think I'll ever be able to think clearly again. He gestures for me to continue.

"Why... How does he keep changing bodies? He's going to find me. I mean, I can't hide forever!" I stutter, trying to swallow my anxiety. Pierce wraps his arms tightly around me noticing my sudden change in breathing. I can't catch a full breath.

His eyes hold anger, but somehow, I know it's not directed at me. "We would be ready if we saw the same person coming for you, again and again, that's why he changes bodies. This is his game. That's why I told you Logan wouldn't be a problem anymore when you were trying to go after him at the club." He looks deeply into my eyes. "Scar, I will never let him get to you. I know you have no reason to trust me, but I swear to you I will protect you with everything I have." He promises.

"I do trust you; you've saved my life multiple times. I just don't understand why?" Confusion overtakes me as the tears wash down my cheeks. He wipes them away gently.

"I don't understand it either, I wish I did. I just know from the moment I saw his body standing over you that I had to protect you," he admits. "I don't do this." he gestures between us. "I don't ever mingle with humans in this way. I'm sorry I'm throwing all of this on you, it's just... I know you will be safer knowing the facts and all I want is for you to be safe." He tells me, his piercing jade eyes bore into me.

His demeanor takes on a darker tone. "As much as I want to hurt the people that are coming after you, it's not their fault a demon took control of their bodies. They're bad people but their lives are not mine to take, only when nature has taken its course, do I step in. I never mess with a person's destiny. It wasn't your destiny for your soul to get dragged to Hell so that's a different, rare situation," his deep voice encases me with a jagged truth. I want to ask him more about himself, how did he end up with this 'job'? Why him, what did it mean? And why am I still sitting here and not running away?

He lets me collect my thoughts for a moment, waiting patiently as I sift through this confusing, impossible situation I've found myself in.

"In truth, this is my fault," he admits. His voice is laced with remorse, breaking through the long silence from the moments before.

I look up at him with tear-filled eyes. "I can hardly believe any of this is your fault, Pierce," I reassure him. Not sure how I'm able to try and console someone else while my body is trembling in fear.

He searches my eyes for what feels like the hundredth time tonight. Trying to find a way to answer in a way that I can understand. He doesn't make me feel incompetent, but the words he's speaking are like a different language to me, foreign to my way of life.

His hard chest rises. "Normally, if I come across this happening, I can stop it and they'll move off to somewhere else, someone else. But I felt a need greater than any need I've ever felt to protect you with every ounce that I could. That was my mistake." He spits.

I frown as I feel the tears soaking my cheeks. I quickly look away from him. Suddenly I feel his warm hands pulling my chin towards him. "No, no Scarlett. Saving you wasn't a mistake. It's... You're a light, I know you don't understand how rare that is or what it even means, but he won't stop until..." He doesn't allow himself to finish that sentence. "He wants you because I'm protecting you." He says, bringing his palm up to caress my cheek.

I allow the rough crashing of the angry waves below to wash over my mind completely. I let myself get lost in the dark, focusing on the nothingness that surrounds me. My mind is blank, my body rigid. I try to forget what he just told me, my brain can't handle any more of his world at the moment. I regret pushing him, insisting that he tell me so much at one time.

Through the heavy fog in my mind, one thing is desperately clear. The instinct to run that I've been waiting for is here. I don't know him; he doesn't know me.

I'm next to a stranger... No, I'm sitting with the Angel of Death, and I need to get away. Fast.

As I look into his eyes, I sense the worry in his face as I frantically push myself off the large rock.

My feet begin to shuffle away, and his hand grabs my side. "Let me go!" I shout. A tingling sense of sadness washes over me when he quickly removes his hand and lowers his head, but I push the guilt away.

"Scarlett, please, don't go." He begs, reaching for me again. I can't stay here; I want to go home and pretend that this was all a nightmare. This is too much for me, this is too much for anyone.

With an exasperated sigh, I turn on my heels and book it. Stealing a glance back, I watch as Pierce's head falls into his large hands. "Fuck!" He roars, his thick voice slicing through the wind. Guilt stings down to my core as I pick up my pace, heading away from him and towards the bright lights of the dock with tears steadily streaming down my cheeks.

Eight

Running

My tires squeal against the wet pavement as I fly down the road, headed in whatever direction my hands take me. Speeding towards the dark unknown. Rain drizzles against the car, making my tear-filled vision worse. An hour passes before I realize I have no idea where I am.

My stained cheeks feel tight when I squint my eyes. I pull over to the side of the road to get my phone for the GPS. Glancing at the radio I groan when I see the time, midnight. I got off around ten, my mom must be freaking out. I unlock my silenced phone, eight missed calls.

I go straight to my text, three from my mother

which I don't dare read, and one from Liv.

'Don't worry, I talked to your mom earlier. She thinks you're here, and boy was she freaking out about you not answering your phone. I told her you were asleep. Text me soon, xoxo P.S. Zack told me you were with the tall guy from the club, I want to know everything!'

She's an absolute saint. As my fingers hover over the screen I begin to type a reply, but the screen goes black. I have to laugh at the irony. What would I even say to her in my frantic state? The only person I can talk to about my problems is Pierce and I need to stay far, far away from him.

The moment he floats into the front of my mind, my pulse quickens. I attempt to shove his memory down and turn my car around, hoping that I drove here in a straight line so I can easily find my way home since my phone is dead and I have no natural sense of direction in the dark.

Frustration sets in when I'm still just as lost as I was thirty minutes ago. The light drizzle has turned into a roaring downpour. I take a sharp turn on a familiar-sounding road, then I lose control of the wheel. The violent sound of my tires screeching as I hydroplane in the darkness makes me scream. I'm spinning out of control when a warm hand grips around mine on the wheel.

"Oh my God!" I scream when I see Pierce beside me. He swiftly lifts my right leg. In the frantic moment, I didn't realize my foot was holding down the gas pedal. He leans over me and takes control of the wheel and in seconds we come to a screeching halt. While his foot is on the brake, he throws the car into park.

My breath is caught in my throat as I glare him down. "Have you been in the backseat this whole time?" I snap.

"Scar, let go of the wheel," he gently demands. My eyes pan to my white knuckles that grip the steering wheel, he pries my fingers from it.

"I wasn't in the car Scarlett, I just got here."

My eyes squint at his undisturbed demeanor. "How can you be so calm! How can you say that so calmly!?" I'm still screaming. He acts like this is normal for me, like people magically appear at my side daily.

A small chuckle escapes from his lips as he says, "I don't know Scar, I'm just comfortable around you." He shrugs and leans back in the seat.

"You tell me some divine secret that I'm never meant to find out and you think I'm not going to freak out?" I stare at him in disbelief.

He runs a large hand through his hair. "I didn't want to tell you." He holds his hands up in defense. "That's the last thing I wanted, but you need to know."

A beat of silence passes through the car, the only sounds are the patter of rain. "Switch seats with me," he demands.

"Absolutely not! You can't just show up here Pierce. I didn't ask you to save me, again." As the words come out, I realize how awful I sound. This is the third time Pierce has saved my life, and how do I thank him?

By yelling and throwing a fit. But to be fair, this is all insane.

My confusion about everything is messing with my judgment. I'm directing my anger towards him when I shouldn't be. But I'm scared, so scared of what's happening to me. I take a deep breath as I watch him open his mouth a few times trying to figure out the words to say.

For the first time, he raises his voice. "What did you want me to do? Collect your soul, Scar?" His jade eyes pierce through.

I lower my head, "Is that why you showed up? Was I about to... die?" My voice is a little weak as he places his warm hand on my arm.

"I could sense you were in danger, so I came. You shouldn't have been driving in this weather. What are you even doing out here?"

I shrug. "I was upset so I just kept driving, my phone died, and I ended up here." I gesture to the pitch-black nothingness in front of us. We haven't bothered to move from the middle of the road. No one is out this late anyway. "I thought you said you don't mess with people's destiny." That sounds very weird coming out of my mouth.

"This." He gestures between us. "This is not part of your destiny, Scar. I shouldn't fucking be here. I shouldn't have made you upset in the first place because I should never have told you about me. You only drove out here because you were upset with me." His perfect lips downturn.

I hop out of the car and he swiftly meets me at the driver's door. "Where do you *think* you're going?" He asks.

"Letting you drive," I say, walking past him. When I climb into the passenger seat, it takes him a moment to get back in. I hear a few choice words as he paces on the wet pavement but finally, he climbs in and cranks it up. We drive in silence for a while. My mind drifts off to the three times I've almost died in the past twenty-four hours.

My life was calm, peaceful even. Simple, until Pierce showed up. In truth, I shouldn't be comparing him with the negative. He's the only reason I'm alive right now. He has done nothing but be honest with me, which seems like a hard thing to do. I glance over at him and he's already looking at me, his face looks torn.

"I'm sorry," he breathes, breaking the silence. I want to reach over and touch his face, to soothe the lines of worry he has around his perfect eyes. But I stop myself. He's still a stranger, why do I feel the need to comfort him?

"I'm not used to any of this, Pierce," I say calmly. "I know this is your world but let me ease in, okay? I just don't understand any of this."

"This isn't something I do either. I never would have told you all of this if you weren't in danger. I feel a need, like I said before, to keep you safe, this is all new to me." I look to his eyes, trying to search for answers. From the outside, he looks like a regular guy. Well, I take that back. He looks like a divine God sent here to drive me insane. But, a human, nonetheless.

I stare out the foggy window, contemplating my life until flashing lights break me from my trance. I glance forward to a familiar sight as we come to a stop. I feel a sense of warmth when Liv's house comes into view.

When we stop, Pierce makes his way to my side to open the door. We stand by my car for a moment before I invite him inside, knowing Liv's parents are out of town and there are still things I need to know. I lead him through the front door and into the back yard. I don't want to wake Liv up if we talk inside, I'm afraid for her to hear of my new reality.

I sit as he stands, watching over me. His eyes roam the large, dark backyard. He seems guarded, not towards me but at the world outside of us. It makes me scared; I fidget uncomfortably in my chair.

"How will I ever be safe? He's going to keep coming until he gets me, Pierce, you said it yourself," I tell him. I wrap my hands around myself for comfort.

Pierce shoves his hands in the pockets of his dark jeans, balancing on his heels in a nervous manner. "Don't be mad, okay?" he pleads, refusing to continue until I nod. "I actually haven't let you out of my sight since the bar." My stomach does a flip at his confession.

I shake my head. "I don't understand. You've been around me since last night? Like at my mom's house? I know you left the medicine and all but how haven't I seen you?" A million questions run through my mind as I realize this is the fastest but slowest week of my life. How much has changed in the past couple of days? It's all a blur. I'm a little worried that he was in my house the very night I met him while I was unaware, my facial expression gives that away I'm sure.

He senses my fears. "No, Scarlett. I wasn't like watching you sleeping or anything," he lets out a small laugh, "I don't have to be next to you to feel your mood. I can sense when you're scared, or happy. Really any emotion you have I can pick up on. I say I haven't taken my eyes off of you but in truth, I haven't broken the bond between us since that night." I jumble his words around and once again, I am clueless.

"The bond?" I question.

He sits down next to me. "When I take someone's soul, I get tethered to them for a few moments as I bring them to the... Crossroads we will call it. I know when they're scared or happy and at peace. It's just something I do." He shrugs. "But, with you, I didn't want to break that bond since you may still be in danger. It's a good thing I didn't, considering you almost got yourself killed tonight." His glare makes me bite my lip.

"So, you've been stalking me?"

His eyes roll, "I was going to keep my distance Scar, but I can sense the energy shifting around you. Something dark is coming, I can feel it..." he looks at me with thoughtful eyes, "but I won't let a damn thing happen to you." There's so much conviction behind his voice that my hands quit trembling.

Nine

The bond?

Taking a deep breath, I try to muster up questions to ask him, and although I have about a trillion of them, I'm drawing a blank. The one thing that keeps running through my mind is, why me? I'm nothing special.

Pierce watches me with a grim expression, "Now there's been two attempts. I need to practice sorting through and understanding your emotions while we're bonded. I wish he would have just left you alone but he's escalated, that's why I needed to talk to you. You needed to be aware. I'm just thankful we have the bond now and I hope you don't want to break it anytime soon, it will make my life a lot easier."

I look to my feet. "So, is that why I feel like you know how I'm feeling all the time? Like when I'm upset about something, you'll know?"

He nods. "Yes, I know when your mood shifts. That's why I showed up in the bathroom. That one wasn't an instinct of you dying." He looks to his hands. "I could feel your fear in my veins, it seeped through me and led me to you."

"Oh."

He leans in closer to me. "I can also sense your emotions when I'm close to you, you react to me." A sly smile rises on his face and I blush a deep crimson. He brings his thumb to my cheek. "I'll keep you safe, Scar." He promises. The sweet moment is interrupted by worry for the people I love.

"What about my mom and Liv? You can't be a million places at once and you shouldn't have to be!" I cry, feeling guilty for how much I need him to protect me. I don't like to feel helpless; I like helping people. I don't want to be taken care of; I appreciate the sentiment, but this is out of my control completely. I couldn't protect myself or my family even if I wanted to.

My breathing becomes uncontrolled, ragged. Ever since my father's passing, panic attacks have plagued my body. Pierce leans in close, placing both of his hands on my face, "I need you to breathe, Scar." He gently demands, I watch his movements as he takes in deep breaths. Following his motions, I begin to slightly calm.

He sees that I'm okay and he leans back in his

seat, "I've checked on your mom and Liv multiple times tonight." He admits and it makes me happy. I know I should be freaking out but knowing my best friend and mother are safe sends much-needed warmth through my rigid bones.

"Your mom invited that guy over tonight," he says, trying to change the serious subject I assume.

It weirds me out that he would know that, but I try to ignore it. "Good! I'm happy for her, she needs someone in her life. She hasn't dated since my dad..." I trail off but regain composure. "I just hope he's a good guy," I say with a small shrug.

"Oh, he is," Pierce states.

I tilt my head. "Did you meet him?" I ask.

"No, no... I think I mentioned some of what I can do earlier. But I can tell good from the bad. Sorry, I know you get freaked out by me. I honestly forget that you don't know everything about this world." His eyes continue to dart around the backyard.

"No, it's okay," I lie, but I'm insanely curious about all the secrets there are to know about Pierce.

He places his warm hand on my knee. "Look Scar, I know you don't know me. You have no reason to trust me. I have thrown your world upside down by acting like this is all normal. But I need you to listen to me, okay?" When I nod, he takes in a quick breath. "I know Zack invited you to that party tomorrow... I heard him earlier when he walked back to his friends, saying that it was cool you were busy tonight since he's pretty sure you're going tomorrow." He speaks slowly and I wonder how he heard them when we were so far away, but I let it go. "Can you please not go?" he asks with hope brimming in his eyes.

I try to decipher why he's asking this of me, "Your reason?"

"Well, simply... I don't trust him, and you can't be around bad people right now," he deadpans.

"Is that why you were so rude to him? You think he's bad?" I laugh hysterically. "Zack's so kind to me. He would never hurt me, Pierce. You don't know him," I say, defending my friend.

"First off, I wasn't rude to him. Second, he's just trying to get you in bed." Pierce stands, his fist clenched.

My jaw drops to the floor. What a bold thing to say! I mean why would he care, he's just doing what he thinks is right by saving someone who is 'innocent' as he says, so why would it matter if Zack likes me. Not that I plan on being with Zack, but still it hardly seems like it's his place to say that.

"Why do you care who likes me?" I question.

Pierce casually leans back on the soft, black patio cushion with his arms crossed. "Umm, I... Look Scarlett just stay away from him, he's bad news."

"Are you jealous or something?" I laugh at the thought and he stiffens.

"What? No, of course not. I could never... we could never-" I lift my hand to cut him off before he can create any more damage. He stands up swiftly, pacing in front of me.

I tilt my head, watching him intently. "So what

was this 'date' then?" I use finger quotes, "showing up at my job, winning me a bear, being so kind to me? We could never, apparently, so why waste your time?"

He bites his lip, looking away from me. I hate myself for admiring the way his jaw accentuates when he's trying to figure out what to say. "Scarlett, I'm no good. I-"

"You saved me again tonight and I'm going to assume you're just paranoid, so I'm going to go to sleep, and you do whatever it is you do." I gesture around him and turn on my heels.

He grabs me at my waist, tugging me toward him, against him. "I wasn't asking Scarlett, you can't go to that party." His voice is deep and I gulp, trying to collect my confidence.

I pull myself from him and walk in the house with an attitude. He calls my name, but I keep walking and simply say, "Goodnight, Pierce."

"If you need me, just say my name Scar."

I crawl in Liv's bed gently as not to wake her and my thoughts go towards Pierce. If I wasn't scared, I would sleep in the guest room, but I would rather be with Liv tonight. How dare he question Zack's motives.

I know Zack likes me, but he would never put me in any sort of harm. Not to mention the fact that Pierce said we could never... whatever that means, I'm assuming he isn't into me. Which is fine, he is the Angel of Death for crying out loud.

I'm sure it's just the rush of the past couple days but I feel so connected to Pierce. I laugh to myself. My anger is quickly taken away as I think of the way he saved me, again. I drift off to sleep with a smile. I'm really beginning to go through some major mood swings.

Ten

Fix me up?

My eyes shoot open, and I'm met with a blinding darkness that seems to creep around every crevice of the room. I attempt to adjust my vision to the lack of light while I lay on the bed, but terror takes over when a source of pressure lays on my neck and I begin gasping desperately for air. I reach my hands out to claw in front of me, but I catch nothing.

The clouds take a break outside the window, allowing the moon to cast a white shadow on the large silhouette in front of me. It's impossible to breathe. As my vision adjust to the faint moonlight and lack of oxygen, I see my attacker with his large hands wrapped tightly around my throat. It's Pierce.

I scratch and claw at him, but he won't stop. I can't seem to hit him hard enough. I look towards the doorway hoping someone, anyone will come in to save me. Through my fluttering eyes, relief floods through me as my hero comes through the door. Then, confusion fogs my sleepy daze as the moon casts light on another Pierce quickly walking towards me. Dressed in all black and looking at me with frantic eyes, he grabs himself off of me in one quick motion.

I gasp as I shoot up from the bed. Warm light fills the room. I'm soaked in sweat, breathing heavily as I take in my surroundings. I'm in Liv's room still, and I'm completely alone. I reach my hand up to my neck, afraid that it's sore from the violent contact, but I feel nothing.

It was just a dream, I say to comfort myself. I feel like my subconscious is telling me that Pierce is both pulling me under while simultaneously saving me. The irony of him coming in to rescue me from himself, makes me dizzy. I throw myself back on the soft bed and stare at the ceiling fan as it spins around.

From the corner of my vision, a tall figure emerges. My frightened eyes dart over and see a scared-looking Pierce. Standing in the doorway and running his fingers through his thick hair with a haunted expression set on his face. The dream isn't over.

He makes his way towards me and I flinch when he extends his hand to me. "No!" I scream, trying to kick him away when he sits on the edge of the bed.

"Scar? It's okay. It was a dream. I heard you

screaming, and I thought something was wrong," he breathes out a long breath of relief. I take in his rough edges and soft eyes as I realize I am in fact, awake.

A sound between a laugh and a cry escapes my lips, "Something *is* wrong Pierce! Look at me, look at what this is doing to me." Tears soak my face as I try to remember when they started flowing.

His jade eyes dart around my body in a frantic pattern and worry lines form between his black brows when he speaks. "I'm sorry, I didn't mean to scare you. Why did you flinch when I tried to touch you?" He reaches for me again, this time I don't move, and he gently holds my arm.

"I... I had a dream, you... you tried to kill me." My voice is at a whisper, but I know he hears me as he jumps back, taking his warm hand off of my arm. The loss of contact makes me grow cold.

"I.. Scar," he looks down, "I would never... all I want is your-" The piercing ring from my phone cuts him off. Liv must have plugged it in when she got up since she isn't in here with me. I reach over and see who's calling.

I sigh. "It's my mom, I'll see you downstairs," I say dryly as I look at his worried expression. I soften my voice as much as I can, "Really, I'm just shaken up from the dream. I'll be fine in a few minutes." I muster up a smile to hide my lie. He reluctantly heads for the door, sneaking a few quick glances back at me as he leaves.

I let the call go to voicemail so I can take a few minutes to collect myself, but no matter of time will calm my mind. I scroll down to her contact in my phone. She picks up on the second ring, "Hey, Mom," I say, my voice brittle.

"Hey Honey, how did your first day go?" she asks, and I laugh involuntarily.

It went great! After work, I walked around with Pierce. I know you don't know him, but there's so much you don't know... Another demon tried to steal my soul, but don't worry. Luckily, the Angel of Death saved me, again. He's pretty cute by the way. I would have assumed a large black cloak and a skull face; the myths were way, way off! I laugh at how crazy I sound and feel.

"It was great!" I lie enthusiastically.

"That's wonderful dear. You had me worried last night. Why didn't you pick up the phone? I thought you were coming home?"

I don't know what Liv said we did last night so I keep it simple. "I came to hang out with her and fell asleep watching a movie. I didn't realize my phone was on silent, I'm sorry," I say as innocently as I can.

"That's okay, just try and call me next time. Look, I know this is sudden, but I figured since Liv's parents are in town that you could stay there this weekend?" She sounds hopeful.

"Yeah, of course. Going somewhere?" I ask, and she snickers a little.

There's a beat of silence. "Brian, he's taking me away for the weekend," she says. They're moving too quickly for my liking, but Pierce said he's a good man, so I trust that. Still, it stings a little from the loss of my father. He should be the one taking her off for a weekend trip. I quickly swallow those feelings down. She deserves happiness more than anyone I know, and dad would want that for her.

"That sounds like a lot of fun, Mom, I hope you have a blast!" I say, hoping I sound sincere.

I can hear the way she's nervously tapping her nails on something. "I hope this isn't weird for you, Scarlett. I would have talked to you in person, but you haven't come home." Her voice is laced with sadness but it's obvious she's been enjoying the free time.

I shake my head, although she can't see me. "I promise it's okay, enjoy your trip! I would like to meet him when he gets back," I request and mean it. I need to see if he's worthy of my amazing mother.

"That would be nice Scarlett, but I want to wait a bit longer before I introduce you to him. It's just so… new. I'll be home on Monday. Call me if you need me, dear, I love you!" she sings.

I hang on to her words, not knowing what my future holds anymore. "I love you too, Mom." I tell her, a single tear falling down my cheek.

I lazily stumble out of bed and hop in the shower. Thoughts of Pierce's words last night run through my head. 'I've been watching you since the first night.' It sends chills down my spine. I slowly reach up to my throat to make sure my neck isn't sore, again.

I haven't once been afraid of the divine being that's been rescuing me before, so why should I be now? I say divine, but I'm not sure if that's the right word.

He looks angelic, but he's always so serious. The harsh edges he creates when he creases his brows make him tougher looking than the angels I imagined in my head growing up. I try to not think about what he may have done to be what he is now. He said he hasn't had human feelings in a long time, so was he once like me?

The harsh metal from Liv's shower curtain racking across the bar makes my heart drop. "Are we going to that party tonight?" Liv asks excitedly as she barges into the bathroom catching me off guard and halting my endless thoughts. I let out a scream, she has no idea how unwelcome surprises are in my life right now.

"Umm, I'm not sure," I say, lathering shampoo into my long locks.

She laughs at my frightened expression. "Funny, we're leaving at eight," she states, closing the curtains back but staying in the bathroom to dab on some makeup.

After a brief moment of thought, I decide that Zack and his friends are harmless, and it makes me mad that Pierce thinks the weird way he can read people tells me what I need to know about a guy I have known my whole life.

I never go to parties; I've been crammed into books for four years and I need a night off. I barely know him. He can't just barge into my life and tell me what to do. Besides, I need a distraction.

"Okay, yes!" My voice is more excited than I feel. "I have to go run some errands, so I'll meet you back here at eight?" I ask, hoping she doesn't want to ride along. I need some time for myself.

"Sounds good!" She squeals. After a pop of her lips from some gloss, she exits with a little pep in her step. I continue to let the hot water cascade over me until it runs cold.

The day goes by quickly and I think about where Pierce may be multiple times throughout it. I figured he would have come back upstairs at some point. Where did he even go earlier? Truthfully, I don't need him to come around right now. He doesn't trust Zack for some reason, and I don't dare call his name, in fear that he will show up and ruin my night before it's even begun.

The sun has fully set by the time I arrive back at Liv's place. I did a little shopping but mostly I just drove around aimlessly.

I walk into her room to find her sitting cross-legged in front of a mirror, mouth open as she places mascara on her already thick lashes.

She grins when she sees me. "Hey! Get ready!" she cheers.

"On it!" I smile, liking this feeling of normalcy. I head over to her massive closet and dig through her collection. Since I'm already breaking the rules, I feel a bit of rebellion creep up into me as I grab a scarlet red dress that makes me blush as I touch its thin fabric and one too many straps.

I stand in front of a full-length mirror and place

the dress front of me, curious if I could pull it off. I hear a squeal and look to my reflection to see Liv making her way to me with a bright smile on her face. "Look at you! You've been an adult for two days and you're already wanting to dress sexier!" She claps her hands and looks so happy that I ignore her remark.

I think about putting it back but decide that I want to feel good about myself tonight. I want to feel sexy; I have been in danger lately. My life has been on the edge and I need to escape from my normal routine. Pretend to be someone else.

I turn back at her and smile. "Fix me up?" I ask and she squeals again.

One hour and a bottle of hairspray later, I barely recognize myself. My long brown hair is curled into big waves, my eyes are dark with a smoky tint around them. Red lipstick to match my fiery red dress.

I begin to wonder if it may be too much. "I'm not sure Liv," I say as I questionably stare back at myself.

She holds her finger up. "No, no, no. You look HOT!" she exclaims. "Besides, we have to get going. Zack will be here any minute!" She jumps up and her eyes trail across my face, checking that it's perfect. She nods her head triumphantly and grabs her purse.

I glare around the room looking for my flats when Liv sticks a pair of black stiletto heels in my face. I shake my head, and she glares me down.

Her tilted head and narrowed eyes tell me she's right. I have a whole new look tonight and a pair of flats would completely ruin that. I place them on my feet and hook the delicate straps around my ankles.

A car horn blares from outside and I quickly but carefully make my way down the stairs in my heels. As I'm walking to Zack's Jeep, I spot something in the corner of my eye. I look back but nothing is there, I must be seeing things.

Zack leans against his car and whistles at us when we come into view. It makes me laugh; I pull my dress down a little as he wraps me in a tight hug, momentarily lifting me into the air.

"Scarlett, you look…" he pauses, taking a moment to rake his eyes up and down my figure after he sets me down. "perfect." he decides. The gesture makes me blush and I quickly become uncomfortable as I shift in my too-tall heels.

I allow the nerves to flow through me, and then I suck it up. I've almost died three times, I truly do need to live a little more. Pierce will never find out.

I laugh when I realize he actually will. But he won't be mad when he sees no harm has come to me or Liv.

Zack slings his arm around me as we walk into his house. His usual immaculate home is dotted with kegs, lights, and dancing bodies with a trail of red cups littering the ground. His mom would kill him if she saw this. Loud music blares through the speakers as we get handed three drinks. I look over to Liv as she sets her cup on the counter, her eyes trained in front of her. She's zoned out, besides not taking her iron pills, we both haven't eaten anything.

I walk up to her and whisper in her ear, "Take your pills."

She pops two in her mouth and after about twenty minutes she is right as rain. "Time to drink!" she cheers.

I watch as Zack rummages through his pantry for snacks, "Hey, Zack do you have any canned beer?" I ask with a smile.

His brows lift. "There's a keg at the front, didn't someone hand you one?" he asks, looking at my empty hands.

I nod. "Yeah, but I don't drink really, so I would prefer a cold can. If you have any? It'll just make it easier for me to get it down." I tell him.

Liv raises her hand. "Make it two if you have them!" I smile at her. We learned our lesson the other night. Even if I trust Zack, you truly never know who could be at this party. The thought makes my chest tighten a little, but I swallow the uneasy feeling back down and ignore it. I need to prove a point to Pierce that he can't control everything, even if his intentions are good. Okay, I need to stop thinking of him, he's clouding my every thought.

Zack brings us two closed cans with a grin and makes his way to a nearby keg stand. Liv smiles at me, taking a swig of the cold beer. "I'm glad to see you loosening up Scar, it's a nice change," she says.

"I'm tired of being boring," I admit with a shrug.

She shakes her head, placing a gentle hand on my arm. "You're not boring; you never have been. I only push you to do different things because I know how much fun you can have. But I swear I will never ask you to go anywhere you don't want to anymore. Are you comfortable here?" she asks, checking on me.

"Liv, you act like you weren't put through the same thing as me at the club. Are you comfortable?" I question.

"I'm more exposed to this world than you, Scar, but this is a nice way to celebrate things with you. In Zack's house where we're safe." she smiles and gestures towards the table where they're playing beer pong.

As I walk with her, I laugh at myself about her comment of 'this world'. If only she knew the world I have been exposed to, she would see how small we all are.

Zack grabs my waist, pulling me to him. "Hey Cutie, you're my partner," he winks. I can feel his weight leaning on me a bit from the sluggish effects of the keg stands he was doing moments ago, to make up for lost time being sober from picking us up.

I watch as they rack the red cups into a pyramid shape and pour warm keg beer into them. "I've never played so I can't promise we won't lose," I tell Zack with a nervous tone, not wanting to embarrass myself in front of everyone. I shrug out of his grip a little, he is a bit handsy, I've just never paid much attention before.

Once the people at the table have finished their game Zack brings his fingers to his lips, letting out a high-pitched whistle to gather everyone's attention. "Any takers?" he challenges with a boyish, all-American grin. With his slurred speech, I begin to wonder if he did drink before he picked us up.

"I'd love to play." A deep, enticing voice sounds to my right. My eyes search for the familiar tone and I see Pierce leaned up against a wall. He's dressed in all black and looking devilishly handsome, with his smoldering gaze trained on me.

Eleven

Goodnight, Scar

"What are you doing here?" Zack slurs as he pulls me a little closer to him. I examine Pierce's stoic expression; he tenses up a bit and steps forward. His sharp gaze pans to me, and he softens.

A small blond girl comes stumbling out of the kitchen. "I invited him!" She shouts, grabbing onto Pierce's arm. Oh, he must have not known that this was Zack's party. I love that he can go wherever he wants, but I'm supposed to lock myself inside like a prisoner.

I can't help but glare at the drunken girl that's hanging on him. Jealousy seeping into me, I try to compose my face. I hope that I'm doing an okay job.

Pierce and his new girl walk over to the table. She's so drunk she can barely stand. She leans on Pierce, but he pays her no attention which makes me laugh a little. She props herself up on the table.

"I don't think you can play," I say to her with my arms crossed. A little surprised by my tone. Why am I being so rude to someone I don't know?

"I can" -hiccup- "I can play." Her high-pitched voice is cut off when her hand quickly flies to her mouth, her porcelain skin turns a pale green.

"I think your girlfriend is about to throw up, Pierce." I state, shooting daggers at him.

He shakes his head, shrugging. "What? No, I just met her tonight," he says as she runs off to the bathroom, alone.

"Liv, let's get started. You can be on his team," Zack suggests, his voice is thick with irritation as he gestures towards an equally angry Pierce.

Zack arranges the cups on the sticky black tabletop. It's coated in a thin layer of beer and I know this is not sanitary. I look around the room for a towel before giving up and not wanting to look like an idiot trying to clean a table that's bound to get dirty again in a few minutes.

The game begins quickly, and no one is talking, I'm thankful for the loud music. I watch as Zack makes a cup and Pierce downs it. They keep doing this back and forth like it's a competition. I grab the ball from Zack's hand and try to make the middle cup, but miss. Zack is quick to replace my empty cans with new ones as I drink them faster than I should but the thick tension in this small living room is making me anxious. I see Pierce eying him disapprovingly as he pops the cold can open for me and I take a long sip.

We're down to the last cup when the annoying drunk girl finds her way back to Pierce's side. He rolls his eyes which makes me happy but irritated. Why keep the charade going? Just tell her to leave.

I decide to annoy him; I have more confidence to deal with Pierce when I'm buzzed. I grab Zack and twirl his hair a bit as I smile at him. Zack swiftly puts his hands around my waist pulling me closer. I know this isn't very nice of me to do to him, but I don't care right now. I look over and see Liv's jaw drop a bit. Pierce has a deep scowl on his face as he takes two long strides and gently grabs me on the arm.

"Let's go," he demands.

"Hey man, chill. This is my house. You can go." Zack gestures to the door.

A challenging laugh escapes Pierce's lips as he looks from Zack then to me. "Scar, do you really want to do this now?" he asks.

I'm about to yell at him, but when I think about it for a minute, I shake my head. This is definitely not what I want to do. Pierce could destroy him with his pinky, I suspect. Besides, I have a burning desire to spend time with him. If he leaves, I don't know when I'll see him again. This alcohol is making me think funny things.

"Uhm, Zack. I'm gonna head out," I say quietly as I turn towards the door.

"Scarlett, you don't have to go with him. You can stay the night with me," he suggests as he grabs the arm Pierce isn't holding, I feel like I'm in a ridiculous match of tug-of-war.

Pierce stiffens at my side. "Thanks, but I think I've had a few too many beers," I admit as I try to pull my arm from him. Zack reluctantly drops my arm when a low growl escapes from Pierce's chest. I look over at Liv who is still staring in shock.

"Want to come?" I nod my head towards the door and see a smile creep on her face.

"No. You two can go back to my place though." She winks as she throws me her keys. I feel a deep blush rising in my cheeks, I glance over to wave goodbye to Zack and he looks away with a scowl. I feel guilty for toying with him, but Pierce drives me insane.

Of course, Pierce's grin stretches all the way up to his perfect emerald eyes as he wraps his arm around my waist and leads me outside. I'm thankful for his strength as I begin to stumble on my feet, I drank too much.

We exit the house and he leads us towards the yard instead of the driveway. "Where's your car?" I ask curiously.

A small laugh escapes him. "Why would I need one?"

Nerves rake through me. "You're not thinking of... teleporting us out of here, right?" I whisper. He bends over in laughter. It's cute seeing such a serious guy laugh like a kid.

"Teleport? Scar, you're cute," he brings up his

hand to brush a rogue strip of hair from my face. "Just trust me." He holds his hand out and I cross my arms, glaring at him with a scrunched face.

"Who was that girl?" I ask with irritation thick in my voice.

He chuckles a little. "Are you jealous?" He leans his head down as he takes one long step towards me.

"No," I lie.

"I came here for you. I knew I needed to get inside and have an alibi, so the first drunk girl I saw I talked to. Are you sure you aren't jealous?" he asks again, and I shake my head, not wanting to admit it.

He begins slowly walking back towards the loud house. "I guess I can go find her again." I yank his large arm back and a glimmer of humor flakes in his emerald eyes. "I was just kidding," he assures me, a hint of a smile left on his full lips.

He holds my hand again and once we are out of view, he opens his arms wide. I gravitate towards his embrace and he wraps me in a tight hug. He looks around one good time and checks to make sure no one is around, then I squeeze my eyes shut against his broad chest.

The distant music is gone, and I inhale the familiar scent of Liv's house, vanilla and cedar. I look up and we're standing in her living room, it's quiet besides the soft winds rustling the large trees outside the windows. The room is dimly lit by the warm lights of the lamp.

"I don't think I can ever get used to that," I gulp. When I look up at Pierce I drink in his hungry expression. I nervously laugh as he gently backs me into a wall. Eying me up and down. I shiver as I feel his hot breath down my neck. He's standing so close.

"What were you thinking?" His voice is deep, but his eyes are filled with the familiar concern he has when he looks at me.

"I.. just wanted to have fun." I say quietly, looking up through batted lashes. My breathing quickens from the feel of our bodies being so close.

"I wasn't going to follow you tonight; I knew if you needed me, I would sense it. But when I saw you in that dress." With a featherlight touch, his fingertips trail the thin material of my dress. I turn my face down to blanket my flushed cheeks with my hair. His fingers wrap around my chin, and he lifts my line of sight to his. "And then the way he hugged you... I knew I couldn't let you be around all of those *boys* like that." He tries to hide his anger under a half-smirk.

"I thought you were just around to protect me, Pierce? Why are you acting like a boyfriend?" My voice is demanding, I need to know how he feels, him acting this way is confusing me. "You told me last night that you could never... Well, I'm not sure what you were trying to say but I get the point that you're not interested in me like that." My voice is small, hiding my embarrassment.

He throws his head back in a deep laugh, then he cranes his neck down, lowering it so when he speaks his warm breath tingles against my neck. "Is that what you want Scarlett? The Angel of Death interested in you?" he inquires in a mocking tone.

I shrug. "You seem human enough to me."

"I'm a monster! I've done horrible things. I, of course, would never hurt you. But that doesn't change what I am," he scoffs, his eyes growing dark.

I bring my palm to his clenched jaw. "From the second you saw me, you've done nothing but keep me safe. You are a good person."

"Person?" he sneers.

"Tell me what you want to say, please Pierce," I beg.

"Scar, I can't..." He's hesitant as he steps away from me. I shiver when a wave of cool air rolls over me from his absence.

I step towards him. "You can't what?"

He bows his head, biting his bottom lip. "I can't see you with him, I... I know it's not natural but I'm too selfish. I want you to myself," he demands as he brushes his fingers against my cheek. My body is on fire. I've never felt this way, maybe it's the alcohol?

He brings his face inches from mine and I have to look nearly straight up to meet his striking gaze. "Do you feel the same way?" he asks as his emerald eyes bore into mine. I'm thankful they've softened.

I do, I do. But I can't seem to make the words come out, so I nod slowly.

"No, I need to hear it," he gently orders.

"I feel something Pierce, I don't know wh-" He cuts me off when his lips crash into mine.

We get lost in each other, melting together as he easily lifts me up, wrapping my legs around his tone back.

Our mouths are still intertwined as he walks to the couch, he gently lowers me against the soft padding.

It feels natural, the way we kiss. The way his tongue dives with mine, dancing together in a heated passionate waltz. When I'm in this position with him hovering above me, I realize how massive he is. He can barely fit on this couch and it's not a small one.

His hands greedily wander around my body and I can't help the small gasp of breath that escapes my swollen lips from his firm, confident grip.

He trails kisses from my jawline down to my neck. I muster up the courage to sink my hands under his shirt, but when I curl my fingers around the fabric to lift it off he pulls away.

He plants a small kiss on my forehead. "You're drunk, Scar," he states.

"I'm sober now!" I lie, ignoring the pleading tone of my voice begging for him to come back.

He lets out a chuckle. "Right." He stands, extending his hand to me. I place mine in his and he securely wraps his fingers around mine, leading me to the guest room.

"Get in," he insists, gesturing to the large, four poster bed against the back wall. My heart rate picks up, having never slept with a guy before but I already know with Pierce, I would feel so safe. I lift the thick white comforter back and slide into the soft bedding. I look up to him as he stands next to the bed. His fingers curl over the blanket and he pulls it up, covering me.

"Goodnight, Scar." His velvety voice drapes over

me as he turns to leave.

"Wait, please stay," I beg. He stops, turning towards me with and adorable grin on his face.

He climbs in beside me and pulls me close to his hard chest. I breathe in his intoxicating scent, my eyes close involuntarily as I struggle to keep them open. The alcohol coursing through me is making my lack of sleep these past few days obvious, but I don't want to go to sleep yet. I place my head on his chest, unable to hold it up any longer. I finally close my eyes as his warmth envelops me.

"I know I act tough and think I don't need any help, but I need you, Pierce," I mumble as I drift off to sleep. I feel a smile creep upon his face as he snuggles against my neck.

Twelve

Road Trip

My eyes flutter open and a thin layer of sweat lays on my face. I bring my hand to my forehead. It's hot, too hot in here. I feel a heavy arm draped over me. Pierce.

I look over and study his face, sleep taking away the hard edges, and making him look softer, younger. I almost forget *who* he is, *what* he is as he takes deep breaths, his chest rising and lowering naturally. When I realize the blazing heat is coming from his tan skin, I worry less about the suffocating warmth and focus on the comfortable way his arm feels around me.

My sleepy gaze pans to the window, soft morning light cascades over the room. I'm curious to know why he doesn't look like what I think the Angel of Death *should* look like, I shiver at the thought.

"What are you thinking about?" His deep tone breaks me out of my thoughts, his voice heavy with sleep.

I glance over and see his head still lying on the pillow. Bright green eyes stare up at me through thick lashes. Perfection.

I take in a deep breath. "Can I ask some… questions about you?" I ask.

His fingers interlace with mine. "Go ahead, just don't freak out and run away again." He laughs but I collect a hint of truth to his words.

My mind flows freely, as do the questions as they fly from my lips. "How are you sleeping? Like, how do you sleep? Aren't you supposed to be a terrifying be-" He cuts me off with a gentle finger to my lips.

He sits up, ruffling his thick black hair with his large hands. "Woah, Scar. Don't overwhelm yourself. Take it easy. We have all day," he teases, stretching his long arms above his head. "I still have a human body, I'm just a little stronger than your normal man and with a few fun abilities up my sleeve," his cocky grin makes me laugh.

"So why don't you wear a cloak and look evil?" I say quietly, tapping my free hand nervously against my leg. He laughs again and I gently push his arm. "Don't laugh at me! I'm being serious."

"I know, I know. It's just, wow Hollywood really does a number on you humans." The way he casually says 'humans' draws me back a bit.

"You just said you have a human body?" I question.

"It's different. I don't know how to explain it; I don't see myself as human. It's been too long..." He trails off and a million more questions pop into my head.

I try to control my frantic insides, but he knows when I'm truly calm thanks to this 'connection' thing between us.

He looks to the window. "Can I show you something?" he asks, and I nod. "Get dressed, wear something for warm weather." He gets out of bed, wearing a pair of basketball shorts that he didn't have with him last night. The black T-shirt I remember, but I wonder when he had time to get the shorts.

I ponder about clothes for a minute before I realize there are much more pressing questions I need to think about. Like where he wants to go and why he would think I would dress for cold weather in summer?

"Of course, I'm going to wear something for warm weather, it's summer," I state. Even the simplest of requests he makes sound so confusing to me.

I hop out of bed and make my way to Liv's room to grab some clothes. She must have stayed at Zack's. I need to text him and apologize for my quick departure last night; I'll do that later. Assuming we're going to the beach or a park I decide on one of Liv's summer dresses. I pick a cute flowy white one.

I do a quick side braid so my unruly hair stays out of my face, I decide to not wear any makeup since the heat will melt it off. With a shrug, I exit the bathroom and find Pierce leaning against the doorway of the room, he's now in a thin white t-shirt. I can see black ink on his skin underneath it. I begin to wonder how he pulls clothes from thin air, but I stop myself.

His eyes are focused on the bruise that was left from my attacker; he sighs. "Grab a swimsuit," he says.

"See, no need for confusion. You could have just said we were going down to the beach." I tease and he gives me a funny look.

I walk back in the bathroom and throw a simple white bikini of Liv's on underneath my dress and head back into her room. As we're making our way down the steps I head towards the fridge and grab some cold pizza out, I gesture towards Pierce, but he politely declines.

After I finish my slice, he grabs a beach bag that's near the kitchen and he throws two towels that Liv and I used yesterday back into it. He's in front of the fridge now; opening the doors and throwing a few bottles of water in the bag before he walks over to me and embraces me in a warm hug.

I nuzzle into his chest and take in his scent. A hot feeling on my back disrupts me from this sweet moment. The sound of waves tells me we're no longer in the kitchen. I take a quick peek around. I first look at my feet and see weathered wood.

As I glance farther to my left, bright colored fish swim underneath us about a foot down from what I assume is a dock. I sense his eyes on me, taking in my expression as I take in the site around me with a dropped jaw. Beautiful clear waters. We're standing on a narrow dock that's stretching far out into the water. We are not anywhere near North Carolina.

I want to be mad at him for tricking me, but I'm in shock. I blush from the way he looks at me when I take his hand. I'm facing the beach, with the tide rolling in against the sand. Palm trees dot the area, and I see no people around. We're about twenty feet from the start of the dock and I desperately want to turn around to see the wide ocean.

Curiosity takes hold and when I turn, Pierce grabs me from behind and props his head on mine. Breathlessly, I take in the gorgeous site of sparkling, clear waters and monstrous green mountains that are in the distance. We must be on an island or something, somewhere very tropical.

"What... where are we?" I question and he holds me tighter.

"Do you like it?" he asks in a curious tone.

As I turn back to face him, I'm sure he can see in my expression of just how much I like it.

A perfect smile spreads up his face, "We're on a small island off the coast of Brazil." An unusual sound comes from me as I jump, suddenly worried that I don't have a passport, but what does that matter? I giggle at myself.

"I've never seen anything like this!" I have to pick my jaw up from the dock. "I've never even been outside of North Carolina," I admit. "Pierce, this is insane! It is so beautiful!" I squeal as I lean down to slip out of my flip flops. I hold onto him for support as my toes dip into the warm water.

He laughs as I quickly pull away from him and

head towards the end of the dock. I wrap my fingers around the bottom of the dress and pull it over my head.

When I glance back at him, he's casually leaned up against one of the wooden posts. Defined muscles bulge through his white shirt, and the sun casts a glimmering golden against his tan skin.

I gesture for him to come to me. He drops his pants and it startles me for a second until I realize he's wearing a black swimsuit underneath; He slips his shirt over his head and throws it on the dock as he makes his way to me.

The warm sun feels so good against my skin, and Pierce's body is glistening from the sweat that's trickling down his chest. I reach out to touch a tattoo he has on his stomach. It's different from the one on his arm, old-style letters spell words from a language I can't decipher. I trace my fingers over the foreign words, but he jerks back slightly, and I put my hand down in an instant.

He sighs as he grabs my hand and guides it back over the tattoo slowly. "I'm sorry. I'm just not used to any of this. I know you're adjusting too, but you have to be patient with me," his smooth tone matches the rhythm of the calm waves.

I haven't thought about that before. He always seems so collected, so sure of himself but I don't know how close he is to any... humans.

As I graze my hand over the ink on his skin his fingers curl under my chin to direct my attention to his face.

"I feel like this is a dream." I admit.

He caresses my face gently. "Me too, but I can assure you, it's all real. You aren't going crazy, okay?" He assures me, knowing what I'm thinking.

It's too hot, from the blazing heat and his touch. I know this will be a wasted effort because of his size but I latch on to him and push with all my might towards the edge of the dock.

With a loud chuckle and one swift movement, my feet are no longer on the dock but dangling in the air as he slings me over his shoulder and jumps off the weathered wood.

A crisp splash is followed by the clear waters cascading around our bodies as we fall in together, a tangled confusing mess. Which describes our relationship, or whatever this is. Normally this would be too fast for my liking but with Pierce, it can't go fast enough.

How long will he be in my life? Will his interest in me go away when he disconnects? I give the thoughts to the water and let them roll away with the waves as he lifts me high above the water with his strong arms. A deep laugh escaping his perfect lips.

I shake my head, getting the water out of my face.

"Did you seriously try and push me in?" He laughs, setting me back down into the warm tropical waters.

I tread the surface, we're way too far out for me to stand. "Come here," he tells me, opening his arms.

I close the small distance between us and wrap my legs around his waist. His hands rest on the backs of my thighs, holding me up.

He nudges his head to the right. "See that mountain?" he asks. I look to the colossal green mountain that's set in the distance; waves violently crash against the jagged rocks at the bottom. I wonder what it would be like to sit at the top of something so beautiful. "It's one of my favorite places." He tells me, nuzzling his face into my neck.

"I'd like to go one day." I tell him and he nods, promising me. As we stare into each other's eyes, endless questions that I want, no need to ask this man, roam through my mind. His smoldering gaze makes my cheeks flush, and I look past him to the open sea. He lets go of my left thigh but keeps a firm grip on the right to hold me steady. With his free hand, he lifts my chin to pull me back into his magnetic gaze.

"Look at me, Scar," he gently orders. "You're the most beautiful girl I have ever seen. I adore it when you blush, you never have to look away from me." he says sweetly, almost in a whisper. Like he didn't want anyone to hear his words. Like they were only for me and the calm waters around us. Even though there is no one around, as far as I can see.

I can't muster the words to express my feelings, so unlike the peaceful waves that lap upon the shore I crash into him desperately. His hands grip me tighter as the water cascades around our tangled bodies.

His full lips gently cover mine as his tongue searches my mouth. Electricity shoots through me as I get lost in him. His hands grip me as he molds my body to his. It's riveting.

I still feel his lips against mine, but we're no longer kissing. I touch my lips as he hesitantly pulls away from me.

The electric tension is still thick between us but I'm in perfect harmony as he stares into my eyes while I bob up and down with the soft waves as he holds me.

His breathing is ragged, his chest rising rapidly. "Why did you stop?" I question through my embarrassment.

He inhales a deep breath. "I had to. I wouldn't be able to stop myself with you," he admits, his thumb rubs circles on my legs. I know he can sense my mood. With those words, my heart quickens, and my body grows even warmer.

I grow courage. "Why do you want to stop yourself?" I ask, batting my lashes.

"Not fair," he shakes his head, a sly smile playing on his lips.

My wide eyes roam his face. "What's not fair?" I question, my voice low and my fingertips trailing along his shoulders.

"Looking at me like that, all innocent and beautiful," he smirks.

I need to break this tension between us, I put my hands through his thick hair, and I can tell it catches him off guard. A half-smile comes up and I take the small advantage I have to push my body weight on his head to push him under the warm water.

"You can't be serious." He mocks me with a deep laugh, his feet planted firmly on the ocean bed.

I push with all my might. "I can put you under!" I grunt, so sure of myself.

"Ready?" he asks, and I tense when I feel his hands move to the soles of my feet and he pushes gently, I know he's holding back his strength.

My body flings out of the ocean, and I fly a few feet above the water. I can't help but let out a little scream before I plunge back in.

The afternoon is spent like this, just enjoying each other. It's been one of the best days of my life with this beautiful man. I finally get out of the water and send a text to my mom checking in to tell her I'm safe and at Liv's. I cover myself in a towel and Pierce joins me on the warm sand.

My stomach growls so loudly that I cover it in embarrassment. "Hungry?" he asks, and the tone of his voice is off, he sounds strangely happy about food.

I look around the bag. "Did you bring something?" I ask, remembering he grabbed some water.

He steps towards me, rubbing his hands together. "What are you in the mood for?"

"Umm... I don't know, seafood?" I decide. "I didn't bring any money thou-" He cuts me off with a gentle wave of his hand.

"Please don't worry about that, I saw how much it bothered you at the pier. I want to take care of you, so just let me please," he begs, hope shimmering in his eyes.

I want to say no, but how can I deny him when he looks at me with those pleading green eyes, so I nod to give him the okay.

He brings his large hand to his chin, thinking. "Okay, seafood it is. Get dressed," he tells me as he throws his dry clothes over his damp swimsuit and grabs the bag. I follow his lead and throw on my dress and flip flops.

Suddenly his warm arms are around me, I take in the sweet moment of his tight hug mixing in with the warm air surrounding us. The sounds change, and I immediately know we aren't near the water anymore. "You have to quit doing that Pierce, at least give me some warning!" I playfully shout, slapping his arm. But really, it's not scary or painful when he does that, just a little jarring.

"I'm sorry," he frowns, but it quickly turns into a charming smile when I send him a grin.

We're standing in a dark alleyway between two almost ancient looking stone buildings, inviting music plays in the distance. I look to the opening of the narrow alley and he grabs my hand to lead me towards it.

As we walk onto the stone street my eyes adjust to the scenery in front of us, we're still near a beach. I hear the rolling waves in the distance, so I feel less weird about us both having damp swimsuits on, but the cobblestone streets are lively, filled with people going out for the night.

I aimlessly lead us through the crowded streets. Songs in a different language fill my ears. Street performers line the roads and I stop to look back at Pierce, I'm in awe of the sights and smells around us. The sun still sits high in the sky, but it's beginning to descend.

I can't believe how incredibly fast the day has gone. Then again, what time is it where we are? More importantly, where are we?

Thirteen

Brazil

Leaning into him, I quietly ask, "Where are we now?"

"Not far from where we were, just on the mainland in Brazil," he whispers in my ear, his deep voice drowning out the loud music and making me forget we're on a crowded street. He squeezes my side, grinning. "I just, I never get to do this with anyone," he tells me, and I realize this is every day for him. But is he normally always alone? That makes me sad for him.

He senses my change in mood and grabs my hand, leading us towards a mass of dancing bodies. I try to keep up with his long stride, but I stumble on the rugged cobblestone floor and clumsily bump into a girl. We fall into a heap on the warm stone, our legs tangled. I profusely apologize, unsure if she speaks English until she responds, "It's totally fine!" Her boyfriend looks concerned, and he helps her up, relaxing when he sees she's okay.

Pierce extends his hand to me, lifting me with ease. We walk through the crowded pathway and he smooths my dress out. "Scar, be careful!" He jokes, teasing me.

We get to the patch of dancing people and I twirl around to the lively music and giggle when Pierce brings me close to his chest. I ignore the rumble of my stomach as we take a moment to get lost to the beat, immersing ourselves with others who are equally as happy as us. I can't believe we're in Brazil right now. My mental state from last night to now is completely different. I feel so comfortable around Pierce. It's like these crowded streets are empty, like it's just him and I dancing to the sounds of the town.

The delicious aroma of spiced food flows into my nose, and my stomach demands attention. I stop dancing and look to Pierce. In unison we both mouth 'Food.' He laughs as he throws his arm around my shoulder, leading us towards a small restaurant just ahead.

We walk past a family with a small terrier who upon peering his large eyes at Pierce, cowers to the ground, whining. We quicken our steps, and I don't question what just happened.

My fingertips trail along the textured stucco walls of the restaurant, bright murals painted on the surface bring life to the small building. The hostess leads us to a back deck and gestures for us to sit anywhere we'd like. We walk on the weathered wood deck and I take in the simple yet elegant décor.

Pierce decides on a small, circular table tucked away on the edge of the deck. He pulls out my seat and I smile as I sit down, taking in the subtle warm light coming from the low hanging globe above us.

He looks simply perfect as he sits across from me, his sharp edges illuminated by the cast of golden light. He smiles at me and my heart flutters as I take in this moment. Unscathed by the threat of looming attackers, I don't worry about my problems right now, all I can see is him.

I reach my hand out and place it on top of his. "I needed this, Pierce. Thank you for doing this," I say. He smiles before moving my hand to place it in his, instead of on top of it.

The waiter breaks our silent moment of staring at each other. I can't understand what he's saying, as I don't speak Portuguese.

"Nos teremos duas aguas, por favor," Pierce says to the waiter. His voice is velvet as the foreign words roll off his tongue. The waiter nods and walks away with a smile.

I throw my hands up. "Of course, you speak Portuguese." I dramatically roll my eyes, earning a small laugh from Pierce.

"I've had a lot of time," he says, his eyes trailing away from mine, looking out at the dark ocean. He's deep in thought and I can't fathom what his version of 'time' might mean. I need to change the subject because I'm not sure if I want to find that out, just yet. I'm blissfully aware of my ignorance of the situation but for Pierce's sake, and my sanity I will happily pretend this is a normal, everyday date.

"So, what did you tell him?" I ask. Pierce's eyes travel back to me. Before he can answer, the waiter places two glasses of ice-cold water in front of us.

The waiter patiently waits as Pierce's eyes roam the menu. "What would you like?" he asks, setting the menu back down in front of him.

"Anything, just make it seafood," I reply with a smile, I'm not picky at all. I just know I want seafood, especially in this setting. He places our order, and the waiter sends another smile before walking away.

I quickly grab the ice-cold water and drink half the glass. Even though I had two bottles earlier, I am so thirsty from swimming all day.

Light conversation flows through us as I eagerly wait for whatever he ordered to arrive. I wanted to ask him what he ordered for me, but I enjoy the surprise.

The waiter walks towards us with a massive tray, piled with all different kinds of seafood and vegetables. He places a plate in front of both of us and I thank the waiter with a smile not wanting to say the wrong thing; I should have paid attention in foreign language better.

"This looks amazing!" I inhale the delicious aroma.

"I didn't know what you wanted, so this platter sounded like a good idea." He places shrimp and crab legs on his plate, and I stack mine full. The hunger from our busy day makes me think I can eat more than I probably can. He laughs at the size of my plate. "Hey, don't laugh, I like to eat!" I say playfully.

"No, I love that you like food. I just don't know where it all goes," he winks, looking over my body. I blush at his subtle compliment.

We enjoy the food with light conversation, and I finish my oversized plate just to prove a point.

I realize how tired I am as we make our way back to the dark alleyway. I look up at Pierce and see that he's on high alert on the dark streets. His carefree smile is gone, replaced with a scowl as his eyes dart around us. I wonder what made him nervous. I grab his hand in mine and wait for him to look down to meet my face, but he never takes his eyes off the crowd.

I nearly trip over my untied shoe a couple of times as we make it to the alleyway, I lean down to tie it once we stop. When I get up, he pulls me into his warm embrace, and I close my eyes. I'm not sure if I would see anything if I opened them but I don't want to find out. This way I can pretend we were already wherever he is taking us.

When I'm sure we're at our new location, my eyes pan upward, and we stand in Liv's driveway. "What if she saw us just appear!" I stutter.

"She's in the bathroom, taking a shower," he tells me.

My stomach drops. "Umm. How did you know that?" I lightly scoff, irritation lacing my voice.

"Calm down, babe." He wraps me in a tight hug. "I left for like one second when we were still in the alleyway and heard the shower running in the bathroom," he assures me with a grin. I'm thankful his playful demeanor returned, because he looked ready to kill moments ago.

I laugh to myself, embarrassed. "You have no reason to be jealous, my eyes are only for you," he tells me, washing away any worries as he brushes his lips against my cheek.

"I know, I mean it's only Liv, but I was just worried you accidentally saw her," I shrug, and he holds my hand tighter.

"No, definitely not. I always choose a safe place when I go to someone's home." He chuckles.

"When did you leave though?" I ask curiously.

He laughs. "You were tying your shoe." *Oh*, I nod at him. Still, in awe of all he can do, and all the things I'm clueless about.

"Your mood changed, what happened back there?" I gesture behind us like we weren't just in another country.

"I'm sorry, I just... the night was going so well I felt like something was going to happen by how happy I felt. I didn't mean to let my guard down." His shoulder slumps in defeat.

I shake my head, caressing his arm with my hand. "Don't apologize, I get it. But I also know that you are capable of protecting me so don't worry about me. If something were to have happened, we could have handled it," I say reassuringly. "Plus, I had a really good time tonight," I add with a shy smile.

He cranes his neck to get a better look at my face. "I have to leave for a couple of days so just spend time with Liv and be safe." My heart sinks at the thought of not seeing him for a couple of days, we haven't been apart since we met. Which was such a short time ago. Days even, but my God it feels like I've known him so much longer.

Fourteen

You look happy

I don't know what he does when he's not with me, and I try not to think about it. "Don't go, why are you leaving?" I ask hesitantly.

"I just have some stuff to take care of." He assures me as he rubs his hand over my cheek. "If you need me, I'll know," he adds as he leans down to place a soft kiss on my lips.

The subtle gesture makes my heart flutter, which in turn makes him smile. I want to know the extent of our bond. Does he know when his slightest touch makes my skin burn in the best way? Or when his deep, but smooth as silk voice runs through me like a warm blanket on a cold day making everything better?

The words fly out before I can stop them. "Do you only like me because of the bond? Is that why I feel so strongly about you in such a short time? I don't understand all of these feelings Pierce, I never let anyone get this close to me. Ever," I admit. I stare into his eyes so that my nerves will calm down.

He wraps me in a tight hug. "My feelings for you are purely natural, I promise. It's not me that you should be worried about," he whispers into my ear, his voice cracking slightly.

I lean back to examine his solemn expression. "Me?" I question.

"I, well, I don't know. I've never held the bond with someone for long and surely not in this way. I don't know how it works long term, but I sense that your lack of common sense about staying away from me has something to do with the bond." He guesses.

That isn't possible, maybe it is? I'm not sure, all I know is that every thought I have had since I met him has been engulfed with everything Pierce. Nothing can change that, not by him breaking the bond. The feelings I feel for him are so strong though, a primal sense to be with him at all times.

I realize I'm just standing here, staring into his eyes. The intimate moment makes me flush. "Nothing will change my mind, Pierce," I whisper to him as he draws me closer once more.

"I hope not," he whispers into my hair so quietly I can't be sure he said anything.

He releases me from his arms, and a high-pitched screech sounds behind me. I look over Pierce's shoulder to see Liv standing on the porch practically jumping out of her slippers, her hair wrapped tightly in a towel and a fluffy plush robe around her.

I playfully roll my eyes and look back at Pierce, he's smiling at me, his eyes never roaming from my face. It's as if he's memorizing every detail as he ignores Liv's embarrassing outburst. I pull him in for a goodnight kiss and soon after our lips part, I hear a whistle come from the porch, that's my cue. I laugh as I pull away, he lets go of my hand but looks at me with a fierce expression.

"I know he's your friend, but could you please try and stay in with Liv and just have girl time for a couple of nights?" It's not really a question, more of a demand. I know he's talking about Zack, but after everything we've been through, I nod in agreement. It's not Zack I'm worried about, but I don't need to go to a party with a bunch of strangers without Pierce. I can just wait for him to come back.

He leans in for one last kiss before disappearing into the night.

I walk up the stairs towards a very enthusiastic Liv. "Tell me everything!" she sings eagerly as she grabs my hand and rushes us inside. The longing in my heart from Pierce leaving for a few days' hurts, but Liv's excitement lightens my mood.

I plop down on her soft comforter after changing

into a pair of fuzzy pajamas. She brings in two big mugs of hot chocolate, our favorite, brimming with sweet whipped cream and a signature chocolate drizzle that threatens to drip down the side. We make this even when it's ninety degrees outside, it's our thing.

I quickly down the sweet drink and set the empty glass on the nightstand. I can't stop smiling and she notices. "So where was his car? I saw him walk onto the street?" Her usual nosy demeanor shouldn't catch me off guard, but it does.

"I umm... He parked down the street?" The words tumble out and sound like more of a question than an answer.

She gives me a puzzled look, "Why would he do that?" *Great, backtrack Scarlett.* I suck at lying.

"Well, I'm not sure exactly. I think he wanted to walk with me a little bit. We had a big dinner," I groan, clutching my very full stomach.

She perks up again. "That's sweet! A little moonlit stroll." She dramatically swoons. "Where did he take you?" She continues being her nosy self. I fill her in slightly, that we ate at a seafood restaurant, the one that's down the street though. Not in Brazil, obviously. We talk for hours about Pierce and summer, it's nice to have a normal human discussion without the looming threat of what dangers lie beyond my safe bubble.

I look over to see her lightly snoring, a smile peels up my lips as I pull the comforter out from underneath us and cover us both up. Almost immediately I'm welcomed to sleep, my dreams consisting of a mysterious man and crystal-clear waters.

I jolt awake from a deep sleep, drenched in sweat. Nausea overtakes me as I race to the bathroom and heave over the toilet, throwing up all of the food in my stomach, I guess my emotions aren't as controlled as I thought they were? Or maybe the food was bad? I'm too tired to think about it. I quickly wash my face and brush my teeth before crawling back into bed.

Every day that Pierce is gone drags by at an agonizingly slow rate. How can I possibly miss someone I've known for such a short period of time? I feel sick the entire time he's gone, and I feel guilty for Liv having to lay on the couch with me for two days straight. She, of course, didn't mind, and I just told her I got a stomach bug.

I'm mostly worried about where he is and the fact that I can't call him. Why doesn't he have a cell phone? I laugh because I forget he isn't exactly a normal twenty-one-year-old.

I wake up to a text on Tuesday morning from Mom to let me know she's home. I gather my things and give Liv a hug bye. I had a good weekend with her, but I miss my bed so much. I normally wouldn't be up at nine am, but I know Pierce should be arriving back soon and it's making me antsy. Will he know I went home? Of course, he will. Does he miss me? Will he even come back? These are my thoughts on my short drive home.

I walk in my house and see mom looking happy

and refreshed as she sips on her morning coffee. "How was your long weekend with Brian?" I ask through innocent eyes and a knowing smile.

She swats my arm before pulling me into a tight hug. "I missed you so much, honey. Did you have fun with Liv? I should call her parents to say thank you for having you over!" She reaches for her phone and I slightly panic.

I let out an awkward chuckle. "Mom don't embarrass me. I'm an adult now, remember?" I say as I stand on my tippy toes, which makes her smile. "We had a great time, mostly stayed on the couch and watched movies. It was fun," I say with a sheepish grin as I tuck my hair behind my ear. Glad that the nauseous feeling in my stomach is slowly going away.

She tilts her head to study me. "You look awfully happy this early in the morning. I figured you wouldn't have read my text until you girls woke up around noon," she jokes.

I take my bottom lip between my teeth, I'm not sure how she will react. I've had boyfriends of course but they were always a quick fling, lasted maybe a month before I ended things. I never let anyone get too close. Liv is the closest person to me besides mom and Zack. Well, Pierce too, now. I think of his name and my heart beats faster in my chest.

"Umm, I met someone?" I say this as more of a question, watching her facial expressions to gauge her reaction.

"Honey! That's wonderful. Who is it? Do I know

him? Oh my God, you are finally giving Zack a chance!" she squeals in excitement.

I shake my head, twiddling my thumbs. "I said I met someone, which means a new guy," I reply. I know she loves Zack, but I have known him far too long and I just don't have those feelings for him. I nervously look up at her and she still looks equally as excited and interested, so I continue. "His name's Pierce." My tone is at a higher octave than usual, what is he doing to me?

"Ohh, that's a cute name." She's practically bouncing on her feet. "How old?"

Not sure, I laugh to myself. "Twenty-One." Her face grows serious and I already know what she's thinking. "He doesn't drink," I tell her, holding my hand up before she can talk. As the words hit her ears, she takes a sip of coffee and smiles.

"Well, I would love to meet him," she grins.

"Hopefully soon!" Hopefully he gets home soon. I miss him so much. "I want to meet Brian soon." I fire back before she can change the subject.

She smiles brightly. "I wanted to talk to you about that. I really like him Scarlett, and I think you will too." She gives me a hopeful look. "He owns a beach house about forty-five minutes away, I was wondering if you would like to come with me sometime?"

Her eyes gloss over a little and I know she doesn't like talking about this around me, but she doesn't need to feel like she has to hide anything. I know how much she and my father loved each other. It makes me happy that she's found someone to make her smile again, even though it hurts me to my core that my father isn't here, I'm happy for her. I feel the tears drip onto my cheeks.

I quickly wrap her into a tight hug. She gasps a little at the rushed contact. "Oh, honey I didn't mean to upset you, you don't have to meet him," she stammers as she sets her coffee on the table to wrap both arms around me.

I shake my head in her hair. "No, mom, I want to, I promise I do. I'm just happy for you is all." I assure her, pulling away so she can see that they're happy tears.

"I love you, Scarlett, so much," she beams.

"I know mom, I love you too," I tell her as I wipe the tears from my face. A beat of silence passes between us before I decide that may be enough heart to heart for today. "I need a shower and maybe a nap," I say as I head for the stairs.

"Okay honey, I'm deep cleaning today so don't mind me! I'll wake you up for dinner if you decide to sleep the day away," she yells out when I top the stairs.

"Sounds good!" I exclaim as I open my door.

The warm water from the shower soothes my stiff muscles. Ever since Pierce left, I have been on edge, not just because I miss him. But what if something happens? What if someone comes after me? I have become extremely paranoid in the last few days and I know my behavior is completely justified.

I leave the shower once the water runs cold and step back into my room to get changed. For the first time today, I look on my bed and a smile forces itself on my tired face. A black t-shirt is laid out for me next to a big, fluffy pink bear. I slide on a pair of boy shorts and place the shirt over myself, inhaling the intoxicating scent of mint and leather. This is one he wore and that makes me happy, I climb into my warm bed and throw my fluffy comforter over me. I wrap my arms tightly around the bear, which I've now named 'Ferris' and drift to sleep.

I wake to a warm hand brushing my cheek, why is mom waking me up so sweetly? She normally shakes me out of bed to go to school. Ahh, school is over. What an amazing feeling. I grunt and throw my pillow over my face, but it gets pulled from my grip. "I want to sleep!" I quietly demand with closed eyes as I wrestle her for the pillow.

"You didn't miss me?" A warm, achingly beautiful voice asks in almost a whisper.

Fifteen

Pierce, meet my mom

I squeal, jumping into his lap before my eyes
are even fully opened.

"Shh, shh, babe. Your mom will
hear," he laughs, keeping his tone low but the natural
rumble in his voice can't be quieted.

"Sorry! Wait, how did you get past her?" As the
quiet words come out, realization hits me that he can just
pop up wherever he wants. I laugh and he gives me a
knowing nod before he brings his hands to hold my face
while he moves toward my lips.

His kiss is different this time, almost desperate as
he holds me tight around my waist. I get lost in the way
his lips melt into mine, the way his hands grip me as his

tongue expertly searches my mouth like we've been doing this for years. Like we were created specifically for each other.

He pulls away from me and looks into my eyes, his piercing green searching my dull brown. "I've missed you so much Scar, that was the longest two days," he sighs in relief.

"Tell me about it!" My excitement is making it hard to whisper. I don't mention that I got sick in his absence, it sounds too desperate. "Thank you for bringing Ferris." I gesture to the bear, and he smiles at the name I chose.

He leans in closer to me, a frown taking over his face. "I wanted to talk to you about why I was gone for so long." He takes in a long, deep breath. "I went on a mission to figure out who this demon is, his name is Preta."

A shiver runs through me and I feel Pierce rub his hands across the chill bumps. "Do you know much about him?" I wonder, not sure I want to know the answer.

"A little." He shrugs. "He's an ancient demon. When he walked the earth, he was a very corrupted and deceitful human. He did terrible things, and when he went to Hell he was the perfect candidate for a demon. After he turned, he was ravished with an insatiable hunger." He gives me an uneasy look, like he doesn't want to tell me. "He is hungry for souls, and with you, it's the best game for him."

A shriek escapes my lips. "How do you know all of this?"

"I went to an old man; I was informed he could tell me about things like this. The library I went to was ancient, Scar. It was the oldest history I've ever seen. I know so many languages, all of them really, but this writing was from so long ago that he had to translate for me." He twirls his finger around mine while he takes in my expression.

"What can we do?" I shiver

He places his hand on my waist. "You can do nothing, I'll take care of this." He promises and when I go to argue he brings his lips to mine. The worries leave my body as he softly kisses me.

His hand clenches the fabric of my shirt. "I like you this," he smirks against my lips. I blush at the contact before I look to the clock and see that it's seven. The aroma of a home cooked meal travels from the kitchen, making my stomach growl, it's empty from throwing up last night.

"My mom will be up any minute to get me for dinner!" I shriek, a slight panic rising in me.

Pierce ignores the fear in my voice. "That smells delicious," he remarks, getting off the bed. "I'll meet you at the door in ten minutes."

I look at him, shaking my head. "Umm.. my mom is here," I whisper, my nerves shot.

"And?" He kisses my forehead, "I want to meet her," he says calmly.

My chest pounds. "You want to meet her here? Now? I've never had a boyfr.. well a guy I'm talking to? I'm sorry I don't know what to call this." I gesture between us and he laughs.

"I'm yours, babe, you can claim me however you want," he tells me as he slicks a hand through his thick black hair, the gesture makes my knees buckle.

My cheeks flush as I look into his eyes. "Okay...." I say shyly and he kisses me on my forehead.

"See you in ten," he says and when I look up to agree, he's gone.

I shake my head in disbelief. Nerves flood through me as I think of what he said. 'I'm yours, babe.' The way he's so comfortable around me, and I with him warms my soul.

I quickly slide a brush over my unruly hair, it's tangled from me tossing and turning during my nap. Luckily, it's dry from the shower I took this morning. I must have really needed to sleep; I didn't sleep much all weekend though. I just kept throwing up everything I would eat; Liv was so sweet making me soup and bringing me Gatorade. Thank God I feel better now. I throw on a pale blue dress and glide down the stairs with a huge smile.

Mom is standing over the stove in her signature blueberry apron. It always reminds me of her pancakes, that's why I bought it for her on Mother's Day two years ago.

"Hey, mom! Pierce was... texting me and told me he wants to meet you!" I chime, filled with excitement.

"Lovely! Maybe this Friday?" she suggests as she stirs the large pot in front of her.

A nervous laugh escapes my lips. "Umm, more

like in ten minutes."

She whips her head back to look at me. "Oh my! I look horrid, is he sure today? I need to get changed." She begins pacing about the kitchen.

I laugh, "Mom, you look great. He's wonderful. Please don't get worked up, I know you'll love him." I say and mean it. They will get along just fine, Pierce is a gentleman and my mom will see that.

"If you say so, I just don't want to embarrass you," she frowns.

"You're joking, right? I should be more worried he will have a crush on you! You're the prettiest mom I know." I smile proudly.

"Stop it, Scarlett! You're making me blush," she turns back towards the food, which now that I'm closer and can smell it, it's her signature dish, chicken alfredo. My dad's favorite, she hasn't made it in so long. Only on special occasions or when she's really happy. I'm beginning to like Brian even more for bringing her happiness back.

The bell chimes and I run for the door. My mom giggles as I stumble over my bag from my sleepover with Liv on the floor. "If you would have put that where it goes..." I hear her mumble in the background. I laugh as I open the door revealing Pierce. Of course, dressed in different clothes than ten minutes ago.

His unruly hair is now styled to perfection, still messy and tousled but in a perfect way. His signature white t-shirt is exchanged for a sleek button-up that covers his tattoo. I'm sure that's why he wore it, considering it's hot outside. Little does he know my mom adores tattoos and has one on her shoulder in memory of my father. Dark blue jeans accompanied by black boots make for a striking sight in front of me.

"Can I come in?" he asks in a quiet voice.

"Of... Of course!" I stutter as I gesture him inside. A blush rising to my cheeks from my lack of not being able to look away from him.

He bends down to whisper to me, "You look beautiful." His hand brushes mine as he walks past me towards my mom.

I walk quickly to match his long strides. "Mom, this is Pierce. Pierce, this is my mom, Stacy," I say with a proud smile, excited for two of my favorite people to meet. He greets my mother with a hug, and it makes me melt.

"Set the table will you, dear?" she suggests, and I grab plates and utensils and head for our small dining room table. I wipe down the dark stained wood with a cloth before setting the plates out. I place myself between Pierce and mom so I can make the dinner less awkward, but from the sounds of them both talking and laughing in the kitchen, I don't think it will be a problem. He fits in so well with me it only makes sense they would get along. A smile is plastered on my face and I can't seem to shake it off, I don't want to.

They walk into the small gray room, both hands full of bowls and pots. Pierce sets the large pot of noodles smothered in garlic alfredo on the table and turns to smile at me. "Thank you," I mouth to him, and he winks.

We take our seats while mom grabs all of us lemonade. I'm worried I'll get sick again, but Pierce is here so my nausea is at ease.

My stomach growls as I scoop a large portion onto my plate. We all quickly dig in, and the taste of my favorite meal warms my heart.

"This is so good!" Pierce exclaims as he shovels fork fulls into his mouth. We both laugh when a dribble of sauce drips down his chin.

"When and where did you two meet?" she asks curiously, I avoid her gaze in fear. In truth, it's a valid and normal question, but I in no way can admit to her, or myself that it's only been what, a week? It feels so much longer. The deep feelings I have for him truly can't be explained.

Pierce lets out a single cough and I look over at him. "I met her about a month ago at the Pier," he smoothly states. I instantly calm, that's a much more acceptable timeline to have him over here for dinner.

My mother nods with a smile. "So, Pierce, what do you do? I assume you're still in college or just graduated? Because Scarlett says you're twenty-one." She gives me an odd look when I spit my lemonade back into the glass.

Pierce shoots me a perfect smile before turning back to her. "Actually, I used to be a soldier," he tells her. My stomach drops. I detect something in his tone that piques my interest, like this was his life before. I scoot closer to listen intently.

"So was my Malcolm." Mom sighs with wonder as

she stares at the green-eyed man in front of her. I'm assuming she's searching through his features and his youthful face wondering his phrase 'used to'.

Pierce looks around quizzically. "Malcolm is my father," I tell him. I haven't told him about my dad or what happened to him, but knowing he was in the military tells me when the time comes, he will understand our loss.

"How long were you enlisted?" she asks, and I give him all of my attention.

"A long time," he laughs, and it raises more questions in my already overloaded brain. Mom gives him a small nervous laugh but doesn't press the issue of his current job which I'm thankful for, what would he even say?

"And your parents?" she wonders, and I immediately go rigid. He hasn't talked about them with me yet.

I shake my head a little. "Mom, I don't think-" Pierce places his large hand on my thigh under the table to stop me, a gesture that it's okay.

"I'm sorry, I don't mean to pry. I'm just interested in you; Scarlett isn't one to bring boys around," she admits with a small laugh and Pierce grabs my leg tighter, almost possessively, but his smile is bright. I place my hand over his and give a gentle squeeze.

"No, truly, it's okay. I don't mind," Pierce assures her and his demeanor seems comfortable enough. He takes in a deep breath, "They're in heaven."

Mom looks away and coughs, Pierce turns to me

and winks. What?

"I'm so sorry, Pierce." She gives him her warm smile. He returns it.

"It's okay, it's been a long time," he states, and I wonder just how long he has been without them. The fact that he even has parents, I'm so confused about him.

"Let's talk about something else," I suggest when the room falls silent.

The rest of the dinner is filled with light conversation. I ask about Brian and she mentions that he has a daughter my age, Kayla she says. She assures me I will love her; I wonder about his family. How will we fit in with them? I need to meet them soon.

I help her in the kitchen with dishes while Pierce sits in the living room. He tried to help but mom insisted he go relax.

"I think I like him," she grins as she places an already clean plate, that she's scrubbed to death, in the dishwasher. My stomach flutters. I knew she would, how could she not?

"I think I do too," I admit with a grin.

"You didn't tell me he was in the military, that would have given him extra brownie points before dinner," she says with a laugh.

I awkwardly laugh back, not knowing what to say since I didn't know myself.

After we clean up, I walk back into the living room and sit with Pierce. He looks huge on our tiny couch and it makes me chuckle.

"What are you laughing about?" he asks.

"I'm just happy. Thank you for coming tonight." I look back towards the kitchen. Our house is small so I can't bring up too much since my mom will hear me. "Do you want to go somewhere?" I ask.

"Where?" He raises his eyebrows and I know what he's thinking.

I hear my mom shuffle into her room, so I know it's safe to talk, quietly. I lean in closer to him and whisper, "Can we do a normal date?" I ask, and when his smile turns to a frown, I quickly backtrack. "No! No, no don't frown! I absolutely love the date you planned for us yesterday. It was the best date I have ever had." I assure him and his face brightens back up.

"I just can't give you anything like that..." I admit as I look at my feet.

He cups my face between his calloused hands. "Scar, you give me everything just by being you. I haven't felt this way before. I'm happy. You have no idea what that means to me, my life was dark before you. Please don't think you aren't exceptional," his gentle tone lulls me.

"So, what are you thinking?" he asks as he leans back into the couch away from me. Seconds later, mom comes into the room.

She dusts her hands. "What do you two want to do tonight?" she asks. I feel guilty wanting to leave but I can't be as close to Pierce as I want. No, need, to be when she's here.

"I think we're going to head to the city," I say as I give her an 'I'm sorry' look. From the corner of my eye, I catch Pierce smirking.

"That sounds nice! You two have a lovely time and be careful!" she says as she gives me a knowing nod. Thoroughly okay with us leaving, I wonder if she's going to go see Brian.

Pierce rises to his feet. "I had a wonderful time Ms. Wells," he says. How does he know my last name? I roll my eyes at myself. Of course he knows it, he knows everything.

"Please, call me Stacy." She smiles, pulling us both in for a hug. I shuffle out with a sigh. I'm not sure how Pierce is with strangers hugging him. I give her a quick smile as I throw on my shoes and grab him to head out the door.

Sixteen

Ice cream

Pierce holds his hand out to help me into the passenger seat of my car. It's sweet he always wants to drive, but then I think about my anger-induced driving that rainy night, and that makes me second guess if it is just him being a gentleman.

I toss him my keys when he slinks into the passenger seat, he presses the button and stares at me while the seat slowly moves back, smirking about my short height.

I playfully swat his arm when he jokingly wipes his forehead to knock off fake sweat from his 'long journey'. He laughs, taking off his button up to reveal a crisp white t-shirt underneath.

We take off towards the city and I find myself

thinking about how nice dinner was, besides the sad story of a glimpse into Pierce's past. I think he had a nice time; I just hope my mom wasn't too intrusive. "I'm sorry my mom is a little much. She's a hugger, like me. I should have warned you." I laugh.

"No, that was really nice. I didn't realize how much I missed family dinners. I would like to come back soon... if that's okay with you?" His warm tone makes me blush.

"Of course," I say simply as we head down the road.

When he places his hand against my bare thigh, chills spread over me. "So why do you want to go to the city?" He asks.

"I just want to get some ice cream and walk around." I shrug even though his eyes are on the road.

"You and your ice cream." He laughs and I playfully swat his arm. "Where is it?"

"This place in the middle of downtown, they have a cold slab and they mix in all the ingredients you want," I smile, but I can't ignore the million questions that float around in my head. Mom already gave him a gentle third-degree tonight, so I'll wait until later to ask him.

"I'll put it on my GPS," I offer, typing in the address and letting the voice from the navigation drown out my racing mind.

After a quick thirty minutes has passed in silence, Pierce's deep baritone breaks it. "What are you thinking about?" he asks, and I flush. I don't want to bring up anything too serious so I keep it light, well as light as I can be considering our situation.

I shift in my seat a little. "While you were gone, did you wonder about me?" I ask quietly, trying to redirect my mind to my earlier concerns.

He places his hand over mine in my lap. "I missed you fiercely, Scar, I couldn't stop thinking about you." I adore his honesty; the way he tells me how he feels about me without holding back.

"I was paranoid the entire time, worried about you and worried about someone coming to attack me," I admit.

I look to him and note his expression is pained, haunted really. "I saw you, I checked in so many times while I was away. I knew you were safe." He admits and it makes me sit up straight. I'm irritated, and when I angle my body away from him, he sighs.

"Why didn't you talk to me? Or at least let me know you were okay?" I snap.

He whips the car into a parking spot, and I turn my face away from him in defiance.

"Look at me," he softly demands. My gaze travels to his jade eyes. They're full of something that I can't put my finger on. The car is dark, so he flips the warm interior light on. He holds a finger between us. "First, you don't need to sit and worry about me while I'm away, okay?" His tone is serious and full of grit. I nod to hide the fact that his cold demeanor makes me shiver.

"Second," he continues as he places his hand on mine, "I knew if I saw you, even for a second... I knew you were safe and that's all that matters," he states, ending the conversation, but I'm not having it.

"But I didn't know," I state flatly, but he cuts me off by exiting the car and coming to my side. He opens the door, but I refuse to budge. It's not fair he gets to see me to check and make sure I'm okay, but he can't even say hello to me.

He kneels down next to the car as I glare back at him. "Look, I was worried sick. Absolutely sick about you." I stammer and his hard expression softens. He pulls me out of the car in a swift motion and wraps me in a tight hug. I begin to wonder if he's about to bring us somewhere else, but I peek through his arm and see we are, in fact, parked near the ice cream place.

"I'm sorry. Nothing will happen to you Scar. I know it did before, but I promise I won't let anyone touch you again." He makes a promise that neither of us can know for sure he can keep.

I shake my head. "I'm not worried about just me," I state.

He leans into my hair as he lets out a small chuckle. "Nothing will happen to me either, I promise you." I don't want to fight with him anymore, so I lean up and give him a sweet kiss. He pulls me farther back to examine my face before he lets out a soothing laugh.

"Why didn't we go to the one you work at?" he asks quizzically as he grabs my hand, leading us down the sidewalk.

"I spend three days a week there." I shrug not wanting to admit that after thinking about my dad during dinner, that I don't think I can handle sitting near all the memories.

"And the real reason you didn't want to go to the boardwalk is?" Damnit, of course. He knows I'm lying.

"I just... talking about my dad tonight. Pop's shop is where we used to go as a family. I know I work there, and it's stupid that I sometimes can't even walk inside the place." My voice is laced with embarrassment.

"It's not stupid, Scar. I get it, I do." His tone is reassuring. "I would love to hear about him one day though," he adds and the fact that he doesn't press on it more, knowing I'm upset, makes me like him even more.

After going inside, we grab two cones and it warms me remembering the night we first met, such a short time ago.

As we walk down the dark streets, I note that Pierce is on high alert. His large hand wraps around my waist protectively as we stroll past the large buildings. "I love the city at night. The lights and sounds of life bustling around even when the rest of the world is asleep." I try to lighten the mood. He gives me a distracted nod, keeping my body close.

We walk around for a while, mostly in silence as Pierce darts his eyes around every dark street and corner we pass. The closer we get to my car, the faster his feet pound on the pavement making me struggle to match his long strides. I pull him down a shortcut between two large brick buildings, it's narrow and dark. A shiver creeps up my spine, but I know I am safe with him here.

A light rain falls overhead, and a few twitching streetlights project a shiny reflection on the wet stones as

I look down to pay attention to my footing. Pierce's large hand squeezes my side and an abrupt pain in my ribs nearly makes me cry when we come to a hasty stop.

"Ouch Pierce, you're holding me too-" I cut myself off when my eyes pan to a haunted expression placed on Pierce's face, staring straight ahead. I follow his gaze to see a man staring back at us, his head tilted and his eyes possessed.

He's slightly crouched down as he stares at me. His body trembles as he bares his teeth, he looks rabid. Quickly and without warning, the demon disguised as a man dashes for us. His bald head gleaming under the fluttering lights.

Pierce places his hand on my stomach and when he tries to gently push me away, he ends up throwing me back with more force than he intended. Causing my body to slam on the wet ground. His emerald eyes look over me with concern, staying on me for a beat too long as the bald man rushes towards him, "I'm fine!" I scream into the night, begging for him to turn around.

But my desperate cries float away with the wind, it's too late. The man's hand clamps around Pierce's throat and he lifts him from the ground. I tremble at the terrifying sight, knowing I can't do anything to help. My fears dissolve when Pierce's knuckles collide with the man's jaw, who stumbles, releasing his iron like grip.

Pierce has the upper hand now; I shuffle on my bottom against the wet stone floor as I back myself into a brick wall to stay out of their way. Tears pour down my cheeks at the lack of power I have.

They both equally thrash each other around, it's a horrifying sight to see. Pierce's massive frame makes for a haunting echo as the cracking of bones bounces off the walls.

Dread courses through my already cold veins as they collide in the small space. I silently chant in my head the words 'no' as I realize Pierce doesn't have the advantage like I thought he did. The man he's fighting now is bigger and stronger than the others and I flinch at every violent punch that is thrown at Pierce. Why doesn't he just kill him? My thoughts are dark but it's true. This man could easily be a serial killer, he has to be something dark to be possessed, so why doesn't he just kill him. All I care about is Pierce's safety and my hope is evaporating with every passing second.

My haunted thoughts look promising when Pierce slams the man against the wall with such force that the stacked brick crumbles at their feet. His large hand covers the man's throat and a sigh of relief escapes my quivering lips when the demon loses strength. Pierce whips his head in my direction, snarling. "Look away!" he orders, but I can't. I can't look away from him, my concern is too high.

The man directs his paling face to me, his black eyes staring into my soul. A sinister smile creeps up his face.

Things play in slow motion as the man reaches into his pocket. "Pierce! Watch out!" I cry, a blood-curdling scream escaping me as I fumble to get off of the wet ground. Determined to protect Pierce no matter the cost. Pierce returns his attention back to the man in front of him, but the pale fingers of the bald man grip the shiny metal knife too quickly for him to react.

I run towards them in absolute horror as the man brings the glimmering knife across Pierce's neck, slicing into his skin with a firm slash.

Seventeen

Oh, no no no

A loud crunch echoes through the alleyway. I halt a few feet away to see Pierce cracking the man's neck with his bare hands. He releases the now lifeless body of the man, while he too collapses onto the wet stone floor.

My knees give way next to Pierce's still body, and I scream at him to get up. I place his head in my lap and watch his green eyes slowly fade out. His golden skin pales before me and I desperately want to hear him speak, move, blink, anything to let me know that he's still with me. But I don't know if he can come back from the gushing blood that pours from his neck.

In movies when someone is dying there's always a few seconds where profound words are said, the last dying words. I am not granted with hearing his voice again as he lays lifeless on my shaking body.

I scream as loud as I can for help, as I try and push his cut skin back together, my hands covered in thick red blood. It's a violent sight in front of me, but I don't care, I just need to put him back together.

"I'll put you back together, Pierce," I promise to him as I close my hand around his neck. Maybe I'm going crazy, I can't tell, all I see is red. His face is covered in it, his neck and white t-shirt are doused in the thick red substance. "Why won't you go back together!?" I sob into the quiet street.

I begin to hopelessly push the blood back in, scooping it up with my palms and feeling pale myself. "You promised Pierce! You promised you wouldn't get hurt!" I scream at him from my anger about the situation. "You can't leave me! You can't!" I cry through muffled sobs.

A lonely, hollow feeling in my chest tells me he's gone; I stare into his lifeless eyes and realize that I have now died with him. I can't move, I just touch his cheek and caress his thick hair in my blood-soaked hands. I could call an ambulance, but he is gone, I know he's gone.

I stare out into the nothingness in front of me, a spine-chilling screech escaping my lips. My throat hurts from all the screaming but I don't care... I feel nothing. Absolutely nothing. All I see is death.

Someone grabs my arm and I flinch.

Through my blurred vision and choking sobs, I hear shuffling around me. I instinctively go to throw my body over Pierce. "No! You can't have him!" I bark at whoever is trying to take him from me as my body crashes onto the hard-wet concrete. My hands search the wet ground for Pierce's body, but he's gone, they took him from me.

I panic as I pull my blood-stained hands into my blurry vision to see if what just happened was real, to see if I'm real.

Suddenly, I'm picked up like a child being cradled. I sob without fighting because I know there's nothing left in me.

My eyes search the dark ground for Pierce's body, I don't want to leave him here alone on the wet ground. My eyes peel up to look to the sky and my body goes stiff. Pierce is carrying me through the rain. He looks down at me with a pained expression.

His haunted eyes rake over my shaking body. I can't speak or move. I look at his throat, the only signs of his violent demise is the mixture of blood and rain as it soaks his shirt.

Comfort fills my stiff muscles, relief that I can't understand. No matter how at ease I am that he's carrying me, the moments I just experienced leave me in a shock that envelops my entire soul in a dark way. Seeing him that way, his throat... I can't breathe or think. I just sink my head into his blood-soaked chest. This isn't real. I'm having a terrible, awful nightmare.

"I'm so sorry, baby, I'm so sorry you had to see that." His voice is ragged in my hallucination.

I can't look back at him, I can't meet his face. All

I see when I close my eyes is him bleeding out. His life slowly but all too quickly draining from his perfect face. If I look at him, he will disappear. I keep my eyes glued in front of me. I don't want to be here anymore. The dark stone streets fade out and the scenery changes before my eyes, we are now walking through a warm room. It looks like a beach house by the pictures on the walls and décor.

His chest rises and falls at a rapid rate. "Scarlett, I'm so sorry you had to see what I did. I'm sorry you had to see me that way, laying on the ground like that. I can't imagine how terrifying that was for you, I never thought it would come to that. I can't die, Scar," he groans. "I didn't think to tell you that when I die, I wake up. I never thought we would be in that situation, but I got distracted. If that would have been you..." he cuts himself off and holds me tighter to his chest. I want his words to comfort me, but I feel hollow.

The only thing keeping me going is knowing that he's okay. I repeat those exquisite words over and over. The movements of Pierce carrying me through a dark room are the last things that I remember before I shut off. Completely and utterly collapsing within my own dark thoughts.

Eighteen

Pierce

I hold her shaking body tight against my chest as I flip the bathroom light on. I have to get her out of this red dress. It was blue, oh my God, it was blue.

As the bathtub fills, I stare at her hollow expression, her eyes never meeting mine. Panic sweeps through me as guilt consumes my entire being. I never would have imagined she would see anything like that. I tried to protect her, I tried. It wasn't good enough. My better instincts told me I should have stayed away; I should have protected her from a distance. But I was selfish, and now she's paying the price.

She needs to recover from what she saw. The absolute horror in her eyes will forever haunt me to my core. While I was healing, I couldn't move. I'm fully aware of the motions of death. The pain and the feeling of losing your life are normal to me, but nothing will haunt me more than seeing her trying to push my open throat back together as I lay lifeless on her lap unable to soothe her worried face.

I felt her small hands frantically pulling the bloody skin back together, screaming my name. That awful, blood-curdling sound coming from her perfect lips will torment me for the rest of my infinite, hollow days. The empty, isolated future I will have to endure without her, that I've dared not to think of until now.

This is so fucked.

After removing the rest of her clothing, I sink her body gently into the tub, noting the bruise that's forming on her back from where I pushed her away. I didn't mean to shove her so hard. My only instinct was to get her away from the black-eyed demon rushing to take her from me. I thought I couldn't hate myself more but the burning ache I feel when I look at her perfect skin being damaged by my hand makes me cringe.

I leave for a swift moment and head to her house, I'm back in one second. Before she can even realize I'm gone so I can grab us some clothes. I quickly rinse myself in the shower, so I don't get any more blood on her. I slip on a clean pair of sweatpants and a t-shirt before returning to her side.

Kneeling by the tub, I see the water is steeped in red from my blood. It cascades down her fragile body, dulling the red color to a faint almost a translucent pink. I have to refill the tub three times until the water runs clean from me gently scrubbing the thick red off of her.

During this process I'm keeping my left hand on her, to comfort her. It's something I do when I bring a soul over, a scared child, or a helpless mother who has been torn from her family and is frightened by me. I help soothe them into transition. I know they're going to heaven and it will only be seconds before they're blissfully happy for eternity, but I don't want them to be scared at all.

My gentle touch seems to thaw her stiff body and her eyes slowly move around the room, taking in her surroundings. To my horror, she never speaks a single word as I get her out of the tub and dry her off.

I slip the T-shirt I left with her to sleep in over her head, careful to not touch the bruise. I couldn't handle it if she winced at my touch right now. This is hard enough to not hold her and cradle her in my arms to soothe her as it is.

Her expression is dark, her face void of any emotion. I want so badly to comfort her, but it's not my place anymore. After what she saw, I don't know how she can stand to be in this room with me. Then again, she isn't moving. She may want to be far, far away from me now. I've broken her.

The only solace I find comfort in is that she's safe.

I'm thankful I've defeated the threat, the demon that was after the soul of the glorious woman I love. Her delicate soul belongs nowhere other than in heaven many,

many years from now after she's lived a long, beautiful life.

I've defeated the threat, but I've lost my world.

She saw me end someone's life tonight, she saw my lifeless body. I have to let her go. She is too pure for me, for my world. I saw the innocence slowly fade from her beautiful eyes when I died on her lap. Thankfully her light is still blindingly bright. I'll miss that, the way I only see her. The way that the rest of the world is dulled in comparison to her. She has no idea how much she colors my world, truly she doesn't.

Maybe Zack can make her happy. My body tenses at the thought. He's a nice kid, but I know what he wants. He may think he likes her but no one, not a single soul, will ever feel the way I do about her.

I can't imagine his, or any other man's hands on her. The thought makes me physically sick. I have to pull myself from my selfish thoughts. I have to, for her.

My job is simple, well as simple as it can be. I bring souls to their deciding fate. I'm never tethered to a human for more than mere seconds before I hand them off. I have never come across a situation like this, I have no one to ask for help.

After I was punished, I woke up knowing what I needed to do, what I have to do to keep the world in order. Like the weight of humanity rests on my shoulders. Nothing has brought me to my knees like this beautiful girl has, she deserves so much more than I can offer.

I want more than anything to keep this bond so I know she's safe at all times, but my fears and selfishness can't keep her tethered to me forever. I have to give her the chance to let go of me.

Tomorrow I will bring her home. I wish she had someone to talk to so she can work through the horrific site she saw tonight. Her mom will be gone to work, and the threat of the demon is no longer looming over her perfect head. I can break the bond, let her be free of me.

For me, the bond won't matter. Breaking it will be like cutting a feathered rope. Nothing will change my feelings for her. Nothing will be the same for me after her, the light and color to my never-ending darkness. My thoughts haven't been in the dark place I'm in now since I first laid eyes on her. Now they are consuming me, again.

She's safe, that's all that matters.

She's safe, she's safe, she's safe... I chant to myself as I steel my gaze from her on the bed, still staring at nothing. I force myself out the backdoor and towards the sand. I can imagine her here, in the daytime, admiring the view. Her love of the ocean never ceases to amaze me. That's why I brought her to Brazil, and now to this beach house that's nestled in the sand overlooking the ocean. It's Brian's. I've checked in on her mom here and I knew no one would be here considering it's a weekend home.

I didn't want to take her too far from the familiar surroundings of her town. If, no, *when* she snaps out of this, I will take her home. I'll fetch her car from the city and drive it back when I know she's asleep tonight.

I stare out at the water she adores so much but I find no comfort in it, they all look the same to me. I've seen them for centuries over and over.

Physical pain shreds through me as I break it. This is it for me, she was my only chance of happiness, but I had to do this, for her. I tell myself over and over again that this is all for her.

I bring myself into the bed beside her one last time. Now that the bond is broken, I can't tell if she feels any different towards me. Her still body is staring out the window as I climb in the bed. I'm desperate for her to put her head on my chest.

I don't push it; I just want one more night with her. I try to comfort her the way only I can, but my heart sinks at the realization that we have no more bond. I can't fix all her problems with my touch anymore. I could but I won't invade her privacy that way, I won't force her to be okay. I simply wrap my arms tightly around her, tomorrow I will have let her go.

Nineteen

What day is it?

Feeling Pierce's arms wrap around me as I lay in bed with him in silence is such a calming experience. I'm immediately engulfed in his comfort. The way only he can heal my aching heart with a single touch overwhelms me.

I continue to stare out into the sea, I can't bring myself to talk. My throat is on fire from screaming but I have no energy to get a glass of water. I don't even have the energy to hold Pierce the way I need to.

I feel slightly better now; the images are still burned into my vision, but the moment he laid down next to me, I felt happy again.

I'm going to let my body heal, I know I'm traumatized. I'll talk when I'm ready. He's patient so I know he won't mind. I just need to be in my head a little longer.

I hesitantly let my body rest, knowing my nightmares will be tormented with blood and fear.

My heavy eyelids flutter open with the rising sun. I no longer feel Pierce's arms around me, my hand frantically searches for his warm body. My heart goes cold when I realize I'm not at the unfamiliar beach house anymore, I'm in my bed.

My body jolts upward and I cringe at the sudden movement. My back hurts so bad I audibly wince when I stand. I glance at my clock to see the time and notice a note beside it, written in black ink.

Scar,

I'm so sorry, I'm so damn sorry. I can't begin to find the words to tell you how remorseful I am. You will be safe from now on. The demon won't haunt you anymore, and neither will I. The bond has been broken since last night, so I'm not sure this letter is even necessary. I may be writing it more for my own sanity than anything. Please take care of yourself.

I will keep you in my heart for the rest of my days, my love.

Sincerely,

Pierce

A loud thud booms through the room and I realize it was my body slamming against the hardwoods, I don't care to wince at the pain that it brings from my sore back. All I feel is the crushing of my heart from Pierce's finite absence, that pain is infinitely worse.

I lay here, on the cold flooring of my bedroom for what feels like hours, thankful my mom is at work, so she doesn't have to see me this way. I need to get out of here, I need to go to Liv's for a few days where I can welcome the darkness without having to pretend. I pull out my phone to text her.

Day One

'Hey Liv, can you come to get me?' I send her, knowing I can't drive in my condition and anyways, my car is in the city. My phone rings almost immediately.

'On my way, your mom thinks you're here anyways. You have to start telling me when I'm covering for you!'

The minutes tick by slowly before I hear her pull into the driveway.

I look down and see Pierce's black shirt on me, I cringe at the thought of never seeing him wear it again. I rip it off of me in haste and throw on another t-shirt and jeans before I head to the car, not worrying about my hair or anything else. I examine the bruise on my back in the mirror, it's large and it stings but I make sure to conceal it with a large shirt. I don't dare look at my face, I know I won't recognize the girl I see staring back at me.

I sink into Liv's passenger seat and she gives me an odd expression. "Why didn't you drive?" she asks as she examines my face.

"My car isn't here," I reply flatly.

"Yes, it is." She gestures to my silver Altima parked neatly in front of us. How did I not see it when I passed it? I guess Pier... *he*... brought it back.

"Oh."

With a huff, Liv crosses her arms over her chest. "What did he do?" She goes into best friend mode, ready to attack. When my response is a tear that trails down my cheek, she frowns. I don't have the energy to explain the impossible or make up some simple lie to explain my zombie-like state.

"Please, Liv. Just let me not think for a while. Can we please leave?" I plead with a small voice. My throat aches from the small amount of talking we've already done, and I can't be near my car right now, knowing he was in it such a short time ago makes my stomach flip. I don't care how desperate I look; I can't help the overly intense feelings that I feel for this man. He broke the bond, but it made no difference. I knew it wouldn't. He was always so worried about it, but it never mattered.

"Yeah, yeah of course." She gives me a small smile as she pulls out of my driveway, but I can see the anger in her eyes, directed at the man who hurt me.

Time passes quickly and I don't know where the day has gone as the sun starts sinking into the earth. Can't I go with it?

Day Two

Liv is propped up next to me, concern laced on her face, but she's been patient all day. I've turned down her request to feed me multiple times, I don't think I can handle anything in my stomach. It will make me sick.

"Can I at least order some Pizza?" she suggests, and I give one nod, I don't have the energy to argue with her. I know she only cares about me and she wants to help but I came here to sulk, why can't she just let me sink into this couch for a while.

I pull my phone out to text Mike and ask for the week off, he's understanding and I'm too empty to care if I get fired. He was my dad's best friend, so I laugh a little inside at the thought of getting fired by him. He replies with a simple, 'Yes, of course, we're overstaffed anyway.'

The food arrives, and as quickly as the pizza hits my stomach it's back on the floor. I shuffle to clean up the mess from the tile in the kitchen but Liv shrugs me off and forces me to go to bed, I don't argue.

Day Three

Mom is concerned, I know she is; I keep telling her that Liv is going through a break-up and needs me. I muster up all the energy I have to talk to her at least once a day. She pretends to believe me.

I can't keep anything down besides water. I refill

my glass in the bathroom to dull the ache in my stomach from lack of food. That's all I've done today, move from the bed to the bathroom for water. Liv is beginning to grow impatient. Sleep lets me forget everything when it graces me with its presence.

With no bond between us and no way to contact him, I let the little sliver of hope burn inside of me that he may visit me and Liv as I pull a piece of paper from the desk in the guest room and a pen. "I saw you in my dreams," I write before I lift the windowpane and place the folded note on the seal, grabbing a bird-shaped paperweight to weigh it down, silently praying it won't fly away.

Day Four

The winds howl, a storm is brewing. I watch as the trees sway outside the window and I remember the note. I rush to yank the pane open, breathing in the fresh scent of the calm before the storm - then I check, the note is gone... but so is the bird, the last ounce of hope fades when I crane my neck down to see the bird didn't fly away but fell off the ledge and shattered into a million pieces. The darkened sky parts as the storm rolls in, headed straight for me. I continue to write pointless letters to a ghost that will never show his face again.

Sleep. Nightmares, was it even real?

Day Five

I step out of the shower, the first one I've taken in days. My hair tugs against the brush as I work the tangles from my thick hair. I don't bother to dry it before I lay my head back on the pillow.

Day Six

It's night again and Liv made me a big glass of hot chocolate and homemade chicken pot pie. I was worried that I would throw it up like everything else, but I ate so much I almost got sick from just simply being too full. She smiled like she won a small victory after an hour of me keeping it down. I went back for seconds a few hours later before heading to bed. My stomach was dancing in happiness because of the comforting food. The hot chocolate soothed my aching throat. My brain and heart still felt useless.

Time is a funny thing; I've always heard the expression, "Time heals all wounds." I heard it from countless people when dad died overseas. That pain is still sharp in my chest, it will never dull. This pain is different, it seeps through every inch of my body, engulfing me with pain. Literal pain. At least I have the hope of seeing my father in heaven one day, I don't have that with Pierce. When I'm long gone, he will still be roaming the earth and that kills me.

On the Seventh day, Liv is over the sulking.

"You have to get out of this house!" She barges into her room; her hands grip the thick curtains that kept the space dark. The ting of the rings sliding against metal hurts my ears, even the setting sun hurts my eyes.

"No, I don't," I reply sharply as I throw the heavy blanket over my tired eyes.

Liv walks to the bed and throws the blanket on the ground. "Up," she demands, and I moan in frustration. "Seriously, get up. We're going out."

"Out?" I ask, a small shock in my voice. "Where?" I ask hesitantly.

"Bonfire, Chad's place. Get dressed. Zack's on his way." A flitter of hope rises in me. If Zack is picking me up maybe Pierce will stop him, I know he gets jealous of him. I internally groan at the thought. I'm being delusional, he's gone, never coming back. But still, I cling to the false hope as I stretch my arms and sit up on the bed.

I stare at her for a brief moment, she looks surprised that I'm agreeing. "Promise if I'm not having fun we can leave?" I ask with a hopeful look in my eyes.

She jumps up and down, "Yes! Anything to get you out of this house!"

I crawl out of bed and hop in the shower, ready to try something different.

"Ready?" Liv asks as she spritzes herself with a large bottle of Pure Seduction, smothering everything in the room with the sweet scent.

"Almost," I say as I twirl the last curl-free piece of hair over the wand. Spraying a strong hold hair spray to mix in with Liv's perfume cloud. I look almost alive, my skin has turned pale over the course of the week but a large amount of foundation and a little blush has livened my features up.

When Zack arrives, I try to hold in my emotions to keep a blank slate on my face to hide what I feel, but he sees me, he always does. He rushes for me, picking me up and wrapping me in a tight hug. I feel comfort in his arms as he strokes my hair, "Did he do this to you?" he whispers in my ear, and I cringe.

Twenty

Burn

I can't hold it in any longer. "He did." I quietly sob into the familiar shoulder of one of my longest friends. Zack pulls me even tighter against his broad chest and I revel in the warm feeling.

Liv coughs behind us, breaking me from my trance. I glance over at her and give her a small smile. I'm so thankful for her.

"She really needs food in her stomach," Liv says, gesturing to me. The thankfulness is gone, I roll my eyes.

"Girl Code." I remind her but she ignores me.

Zack's eyes drink me in for the first time. "Shit, Scarlett, I saw you last week. How do you look so thin?" He places his hand over his mouth as he assesses my fragile state.

"I did eat," I state, darting my eyes to where Liv stands.

She takes a dramatic breath. "You ate chicken pot pie, that's the one thing you've had in days that you could keep down," she says in a worried tone, like a mother hen. She directs her gaze towards Zack. "I ordered Chinese, pizza, even Thai food!" she exclaims.

I want to comfort her; I feel awful that she's been trying so hard. For days she's been ordering everything trying to make me feel better and I try every time, but it just makes me sick. When will I ever be able to keep food down?

"Can't you just make what you made last night? We can stay here." I beg, realizing maybe I shouldn't leave.

She shakes her head, stomping her foot into the ground. "No! You are going to get out of this house. You barely know this guy, he shouldn't be affecting you like this!" She scolds and I flinch at her harsh words, she doesn't understand. Doesn't she know I love him?

She notices my sad expression. "If you can't keep what we eat down, I promise I'll make you chicken pot pie again," she assures me.

Sliding into the front seat of Zack's jeep, I look in between my two constants. I'm so thankful for them sticking by my side, not judging me when I've fallen into this dark hole. Zack was here for me at another hard time in my life when my dad passed away, never failing me, never judging.

Liv hadn't come around yet, but I know she would have been there for me too. I reach over and put my hand in Zack's, addicted to the feeling of needing to be comforted by someone familiar.

We stopped by Panera and ate, I opted for the soup so it would be easy on my stomach. I felt fine afterward, hopefully my stomach has fixed itself.

The ride to Chad's was short and as we pulled up to the party, I saw the mass amounts of people surrounding his house. Chad is a guy from school, I don't know him well but it's a small town and we've all been in the same class since Kindergarten.

Kegs line the sand and half of the guys from the football team flip people upside down to get a drink. I've never understood that, why don't they just drink from a glass or take a shot?

I sit down on an abandoned blanket in front of the massive bonfire to warm up. The ocean breeze makes it a little chilly. Zack gives me a sheepish smile as he scoots in close to me on the small blanket, receiving an eye roll from Liv who thinks he's always a little too obvious. Normally I would protest but I don't mind the familiarity right now, it's nice.

"Keg stand?" Liv asks with a mischievous grin.

I laugh a small laugh, shaking my head. "I'm fine."

"Zack?" she asks, and he sighs before getting up. His absence leaves a cold spot in the blanket, but they return quickly with drinks in their hands.

"What's this?" I ask as Zack places a cup in my hands.

He shrugs. "I don't know, something sweet." He laughs as he returns to my side. Always loyal.

The cool sweet liquid slides down my throat as I take in my first sip. I revel in the feeling I get after one glass. It almost makes me not care anymore.

It's been a couple of hours since we arrived. The drinks have been flowing and I've been happily accepting them, desperate to feel anything besides this sadness that's taken residence inside of me. The fire has grown larger, people are haphazardly piling random things on the burning embers to keep the party going. I watch the red-hot pieces fly up in a hypnotizing fashion as they dance above the burning wood.

I feel a soft pressure on my knee, and I direct my gaze to Zack. He's watching me, admiring me. His eyes twinkle from the flames as he brings his lips close to my ear and whispers, "Wanna go on a walk?"

I look around at the partygoers dancing, and twirling. I feel good, better than I have in a week, thanks to Liv and Zack and the sweet cherry drinks I've been sipping on. A walk to the ocean sounds amazing right about now. I smile at him. "I'd love to." I wait for him to invite Liv but when he extends his hand out to me, I give her a shy smile before telling her we will be right back.

Confidence, presumably from the alcohol, makes Zack's demeanor different. He's even more comfortable with me as he throws his arm over my shoulders as we walk away from the fire and towards the water.

"You look very pretty tonight," he says as he takes my small hand in his. I smile as we walk side by side towards the dark waters.

"Thank you," I respond in a quiet voice. The moon casts a white shadow across the water, I take a moment to stare as the waves crash onto the shore.

He stumbles a little as he stands next to me and I notice the flask he pulls from his jacket. "Want some?" he asks, and I grab it before he brings the liquid to his lips.

"You're driving," I remind him, and he shakes his head.

"No, I paid a freshman to drive us home." He tells me, his eyes roaming my face. "Scarlett, you know I would never put you in harm, right?"

I know he would never harm me, no matter what Pierce may think. *Pierce...* I take the flask and bring it to my lips, hard liquor. The burn slides down my throat and I scrunch my face in disgust.

Zack laughs as he takes the flask back and brings it to his lips. "It's just whiskey, Scarlett."

He sits down on the sand and pulls me down beside him. I nervously rub my hands against the tiny grains, enjoying the warmth they hold from being scorched by the sun all day. But the air is chilly this far from the roaring fire and I shiver at the cool breeze.

He wraps his jacket around my shoulders before putting his arm around my waist and pulling me closer. "You know you deserve better than him, right?" he asks, his eyes searching my face.

"I don't want to talk about him, please," I beg, and he nods. We sit in silence for a moment, staring into the obsidian ocean.

"You really do look beautiful tonight." He tucks a strand of hair behind my ear as he brings his face closer to mine. I blush, and then suddenly he brings his lips towards me. They touch for a brief moment before he abruptly jerks away. No wait... he didn't jerk away; he was pulled away from me. My eyes try to adjust to the midnight darkness around me to find out what happened.

When Zack lands in the ocean about ten feet from the shore I gasp and stand on my feet, my toes dig in the warm sand, rooting me in place.

Zack quickly regains his composure as he shakes out his hair and heads back towards the shore.

There's a man at the edge who is waiting in a stiff, almost animal-like stance. The silhouette comes into better view and my stomach drops as I realize it's Pierce.

Pierce's sharp jaw turns towards me and a worried expression sets on his face as I step towards him. To my dismay, he holds up one finger and shakes his head before turning back to Zack.

The thin sliver of moonlight showcases Zack's angry expression. "What the hell, man. What's your problem!? You left her. Left!" Zack's voice slices the sounds of the waves and I stand in place, frozen. Pierce lifts his hands to Zack's shoulders, for a moment I cringe wondering if he's going to hurt him, but I calm when Zack simply looks at me and then walks back towards the party.

My heart begins to thump violently as Pierce turns, making his way towards me in a few quick strides. Is he coming back to me?

He lets out a deep sigh, he's so close I can feel his minty breath against my face. "I'm so sorry, Scar." His tone is remorseful as his green eyes bore into mine, the moonlight is not giving me enough of his features. I dart my eyes around his perfect face.

"Pierce," I whisper, my eyes brimming with tears. "I didn't think you would ever come back." My voice cracks.

His expression goes grim, he tilts his head sideways and places his warm hands on my shoulders. The comfort I feel at that moment is overwhelming and I lean into him. He looks into my eyes and I feel a calming trance wash over me.

His tone is pained, laced with so much grief it's unexplainable. "I would suffer by your hands for a thousand years, but I will not allow you to suffer at mine for another second."

He takes a deep breath, and I fall into a trance at the sound of his voice. "You will forget this ever happened. You came down here with Zack and wanted a moment to yourself before returning and having a wonderful night with your friends." He emphasizes the last word before he nods his head towards the distant party. His voice is calm and calculated but I hear a small crack in his resolve. "You have to forget you saw me, it's for the best." I look into his eyes and they are full of sadness. I try to move my hand to smooth the lines of worry on his face, but I can't remember why I'm concerned.

He plants a lingering kiss on my forehead as he

brings his free hand through the back of my hair. "Be happy, Angel," he whispers in my ear before returning to rest his head on top of mine.

The warmth is nice as I peek around his shoulder, glancing my eyes forward to stare up into the moon as it cascades its silver light over the dark waves.

I admire the ocean for a moment longer before the warmth disappears. I skip back towards my friends, feeling a sense of happiness as we celebrate throughout the night.

Twenty-one

Bridal style

O n the way home, Zack slides into the backseat with me. His clothes were soaked after he randomly jumped into the water, so he's been shirtless since then. True to his word, he paid a freshman to drive his Jeep. Liv sits in the front with him.

At this point, it's been hours since his last drink so Zack would have been okay to drive but I'm thankful he's taking extra precautions. I'm feeling much better than I have in days, mostly thanks to the alcohol but I'm feeling really hungry.

With the windows down and the radio turned up we all sing and laugh, I let the warm air surround me as my long hair blows around the back. It hits Zack in the face a few times and I laugh as he swats it away.

Liv turns the radio down a notch so I can hear her. "Hey Scar, do you want to go with me to the Pier tomorrow? I need some new summer clothes."

"Yeah, of cou-" My body begins to violently heave. I throw up on the metal floors of the Jeep.

"Oh my God!" Liv squeals as my body thrust forward. The sweet liquid burns as it rushes out of me so fast that I can't catch a breath.

"Pull over!" Zack yells to the random kid that's driving, and he holds my hair out of my face as I empty the contents of my stomach all over his car. Always patient.

I didn't realize we had started moving again until we come to a stop in Liv's driveway. Zack walks around and picks me up to carry me inside. "I'm so sorry! Let me clean it up!" I plead, trying to wiggle from his grip.

He flips his blonde hair out of his eyes and looks down at me with an amused expression. "Don't even think about it," he grins. "It's metal flooring, I'll just run a hose over it in a minute." He shrugs and I don't argue.

"I think we should take her to the hospital." He suggests to Liv but doesn't take his eyes off of me. I say 'no' in protest, but they ignore me like I'm a pestering child.

Liv nods in agreement. "I mentioned it to her a few times, but she doesn't want to go. She just keeps saying she has a stomach bug," she replies in a defeated tone as she unlocks the front door.

Zack carries me bridal style through the doorway.

Always strong. "If she isn't better soon, we will," he states and I don't argue, maybe I do need fluids in my system. Maybe they have drugs that will mask a heart that's been ripped to shreds.

He sets me down inside and I hobble to the bathroom to brush my teeth and change, my body feels so weak. I hear the hose running and I cringe at the thought of Zack having to clean that up.

After washing my face one more time I head back downstairs to find them talking with one another about their master plan to fix me. Don't they know I can't be fixed? They have no idea how hard it is that I can't tell them what is going on, what's really going on.

"I'm staying the night," he tells us, and Liv's expression lightens up.

"Movie night!" she exclaims as she rushes to grab what I'm sure is popcorn, but I'm not going to eat a single thing until my stomach feels better.

"Don't forget to take your iron pills," I say to her out of habit and she smiles before grabbing her bottle. I don't want her to have a blackout in front of Zack. It was already embarrassing enough that I threw up in his car, no matter how much he acted like it was okay.

I sit down on the smaller loveseat that Pierce and I kissed on for the first time. It makes my heart ache to be thinking about the ghost of him.

Zack had a bag from his car, and he exits the bathroom in a crisp white t-shirt and gray sweatpants. "Scoot over," he says as he grabs a blanket and sits next to me. His arm slings around me, and I sink into his familiar embrace.

Liv walks back into the living room. Sure enough, popcorn and sodas in hand. She hands me a glass of sprite and I slowly drink it; it feels good going down my sore throat. I ended up eating popcorn during the last half of the movie she chose.

"I'm only eating things you make from now on Liv." I joke as I snicker to myself, grabbing another handful of popcorn. She doesn't respond so I peek back and see her fast asleep.

I grab the remote and turn the T.V. off. I hear a light snore coming from Liv and I giggle a little at her sleepy sounds. Zack being the gentleman he is gets up and carries her to her room. He quickly returns to the living room and helps me to the guest room.

I'm still fairly intoxicated and all I want is to sleep, it has to be at least three in the morning. I walk in and plop down on the comfy bed. Zack takes his shirt off and climbs in next to me. "You don't have to sleep in here," I assure him.

"I'm not leaving you alone," he tells me, and his promise is all I need to feel a little safer.

I get in and lay my head on his bare chest, it's not Pierce but I don't think I'll ever find that level of comfort in my lifetime again. I'm instantly sleepy when he begins to run his hands through my hair, it's twisted and tangled from the salt air, but he gently plays with it.

His chest is radiating heat and it feels so nice. Zack has always been so good to me, he's always a constant. Always patient. Always strong. Always loyal.

"Always perfect."

"What was that?" he asks, and I straighten. Did I say that out loud?

"Nothing," I mumble as I sink further into his chest, falling asleep against his warmth. Thankful that he can't see the blush on my face.

At some point, the sweat coming from my forehead and the familiar nauseous feelings have jolted me awake. Zack sits up as soon as I do. The room is incredibly dark, it can't be morning.

"What's wrong?" he asks, his voice thick with sleep.

I wipe a thick sheen of sweat from my brows. "I don't know, I'm really hot. Like my skin is on fire." I wince as my stomach turns in knots, letting out a small shriek.

"That's it. We are going to the hospital." He turns on the lamp and looks at me. "Fuck, Scarlett, you're as white as a ghost," he gulps, lifting his long arms through his white t-shirt quickly before moving to my side.

His eyes are wild as they rake over my body. I lift my oversized t-shirt and wipe the sweat from my face. A loud gasp escapes his lips and I turn to see his face contort. Anger and concern fill his eyes as he lightly brushes his fingertips against the faded bruise.

"What happened?" He sneers as I tightly pull the shirt down to cover myself, but it's too late. "Did he do this to you?" He can't believe the question he's asking as he covers his mouth with his hand and uses his other to run through his hair. How do I explain it?

A tear falls down my cheek, "No! Of course not," I lie. He won't understand that he was trying to protect me. There was a demon coming after me, how can I explain that. "I... I fell," I lie again, but he doesn't believe me, I can tell by his eyes that he doesn't.

"I'm going to fucking kill him." His tone is full of venom. He lifts me from the bed as I try to hold back the wince from the pain that courses through my body as we head down the stairs.

"Liv," I protest, and he shakes his head.

"Let her sleep, I'll text her soon," he whispers as he opens the front door quietly, turning to lock it behind him. At some point I pass out in his Jeep, all I can hear are his muffled cries of my name as blackness overtakes me, yet again.

Twenty-two

Fluorescents

The persistent tick of machines beeping and a nagging sharp pain in my arm clouds my thoughts as my mind begins to stir. The sound of Zack yelling makes my heavy eyes shoot open. It takes a moment to adjust to the bright fluorescent light overhead.

My gaze pans to a sharp, shiny needle that's embedded in my skin. Another voice -velvet and deep and angry- floats through my clouded ears. A dark, beautiful tone that makes my dead heart flutter back to life.

Pierce stands firm with tattooed arms across his chest glaring down at Zack. What is happening?

"You weren't there! I was," Zack screams at

Pierce with a prideful grin plastered on his face.

Pierce rolls his eyes, speaking back in a calm but stern voice. "She needs me. Infinitely more than she'll ever need you." So smug, so arrogant, so correct.

Now it's Zack's turn to laugh, apparently. "She doesn't need you! Did you see her back? Did you do that to her?" he spits.

Pierce's smooth demeanor falters as he bows his head. "What? No, it was an accident- I-"

Zack cuts him off. "I didn't leave her; I comforted her last night. If I wouldn't have been in bed with her when she woke up, she could have died!" he roars, throwing his hands in the air.

The muscles in Pierce's jaw twitch. "You were in bed with her?" he fumes, taking a threatening step towards Zack. "If you touched her," Pierce brings a hand to Zacks's throat, "if you even thought about touching her I will destroy you." He sneers.

I can't bear to witness another smidge of violence. I attempt to muster up a sentence but all I can get out is a low whimper which makes both of their heads turn to me.

I look into Pierce's smoldering jade eyes, flecked with a smoky swirl of black, and watch as relief floods through them, turning them back to his normal glimmering emerald.

He runs to my side, his height towers over the small bed so he gets on his knees to be level with my face. Zack chimes in behind him. "Do you want me to make him leave?" he asks me, his voice is filled with irritation.

Pierce answers for me. "Thank you for taking care of her, but please go." He tries to sound sincere, but I hear the venom in his voice.

Zack ignores him, "I'm not leaving him alone with you," he states in a threatening tone and Pierce stands up and makes his way back to Zack.

Pierce narrows his eyes at him, "You will," he tells him. Zack nods once before he exits the room quietly. *What was that?*

Pierce walks back to me and sits on the edge of the hospital bed. "Baby, why do you look so sick? Earlier-" His eyes soften as he trails off and reaches his hand out for me, I look at it, feeling betrayed. Where has he been? I've wanted nothing more than for him to be next to me since he left. But he did leave, he left me, alone.

I flinch at his touch and he inhales a sharp intake of breath like I physically hurt him. It makes me laugh.

He raises a brow at me, not finding any of this humorous. "Why are you laughing?"

I throw my arms up a little and feel the sting of the needle inside my arm. "Because you act as if you care. Just so you know I haven't stopped throwing up since you *left* me." I emphasize the last few words.

He reaches to my face and opens his mouth to speak but I stop him, no matter how bad the urge I have to feel his touch, he hurt me. "You broke me, Pierce, and Liv took care of me. She was there for me, and Zack... he picked up the pie-"

He cuts me off with a haunted look. "Please, please don't," he pleads in a defeated tone. I can't be mad

179

at him for long, he looks so desperately lost. "I can't think of anyone else comforting you. I can't, and I won't. I know that may make me selfish, but God, I can't help it when I look at you." His head drops into his hands.

I reach for his soft hair and sink my fingers through the thick dark strands to comfort him. My heart flutters when his hand softly slides around my wrist, and just like that, all is forgiven.

"I missed you," I say to him and feel his body shake under my touch as he swiftly clasps my face in his large hands.

"I missed you, too, so much," he replies with a smile that melts the block of ice that was my heart.

The door creaks and Pierce quickly jumps up to protectively stand in front of me, he relaxes when the doctor walks in. He looks over at Pierce and then back at me "Miss, I can only talk to you or your family members," he says and I sigh.

Pierce walks over to him and places a firm hand on his shoulder. I begin to worry that he's going to punch him from the way his jaw is clenched. "Look at me, it's okay. I'm okay to be here." His voice is velvet and calculated as he speaks calmly to the doctor, who to my surprise gives him a nod and a smile before continuing.

He walks to my bedside and Pierce follows. "Ms. Wells, I am going to tell you something, it's going to be confusing but it's best we talk now. After this, I will call the proper authorities so we can start an investigation if it's necessary." His serious tone makes my body go stiff.

Investigation? For what? He places his hand on

my arm and I see Pierce flinch. "You have large amounts of poison inside of you, arsenic to be exact," I gasp as loud as Pierce does at the doctor's words.

Pierce looks up to the speckled ceiling for a moment, his veins bulging from the way he tenses up. "What?" He snaps, his deep tone bounces off the walls. The doctor still looks calm as Pierce paces back and forth across the small room with large calculated steps, rubbing his hands through his hair.

"Clipboard." Pierce politely gestures to the doctor and to my surprise again, the doctor obeys. He turns to smile at me before handing over the wooden clipboard to a pissed off looking, Pierce.

With every flip of the page, Pierce's rage seems to dissipate. Not into a calm state, more of an emotionless glare with every word he retains. His hollow voice breaks the thick silence, "I know what's happening," he flatly states and the doctor looks to him. He gently places his arm on the doctor again. "You have told her everything you need to, please come back later to run the rest of her test. Don't call the cops and tell everyone it was the flu," he calmly says. The doctor nods with another bright smile before exiting the room.

Silence fills the small space as I try to figure out just what else is going on in my life. Pierce is staring off onto a blank white cement wall, a tortured expression resides in his eyes as he turns to me, still not speaking.

After a long torturous moment, his deep voice rips through the quiet room. "Preta's not dead," he snarls, the words send a cold chill through me. "He's not dead. I didn't kill him, Scar."

The metal rails of the hospital bed rattle from my shaking limbs. "You killed him." I cry.

This is the first time I've ever seen the calm and collected Pierce take on a panicked edge. "This is a new angle. I... I must have just killed that man. The demon left his body. I should have never left you!" he roars, smashing the clipboard against the hard wall. The wood splinters and cracks in half, colliding with the ground. We both watch the papers float down to the floor.

He makes his way to me in two long strides. Placing both hands on either side of me as he hovers above. "Scarlett, look at me," he demands through clenched teeth. "I'm so sorry, I thought you would be better off." His tone is drenched in regret and worry.

"How did he poison me?" I ask quietly, not wanting anyone to hear, even though we are in a private room.

Pierce lets out a long sigh, "I'm not sure. When did you begin to feel sick?" he asks as he searches my eyes for the answer.

"When you left," I admit.

His head ducks lower and I feel his hair tickle my forehead. He audibly winces, "More specifically."

"I'm not sure, every time I ate, I would throw up. The only things I kept down were foods that Liv made for me." Realization floods through me. "We ordered a ton of food to the house, all kinds of different places. Do you think... the delivery guy?" I wonder.

He nods, "It's possible. Did Zack give you any food?" His accusing tone makes me feel the need to defend my friend, he's been so sweet to me.

"Don't Pierce." I hold up a shaking hand. "I know you don't like him, but he would never hurt me," I say confidently. "Besides, he was just in the room. Did you see the blackness or whatever around him?"

"No, but-"

"But nothing," I reply, changing the subject to the issue at hand which is definitely not Zack. "I got sick tonight after the party; do you think he's watching me? Oh my, God, was he following me and Liv around? We've been alone for days!" I squeal and he grabs my hand tighter. "Zack just stayed with us last night, he could have been hurt. They both could have been hurt. What if they would have eaten the food intended for me?" My thoughts are muffled, and my breathing is ragged.

"She's okay," he assures me, and I look up at him.

"She's home alone, Pierce," I say through my teeth.

He rubs his hand over my cheek. "I just checked on her, she's still asleep. I didn't walk in her room, but I heard her snoring from the hallway." He laughs and my breathing begins to soften.

"How did you know I was here?" I quietly ask.

He looks down to our tangled hands. "I... we can talk about that later," he says, changing the subject. "The paperwork says you have to stay for eight hours."

I slump on the uncomfortable bed. "I want to go

home!" I groan.

"I know baby, but you need the fluids and monitoring." He stands up and walks away from me.

I grab his arm before he gets too far. "Don't leave, why are you leaving me again?" I nearly cry.

He turns his head to look at me. "I'm never leaving you again, I will always be with you now," he states with conviction in his tone. "I was just going to get your phone and call your mom."

Panic floods through me, once again. I want to get off this roller-coaster of emotions, when will it end? "Please don't," I beg.

"Don't worry I've already told the doctor it was the flu, that's what I'll tell everyone," he assures me. "You need your mom right now; I know you do."

He's not wrong. "Is it safe? For her to come here?" I whisper.

"Yes." He nods as he steps out of the room. I calm when I hear him talking on the phone near the door, not far away.

When he returns, I bombard him with questions, per usual.

"What do you mean by 'you told the doctor'?" I ask with air quotes. "You did it to Zack, too. He just listened to you, which was very confusing considering he was thinking of ways to kill you after he saw my back in bed." I cover my mouth realizing how awful that sounded.

Crossing his arms, his brows lift in inquiry. "Why did you not have a shirt on?" he asks, ignoring my other questions.

"When I woke up earlier and Zack flipped the light on, I wiped the sweat from my face, and he saw it..." I trail off.

"I'm sorry. It doesn't matter, can I see?" he asks but he doesn't wait for me to answer before he gently lifts me up and pulls my shirt up. His finger gently trails along my skin, and he sighs.

"I'm so sorry Scar, I never meant-"

I cut him off. "Pierce, I know that, you don't have to explain it to me. Now back to my question. What do you mean when you 'told them'?"

He nods but his eyes are glazed over. "You could say I coaxed them, I calm people and make them believe what I want them to." He shrugs.

"Do you do that to me?" I ask nervously.

"What? No, of course not." He scoffs. "Well, I did...." His tone is remorseful as he gestures into the blank air in front of us. "When you were in the state you were in... that night... When I gave you a bath. I comforted you a little, but I would never make you like... do anything," he adds.

I jump at his words. "When did you give me a bath?" I ask.

His eyes search my face and I see the green begin to gloss over; he shakes his head to steady himself. "Do you not remember what happened the other night?"

"Yes. I do, but I don't remember that," I stutter.

"Don't worry love, I had no other choice, you were in shock and I just wanted to make you more comfortable."

My mind rolls through the terrible memories, but I'm left with large gaps. "I remember what happened... And then I remember your arms around me before I fell asleep. Everything in between is a blur. But when I woke up, I was in my bed and you were gone." I start sobbing against my arm that I raise to cover my face. He gently pulls it away and crawls in the bed next to me.

"I would have never left if I knew that Scarlett, I swear, I wouldn't have. I thought when I broke the bond and I laid down next to you... and you didn't react to my touch... I thought you were disgusted by me. Then, I decided you would be better off without all of this in your life." He gestures to himself.

I give him an incredulous look. "When you put your arm around me it was the only thing that was holding me together, I just couldn't speak or move. I was in shock," I say through tears. I'm drained, absolutely drained.

"Shh... Come here." He pulls me against him. I can feel the rapid pounding of his heart against his solid chest. What happened was violent and gruesome and it did break me but not even for one second did I blame Pierce or think less of him for what he had to do.

"Don't be ashamed of what you did for me, Pierce. You had no choice," I assure him. He holds me until I drift off in his arms.

Twenty-three

So, it's the flu?

"**N**o, don't move Pierce, please. She looks so comfortable." My mom's attempt to whisper wakes me, I peer up to see two unfamiliar people behind her worried face. Brian and Kayla, I'm assuming. I wipe my eyes and look over at Brian, he's clean-cut and looks nice, non-threatening.

Short, cropped darkish blonde hair sits atop his head with blue eyes and slight stubble along his jawline. He's wearing dress slacks with a button-up. He looks to mom with a worried grin.

My eyes pan to his daughter, Kayla, who is smiling from ear to ear. Her energy makes the drab room a little more alive, she's dancing on the balls of her ballet flats, a bouquet in her hands. I give her a small smile and she dances over to me.

"I'm sorry we have to meet this way," she sings, handing me the colorful flowers. Tears well in my eyes at the kind gesture.

"Tha... Thank you," I wipe a tear from my face. The sweet gift mixed with the pure exhaustion I feel is making me emotional. She nods as she tucks her short black hair behind her ears. Her dad walks up beside her, his worried expression is gone and replaced with happiness.

"Hello, Scarlett, I'm Brian. It's so nice to meet you. I'm sorry you're not feeling well, are they treating you good?" he asks, genuine concern in his tone.

I nod. "It's good to meet you too," I say through my sleepy daze.

Pierce gets up and I whimper from his absence in the bed. He reaches his hand out to Brian. "It's nice to meet you, I'm Pierce."

Brian smiles, returning his handshake. "I know who you are, Stacy here loves you." The men exchange a laugh and Pierce gestures for them all to go in the hall to give mom and I a minute.

When the door shuts, we both look at each other, tears welling in our eyes. "Why are you so pale, honey? What happened? Pierce said you have the flu?" She questions me with worried eyes.

I look around the bare room. "Well, Liv is going through that breakup, you know, so I was worried about her," I lie "and I didn't realize I was getting sick. I've barely eaten, and I kept getting nauseous." I sigh.

She brushes a rogue piece of hair from my face. "Well, honey. You will feel much better soon; you can't let yourself get that sick again!" She lightly scolds me. "And why didn't you go to the doctor?" She looks puzzled and now that I realize how serious this is, even if it was just the flu and not poisoning, I can't help but wonder why I didn't. I truly thought I was just so heartbroken that it was making me physically ill.

"I thought it was just a cold or something," I shrug, wanting to get off this topic. " Kayla was so sweet bringing me flowers. You can tell them to come back in whenever."

She shakes her head. "I don't want to bother you, honey, I'll send them home and you can rest. I'll stay here," she tells me.

"It's okay mom, really. I'll be leaving soon and I'm about to go to bed anyway," I assure her.

She laughs but there's no humor involved. "I'm not leaving you in a hospital alone." She gives me a knowing look.

"I have Pierce," I say quietly.

"Pierce isn't your mother." She counters, but a smile plays on her red lips. "I do like him though. Why didn't Zack call me? I should wring his neck!" She jokes and I laugh, thankful Pierce thought of that one first.

She rubs my head for a while as we sit in silence in the bright room. My eyes flutter closed, and mom gets up to leave. As soon as she opens the door, Liv comes frantically rushing in, will I ever get to sleep?

Her worried expression makes me feel guilty about everyone being here at this hour, they all care so much for me. "Hey, Liv," I smile, sitting up a little.

"Don't get up!" she gently orders, "Hey, Ms. Wells." She wraps her arms around mom, squeezing her in a tight hug.

"Hey, Liv! Scarlett, honey, I'm going to tell Brian and Kayla to head home. I'll be back soon." She promises as she closes the door behind her.

Liv's flip flop taps against the linoleum floor. "I just finished cussing Zack out, I can't believe he just let me sleep while he took you here! I was worried sick when he called and I realized you two were gone." She sighs as she sits down on my uncomfortable bed.

"Everything is fine, I have the flu," I lie, and she looks to the needle in my arm.

"The flu?" she says with a raised brow. "Is that why you've been throwing everything up?" she asks, tilting her head to examine me.

"Yeah, it is," I lie, again. "I thought I was just upset but Pierce rushed here when he found out," I say the words, but they frighten me. If the bond was broken, how did he know I was here unless I almost died tonight. A shiver rakes down my spine, a familiar feeling nowadays.

She pouts her full lip. "Aww, Scar! We could have avoided all of this by going to the doctor, and wait! Did you say, Pierce?" She dramatically opens her mouth, and I use my index finger to close it.

190

My breath catches in my throat, "Yeah, you didn't see him outside the door?" A slight panic rises inside of me.

"Zack was by himself, but I didn't look around too much. I gave him a few choice words and rushed in here." She shrugs.

I throw my sweaty hand to my forehead, wishing what I was saying was true. "I hate that everyone is here worried about me and all I have is the damn flu."

She looks around the room, "Are you going to explain the Pierce thing?" she questions.

I hear no judgment in her tone, so I don't mind explaining a half-truth. "He works out of town a lot, so he didn't want to get too serious, but he changed his mind."

A cheesy grin creeps up on her face, "Well good! You two seem cute together, I'm happy for you." She yawns.

"Go home, please. I'll text you as soon as I leave but I know you're exhausted." I plead with her.

She mulls this for a moment before finally nodding, "Okay, okay. But only because you aren't alone. Text me when you can." She hugs me before making her way outside, I hear Zack talking to her as the door closes. She wants him to go with her but of course, he's stubborn and refuses.

The voices are drowned out by my tired mind as I go to sleep. It feels like seconds have passed when I open my eyes again. I can't tell the time, but I see the bright fluorescents on overhead. Mom holds my hand as she sleeps in the chair she pulled up to my bed. Pierce has a chair facing the closed door, on guard with his eyes scowling forward. I gently let go of her hand and notice the needle that was in my arm is now gone, they must have taken it out while I was sleeping.

I quietly tiptoe towards Pierce and he cracks a grin when he sees me, pulling me swiftly onto his lap. "When did you sleep?" I whisper, looking over his bloodshot eyes.

He nods his head to the door, "I haven't."

"Where's Zack?" I ask curiously, I know he refused to leave with Liv earlier.

"I sent him home," he replies flatly.

I nod, "Oh. Well, you need to get some sleep." I run my hands through his messy hair.

His defined dimples melt me when he smiles. "Don't worry about me. Please go back to bed. It's six in the morning," he whispers, pointing to the clock above the door.

"I feel better than I have in days, I can't go back to sleep," I give him a pleading look. "Can we go?"

"It hasn't been eight hours."

I can't help but laugh. "You know better than they do, am I dying?" I ask. I know I'm fine but I'm trying to get my point across.

His body goes tense under me and he pinches the bridge of his nose. "Bed," he states, gesturing his hand behind us.

"Not tired," I tell him, but he rolls his eyes.

His eyes bore into mine. "I wasn't asking you."

"Fine." I quickly jump from his lap, annoyed that he's demanding me.

He grabs my arm before I can get too far. "Please, Scar, it's been a long night. I just want you to be well-rested." He pulls me down for a quick kiss before I climb back on the cold hospital bed. I may have been more tired than I thought as I drift off quickly.

This past week feels like a dream, especially now. Everything is a blur.

What if I wake and he's no longer here?

Twenty-four

Pancakes

I wake again, this time in Pierce's arms as he places me in a car and buckles me in.

Mom's chipper voice lets me know I'm in her car. "I checked her out, they told me to just watch her and give her plenty of water and food." She pauses. "Also, Pierce, you're more than welcome to stay. On the couch, of course," she adds.

I wonder why she's okay with that? Did he make her okay with it? I don't think he would do that to her since he won't do it to me, but I'll ask him later.

I shift in my seat and open my eyes, for a moment I'm blinded by the bright natural light. My eyes got used to the faux lighting in the hospital room. "What time is it?" My voice is thick with sleep.

"Hey, sleeping beauty," Mom says. "It's ten," she adds with a smile.

I wipe my eyes. "Where's Pierce?" I hope my voice doesn't sound frantic.

"Right here," he reaches up from the backseat to touch my shoulder.

"Good," I say under my breath which earns a laugh from Mom.

She looks both ways before pulling onto the empty street. "Feel better?" she asks.

"Much," I reply with a smile.

She sighs, "I have to work honey, I hope that's okay; Pierce can stay with you during the day." She looks towards the backseat. "If you aren't busy, of course," she adds.

"No, it's fine I'll take care of her," he reassures her. It warms my heart listening to the two of them talk, she must like him.

We arrive at the house and Mom heads off to get dressed for work.

Pierce walks me to a wooden bar stool in the kitchen and helps me up. "What do you want to eat?" he asks, his face buried inside the fridge.

"Anything," I beg. My stomach hurts from lack of food.

He starts pulling out random things from the kitchen, a few pots and pans are set on the stove with the burners off. He pours a cup of water for me and slides it across the granite countertop. I see my reflection in the clear glass, unfortunately, mom is a perfectionist about scrubbing so I have a clear yet transparent view of my tired face. Dark bags take up residence underneath my brown eyes while my unruly hair matches my mind, tangled.

Thin heels click against the tile, my eyes pan to mom who is trudging through in a hurry, still clamping in her earrings. "Hey you two, I'm heading out now. Call me if you need anything," she looks between us. "And I know you're an adult but let's not be in the bedroom alone," she adds, and I bury my hands in my blushing face. She laughs as she walks out of the door.

Pierce leans up against the counter, a mischievous grin set on his face. "You really have to clarify 'anything'."

"Umm, is it lunch?" I look around the room for a clock "I'm not even sure what time it is," I admit.

"It's breakfast," he replies.

"Pancakes and a cup of coffee sound amazing," I smile, wondering if he can cook.

"Any toppings?"

"I think we have some strawberries!" I exclaim as I flip my head over to tie my hair with a scrunchie. I lift up to catch Pierce watching me, his head tilted. "Why are you looking at me like that?" I ask as he grabs my hand and brings it up to his lips, he gently places kisses on the tips of each finger as he continues to stare into my eyes. Making me blush fervently.

"You're just so beautiful in the morning, I had to admire you."

I let out a small laugh. "Okay, maybe you need

some sleep. And I need some coffee." I stumble over to the coffee maker and impatiently stare at it while it drips, desperately needing the fuel. I fill my mug to the brim with the hot, bitter liquid.

The sound of plates being sat down catches my attention, and I turn to see Pierce's back leaned against the bar top. A vast selection of pastries, crepes, and a clear mug filled with a frothy mixture that looks like a latte is laid out behind him. I set my boring coffee down and sit at the table in awe.

He gestures towards the items as he speaks. "Strawberries and Cream Crepes, a ton of pastries, and a French Vanilla Latte."

I can't help but bend down to smell the array of sweet scents. Fresh from the brewer, and too hot to drink, I simply perk up by breathing in the aromatic aroma of the latte. "Where did you go?" I ask.

"Paris." He shrugs.

"Oh my God! Pierce, this is incredible! I told you to stop spending money on me but, wow." My eyes pan over the assortment and unable to wait another second I cup the warm mug in my hands, bringing it to my lips. The creamy liquid slides down my sore throat and I moan because of the rich taste, it's nothing like the store brand coffee I'm used to. "This is delicious!" I squeal.

"Glad you like it. You deserve something good after what you've gone through." He frowns.

"So what's it like?" I ask, digging my fork into the creamy crepe.

"Paris is beautiful."

"No, the teleport thingy you do. What's it like to go wherever you want?" I ask, peeling a flaky corner from a pastry and taking a bite.

"Oh, well. It's hard to explain, but when I'm gone it feels like seconds to you but it's much longer for me, when you flipped to pull your hair up, I left and placed the order. I came back and talked to you for a moment before returning quickly when you got up to get your coffee." He smiles. "I didn't want to risk you taking a sip of that." He gestures. "When I can give you this."

"Thank you," I say with my mouth full. "But is this safe?" I gesture towards the food. Suddenly chewing slower.

"Yes. I'll be able to tell now. I saw the chefs preparing it and none of them had ill intentions," he replies, sitting down beside me to dig in. "But in general, I wouldn't take any food from outside your house unless I am there with you. Trust anything here unless someone you don't know comes to visit. I will watch over you as much as possible, but you can't take food from strangers."

"Okay, mom," I joke.

"I'm serious," he states, and I plop a dollop of cream on his nose to soften his hard edges, it works. His emerald eyes widen in disbelief, and he returns the funny gesture by doing the same to me, and then licking it off my cheek. After last night I didn't expect to feel so good, so alive. I thank Pierce for that.

We both enjoy the rich crepes and sweet pastries together and I realize I may need to just rest today; I really need to think about what I'm going to do with my job. I love working there but it's more difficult now.

I look at the empty plate as I clutch my full stomach. "You have to take these dishes back," I joke.

"I will, I promise." He crosses his heart.

"Can we go lay down?"

He puts his hand on his chest dramatically. "Scarlett Wells, your mom told you no boys in your room." He playfully scolds and I laugh at his stunned expression.

I walk over to him and lean my head against his chest, slipping my hands into his hoodie pocket. The crunch of something I touch surprises me and I pull out a crumpled piece of paper. A familiar piece of paper. His eyes widen when I unfold it.

"Don't read that," he pleads.

I pull the paper behind my back as he chases me, a nervous smile creeping up his face.

He tosses me over his shoulder, obviously trying to distract me from reading it, but I do anyways.

I see my handwriting; *I saw you in my dreams.*

Underneath it, in cursive ink that's been smudged is simple and sweet. *I saw you too.*

He can feel the warmth that goes into my soul from the words as he sets me down and looks deep into my eyes.

No words are said as I bring myself on the tips of my toes to kiss him. He leans his head down and we kiss deeply as I hold the sweet letter in my hand with a tight grip. "When did you do this?" I ask, my voice smothered in adoration.

"I came to check on you, but I never came inside. I just saw you set this out and I was hoping you would think the wind took it." I can tell the gesture isn't something he's used to, but it means the world to me.

"Well, I thought it did." I don't hide my smile as he wraps my hand around his and leads us towards the bedroom.

Once I sit on the bed, he takes off his hoodie and hands it to me. "Wear it?"

He grins when I slip it on and we both crawl under the covers, he spoons me against him.

Laying here in his arms feels so natural. I run my hands through his hair, hoping he will feel the desperation in my touch. Doesn't he know how much I need him? Does he need me, though?

I kiss his neck for a moment and note that his breathing grows more rapid. I climb on his lap and his hand grips the back of my neck, pulling me into him. I'm lost in his kiss, his touch, his warmth.

He lets this tangled moment of passion go on for a moment longer before his hands grip my waist as he peels me off of him. I can't help but pout. "So you don't want me?"

His hands cup my face protectively, passionately, as his eyes bore into mine. "Don't ever say that Scar. I want every inch of you, every second of the day" His hand slides through my hair, making me melt under his touch. "But you forget so quickly you were just in the hospital for God knows what."

200

At the worst timing possible my phone starts ringing, and I see Liv's name flashing on the screen. Guilt covers me and replaces the moment I just had with Pierce as I send her to voicemail. Pierce, of course, senses this change in mood and he wraps me tighter.

"What's wrong, babe?" he asks and my heart flutters at his words.

"It's Liv, I know she's worried but I'm so scared Pierce. What if something had happened to her or Zack?"

"She will be safe. I promise, so will Zack," he says the last part with annoyance and I gently swat his arm. "It's for the best. I don't want to keep you from her so we can arrange a meeting time and I can keep you safe as well as Liv."

Realization dawns on me, Liv will be far away from me and safe very soon. "She leaves next week for her summer trip. She'll be gone for two months but what about mom, though? Now, Brian and Kayla, they seem so sweet I don't want to bring them into this mess." The tears slide freely down my cheeks.

He places a strand of hair behind my ear. "I wish you would let me just take you away, we could go anywhere in the world you want. Fewer people would work best, so I wouldn't have to worry about you while I hunt down this demon." The grit is heavy in his tone.

"That wouldn't protect my family, I would rather have you here with me and my mom just in case."

"My main priority is protecting you," he tells me. "Everyone else be damned." I narrow my eyes at him, and he rephrases his statement. "Okay, everyone be damned besides your mom, Brian, and his daughter." He smiles, "Since Liv will be gone, she's safe and one less thing for us to worry about."

I swat his arm, "And Zack, fine."

Twenty-five

We leave Friday

I bury my face into his chest. "One more question?" I ask hesitantly, not sure I want to know the answer. He rubs my back as I continue, "Earlier at the hospital, you said twice... that you've coaxed me or whatever. I now know the bathroom thing but what about the first time?"

He stiffens beside me. "The bathroom was the first time."

"What?" I raise my brow in inquiry, but he can't see my face, so I lay down on my back, trying to remember. He leans on his side, looking like a sculpture with no shirt on, and his lean body sprawled across my bed. No, get it together, Scarlett.

He runs his hand through his hair. "The night before last, at the... bonfire."

"You were at the Bonfire?" I snap. "What did you coax me into believing?" I ask in disbelief.

He places his hands out in front of him. "I had just gone to check on you very quickly to make sure the party was safe. When I found you sitting on the blanket next to-" He takes a deep breath, "A guy was making some advances on you that were unwanted, so I shoved him into the water." He laughs, reminiscing about something I have no memory of.

I spring up. "You what? Who was it?"

"Who he was doesn't matter, I took care of him."

My breathing grows ragged. "Did you... did you kill him?"

"What? No!" He laughs. "I saw him kissing you and so I stopped it."

A small laugh escapes my lips, "So you didn't want me anymore, but you wanted to control who kissed me?"

He scoffs, "It's not like that Scar, and you know it."

"Make me remember," I state, curious if that's even possible.

He shakes his head, "Hell no."

I narrow my eyes at him. "Pierce, they're my memories." I remind him but he pinches the bridge of his nose. "Why don't you want me to remember you?"

He lets out a small laugh, "It's not me that I don't want you to remember. It's Zack." He states.

"Zack?"

He sits up and places his hand on me, bringing his face close to me. I become disoriented as he whispers in my ear, "Remember," he whispers in an echo. With a rush, similar to a storm rolling over my body, it all comes back.

"Oh my God." I stare at my headboard in disbelief. "He almost kissed me."

"No Scar, he did kiss you. His lips touched yours for a brief, awful moment. I hesitated; I wasn't fast enough because I didn't know if I should stop it. I hate that I allowed him to even get close." He spits.

I huff, "You know... you left."

He sighs, not responding.

"I could have kissed Zack and it wouldn't have mattered," I remind him.

In a swift movement, he's on top of me. Quite literally hovering over my bed. My breathing hitches in my throat as he gently pins my wrist above my head.

"No one." He tells me with a passionate glint beaming behind his jade eyes, "No one, besides me will ever have the luxury of touching you." His body is suspended in the air and I stare at him in awe.

I cough, "Pierce..." I look at the distance between our bodies, "You're... you're floating!"

He smirks, lowering himself down onto me, "Not floating sweetheart, flying." His cocky grin melts me, "I'll take you one day. Zack would never be able to take you soaring through the sky."

I playfully swat his arm, still speechless from

seeing him move that way. Needing a subject change so I don't freak myself out I ask, "So what you're telling me is you were just going to watch me until I grew old and died and never let me find love?" I laugh, "Just throw every man that got near me into a nearby body of water?"

"Yes." He shakes his head, "I don't want to think about that, okay? But just not with Zack, not when he was drunk. You were drinking too. He should have known better than to try and take advantage of you."

A sly smile creeps up my lips, "If you leave again, I'm going to kiss every guy I see." I joke, laughing when a smile cracks on his lips.

Then he attacks, tickling me until we wear ourselves out.

I leave Pierce sleeping on my bed, thankful he doesn't snore because mom would kill him if she found him in here.

I change and head downstairs. "Hey, mom," I say as I stretch my sleepy body.

"Hey, honey! I'm glad you're up, I wanted to talk to you."

Does she know he's upstairs? Trying to hide my nerves I ask, "Yeah, what's up?"

"I know you only got to meet Brian and Kayla for a brief moment and we need some time away, would you want to go to the beach house for a little vacation? I know it's last-minute, but I think you could use the rest and relaxation."

I want to scream 'Yes!' but I have to think about the safety of everyone. "I would love to, but Pierce-"

My stomach drops as she holds her hand out in front of her, "About that," she says, with a smile. "I wanted to invite him too!"

"Really?" I squeal.

She points an accusatory finger in my direction. "He sleeps on the couch, of course."

"Yes!" I agree.

She sighs while pulling a loose strand of hair behind my ear. "I know you're an adult now and I respect what you two have, he seems like a great kid. Well, man." She laughs at herself. "And you will be leaving for college so soon, I just will miss you so much and I want to spend as much time as possible with you."

I'm beaming. "I think it would be good for both of us to get away."

She claps her hands together "Then it's settled, we leave Friday!" Friday, oh man. I need to go back to work.

I shrug in her direction. "I need to call Mike," I say quietly.

"Already talked to him." She admits with an innocent smile. "Don't freak out though, you have to remember I've known him my whole life Scarlett. He was your dad's best friend and he's so understanding. He's overstaffed with all the high schoolers trying to make quick cash and I know you don't need the money; you save like crazy. He said if you want to take any shifts just to call him."

I playfully roll my eyes. "I appreciate that mom, I

could have called him myself, but I am thankful."

"I'm going out for the day, call me if you need me." She grabs her purse off the counter and heads outside. When the garage door closes shut, I rush up the stairs. I'm too excited about this vacation for him to be sleeping.

"Get up!" I yell as I jump on top of him.

"Your happiness woke me up minutes ago, what's going on?" He beams.

I smile at him, a cheesy grin. "Do you want to go on vacation with my mom and Brian?" I squeal.

He sits up and stretches his arms out wide. "Of course, where to?" he asks.

"He has a beach house," I say, bringing myself closer to him.

"Sounds like fun." He yawns but I notice his jaw twitch.

A frown takes over my face, "Are you sure? You don't seem too excited." I pout and he playfully flips me underneath him.

"You... in a bikini for a week? No distractions? I'm all in." He plants a lingering kiss on the crook of my neck.

Twenty-six

Vacay

I glance at the calendar as I pull a brush through my wet hair, failing to get the tangles out but too excited to pay too much attention. It's already Friday and I'm so thankful the past few days have been safe. I haven't left the house out of fear but I'm excited about going to Brian's beach house today.

Pierce is sleeping soundly on my bed; his dark hair is tousled against my pink pillowcase which makes me giggle. He's been here every night; we haven't left each other's sides. The only time he goes to work - if that's what you call it, I keep telling myself it's work so I don't worry myself more – is when I'm asleep.

I tiptoe around the quiet room, so I don't wake him as I get dressed and meet Mom downstairs for breakfast. I'm so thankful Pierce doesn't snore, or our charade would be up.

"Honey! Liv is here to say goodbye." Mom's words make me frown, but then I smile knowing Liv will be safe away from me. I always miss her so much when she leaves every summer. I rush to the kitchen and practically knock her over with a hug.

She smiles, "I'm going to try to come back soon this time!" she promises.

"I wish you didn't have to go at all," I lie, I know that her being far away will bring so much peace to my soul. If only I could send everyone else I love far, far away from me they would all be safe.

Mom eats with us and heads out shortly before Pierce 'arrives' at the front door. We leave, following behind her in my car.

She told me I would be impressed with the beach house, and I already am from the looks of the manicured lawns as we roll through Brian's street. I enjoy the salty breeze that circles through the open windows, hoping this trip will help to relax us both.

Pierce is oddly quiet as we pull down the driveway that's lined with palm trees towards the yellow beach house at the end of a circular drive. He hasn't spoken much on the ride here and that worries me. He's been content all week as we stayed in and kept a safe distance from anyone other than Mom. I pray everything goes smoothly and nothing bad happens when we're here.

Pierce's warm hand clamps onto my leg, his thumb gently rubbing back and forth to soothe me. The gentle, yet firm touch brings a smile to my face but as I look at him I note the scowl that has taken place where his dimples normally sit. Eyes focused strictly on the scenery ahead, his face slightly contorted. What has him so worked up?

I study him, but I can't understand his expression as we come to a stop. He seems on edge. I'm about to ask him what's wrong when Mom rips my door open, causing a small scream to escape my lips.

"We're here!" she sings, laughing at the jump scare. I step out, and she places her slender arm through mine. I look around at the exotic flowers that make up the landscape. I smile at the familiar seashell wind chime that's hanging on the porch, I bet she made it.

She claps her hands together once, her enthusiasm evident. "We'll get your bags later." She gestures towards my parked car; Pierce is leaning against it watching us with a small smile.

He shakes his head. "I'll grab them."

Arm in arm, Mom and I walk towards the front door, "Why do you two always take your car, where is his?" she asks quietly.

"At the shop," I mumble.

She nods, "Oh, that's a shame. I hate when mine breaks down," she says as we walk into the foyer and head towards the kitchen. The walls look familiar, but I can't put my finger on it. I grew up at the beach so I'm guessing ocean décor is a familiar sight.

"This will be your room for the week." She gestures towards a room further down the hall. "I'll be staying across the house in another guest room." Her voice is quiet.

I hesitate, "Are you not staying in Brian's room?" The words sound weird coming out of my mouth.

She shrugs. "It doesn't seem appropriate." She twiddles her thumbs and I want to tell her it's okay, Brian seems great.

But it's just too soon for me to think of her in another man's room so I'm thankful she's taking me into account. This is new territory for both of us. I give her a wide smile, but it doesn't quite reach my eyes as we continue down the cream-colored hallway.

Our feet pass the slight lip of the threshold through an arched doorway into a large room. A driftwood bed frame catches my attention, decorated with a white plush comforter. Large crystal-clear glass doors lead out to the water. A familiar bathroom to my left.

I bring my trembling hand to cover my lips, trying to shove back the gasp that escapes them. I remember why this looks so familiar. I've been here, I was here...

"It's beautiful right! I knew you would love it." She squeals as she looks around the room. I'm thankful she's mistaken my horror for a positive shock.

"It's something," I mumble as Pierce walks in, a look of guilt on his face raises so many questions about why we came here of all places, and how he knows about it.

She gives me a small frown, "Kayla won't be coming until Monday, she had to work this weekend."

She looks pointedly between both of us, breaking our curious gaze at each other. "You can have the guest room across the hall, Pierce. Please make yourselves at home. I'm about to start lunch so I'll come get you when it's ready!"

When I hear her heels clicking against the kitchen tile, I close the gap between Pierce and I. Before I can speak, he does. "Outside?" He suggests and I nod.

He opens the familiar doors that lead to the sand. My stomach drops at the sight of him at the doorway just like before, my brain was foggy and I was a mess but I'll never forget the way he looked at me for a brief moment before peeling his gaze to the water, not knowing at the time he was debating with himself to leave me.

I slip out of my flip flops as we near the sand. Pierce follows, stepping out of his boots. He keeps one hand on mine which makes it harder for him to remove them, but he refuses to let go.

The only sound that takes over is the wind and waves as we make our way straight out towards the ocean. He sits on a long piece of worn driftwood and brings me down to sit on his lap.

"I brought you here because I've checked on your mom here a few times." He admits and I nod in understanding, my hands still trembling from the vivid memories. "I thought you would want to be close to your house, I truly thought when you calmed down that you would want to be nowhere near me and I know you've never been here before but the familiarity of somewhere your mom has been was a nice place, I think."

I nod, "I get that, it's just hard to see. You made the choice to leave me here. My worst moments were spent in that room." I gesture dramatically towards the glass doors.

"I know, babe. I'm sorry." He brings me closer to his chest and places a kiss on my hair, lingering longer than normal as he holds me tight. We sit in an understanding of silence for some time.

A sing-song voice takes off behind us, "Guys! Food is ready!" I turn to Mom's direction to find her giggling to Brian as they stand on a light wood porch that's placed in the center of the house, higher than the room I'm in.

"Coming!" I yell back as Pierce stands and holds his hand out.

His eyes look at me cautiously as we make it back to my room, "Are you okay staying here?"

"Yes, as long as I don't have to sleep alone." I wink.

He slings his arm around me, covering me in his warmth, "I'll sneak in every night."

Twenty-seven

Look, we need to talk

The kitchen table is set for four which makes me anxious, it's always been just two placements for so long. She's been so welcoming with Pierce that I was beginning to get used to three, one more may be too many.

Pierce's hand is firm against my back and his fingers reassuringly circling my skin letting me know it's alright. He feels it, too. He feels what I do. "Is this the pasta salad you made the other day Ms. Wells?" he asks, saving me from speaking. My voice would crack if I did.

"I've told you to call me Stacy." She points an accusatory finger at him, "And yes. I knew how much you liked it after you ate three plates," she snickers.

"He eats so much!" I joke trying to break the tension I feel inside. But it's true, Mom and I have been cooking nonstop since he comes for dinner every night. It makes me happy that he loves to eat family meals with us.

Brian sits quietly at the round table, I'm thankful it's not rectangular so there is no definite head of the table. I try to imagine Brian as a parental figure, making decisions about important things with her.

I'm leaving for college soon and I don't want her to be alone. I need to work through my feelings of seeing her with someone else. It's not that I dislike Brian, I think he's very sweet, but their relationship only reminds me of the loss of my dad.

He was such a great man it's hard to think of anyone better suited for her, than him. I can't deny her shift in life since she met Brian though. Random bouquets sent to her at work with thoughtful cards attached that I've peeked at. It warms my heart to know she's happy again.

I don't realize I'm moving noodles around my plate absentmindedly until Pierce reaches under the table to grab the hand I've left resting on my right leg. I look up at him and muster a smile.

Mom clears her throat, "Brian and I will be heading out for dinner tonight, would you two like to come?" she offers.

I slowly shake my head, "I'm okay, we can make something here," I tell her, so I can give them their alone time and get some of my own as well. I glance at Pierce who brings a glass of lemonade to his lips to hide a smirk.

Brian straightens out in his chair. "Please, make yourselves comfortable. You can have whatever is in the fridge and pantry. Your mom mentioned you like ice cream, so I grabbed a few tubs since I wasn't sure which flavor you prefer," He smiles and Mom reaches for his hand, but hesitates when she sees me looking at them. I smile at her to say it's okay and she beams as she interlaces her fingers in his.

"Thank you." I smile at the thoughtful act before I return my attention to the pasta salad.

Like the true time warden she is, the second it reached eight o'clock she was hugging me to head off to her dinner with Brian. When the coast was clear I gestured for Pierce to follow me to the upper back deck.

Hand in hand we walk through a set of French doors and out onto the large upper porch, a floating swing that looks the size of a queen-size bed hangs from the white ceilings. I climb in and gesture for Pierce to follow. I want to explain to him why I am quiet towards Brian. Why this is all odd and new for me.

I look into his green eyes and see a flicker of light pass through them as he looks back at me. "I wanted to talk to you," I say quietly, and I note the way his muscles go stiff at my words. "It's okay, it's not about anything bad... It's about my dad," I admit as I look towards my feet.

He gently places both of his hands on mine. "I would love to hear about him, Scar, but if it gets too hard please stop yourself. I want to know everything about you but not at the expense that it hurts you." His reassuring smile sets me at ease as I nod.

I lay my back down against the soft cushion and he follows, we lay staring at the ceiling for a while so I can build up my courage. I turn on my side and see that he's already facing me, with a sweet smile playing on his lips. His dimples deep, his hair shining. It's so hard to concentrate when he looks at me this way.

"I don't know where to start." I breathe.

"Start wherever it makes sense to you."

I use my hands to help me talk, showcasing the story with gestures. "As you know my dad was in the military," A beat of silence passes between us. I've never had to tell this story to anyone, most of my friends were there when everything happened so this is beyond hard for me, but I want him to understand me more.

"He graduated from college and promptly joined the Army." I smile, then frown, then smile again. "Lieutenant Colonel, Mike Wells," I beam proudly. Pierce lets out a low whistle as I continue, "While he was in the Gulf War he earned a Silver Star for saving the lives of his men during an ambush, they were surrounded and he exposed himself to call in artillery fire to keep them off his men, they all lived." I smile, remembering him telling me of his war stories. He would always be so animated and alive when he spoke of them.

My fingertips drag along the chains that hold the bed up. "He was a Man of War. My other friend's dads would come back different but not mine, it never affected

218

him." I shrug. "I never thought about it until I got older but it's just how he was built I guess," I say, and Pierce nods his head. "On his last deployment, he was in Afghanistan for two years." I take in a deep breath to steady myself.

"Ten-year-old me didn't understand what was truly going on over there. My mom shielded me as much as she could but there was only so much she could do. She put on a brave face, but I heard her quiet cries every time she would watch the news in her bedroom. I would sit on the other side and listen to see if any soldiers had perished, crying myself every time." I try to keep my voice strong.

"A few weeks before he was set to return home the house was in a frenzy. Mom was deep cleaning every day, anxiously waiting for his arrival. She was smiling for the first time in years, she was so happy. She bought me a few new dresses for the trip to the airport and I tried them on."

"My favorite was a light pink one that flowed with lace, and I was admiring it in my bedroom mirror when I heard a loud thud and a piercing scream ring through the house. I ran down the stairs to find her at the front door with a paper crumpled in her hands, she was clutching it so hard that when the uniformed men in front of her went to help her up they had to hold her by her shoulders instead of her hands." My voice is muffled by the ache in my throat and the tears slowly streaming down my face. The deep pain of reliving this nightmare.

Pierce gently wipes away the tears. "You don't

have to continue right now," he assures me.

"I need to," I say, knowing I needed to pull up the strength to explain this to him. "The men spoke to my mom for a while, they ended up in the living room and mom held me against her while she wept. She told me to go upstairs and I walked to the end of the staircase out of sight as I listened in." I look up for a moment, trying to roll the tears back in but there's no use. "He had gone out to check on a unit and was on the way back when his Humvee ran over an IED, it was such a high explosive there was nothing left. We buried my father, but it was just an empty box with a flag draped over it." The sobs wrack my body. I wish I had my father's strength and courage so I would be able to talk about him without breaking down.

He holds me against him fiercely, soothing me as he rubs his hands through my hair. I think about Pierce. He was in the military too. I don't know what he did, but my dad always said that his men were like family, it comforts me knowing Pierce is like family to my dad even though they never met.

I pull back from his chest and look into his glossy emerald eyes. "He was a hero, like you."

His expression grows grim at my words. He shakes his head, his hard edges darkening. "I'm not a hero," he states, his tone cold as he pulls me closer to his chest.

"Want to go on a walk?" he suggests. Something to take my mind of the hurt sounds nice. The summer air is warm as we make our way back out to the white sands again. A familiar setting, I will never get over. The way the waves come in at night from the tide. The pink skies as the sun begins to fade below the endless water. I adore the ocean so much.

I study Pierce's stiff expression as we make our way back to the long piece of weathered wood. We sit down and I angle myself towards his body, but he keeps himself faced out at the ocean.

"What's going on?" I ask curiously.

Twenty-eight

I need to talk to you, too

His dark eyes still pointed at the water, he places one hand on my shaking leg to make it stop. He turns his attention to me, a haunted look on his face. "I need you to understand why you can't compare me to someone like your father. He was an honorable man. I am not."

I place a hand on his leg for encouragement and he opens his mouth to speak, then closes it for a long moment before continuing. "I was created for a sole purpose, Scarlett." His chest moves up and down steadily as he contemplates his next words. "I've never been like you, a human. I actually have never felt the emotions you feel, until I met you." I blush at his words but listen intently as he continues.

"The bond is only there for such a short moment, I only have ever felt fear through other humans. Fear of me, the unknown, their death. But with you," he caresses my face in his large hands, "I feel happiness, adoration, want." He tries to fight it, but a crooked grin appears and makes me melt.

He returns to his serious demeanor, "A long time ago, back when monsters and demons wreaked havoc on earth, God created an army." He stops talking for a moment as he sweeps his hair from his face.

"So, the archangels?" I wonder out loud.

A dark laugh escapes his lips. "No, not like the archangels. Me, my men. We were created for one reason and we were sent to earth to fight. I was the leader of the Shadows." I look at him in confusion.

"We were the men the angels turned to when their moral compass was too high. There always has to be darkness even in the light, but I was loyal to all that is good. An angel of the shadows that was never seen nor heard."

"You had parents though?" I ask, remembering him talk about them at dinner when he met my mom.

He shakes his head. "No. But what else am I supposed to say when someone asks about them, ya know?" he chuckles lightly, "Parents make you weak, having someone to care about makes you weak. So we were created without them." My heart lurches, no wonder he enjoys family dinners with us so much.

He looks out at the water, then back to me, his emerald eyes narrowed. "I'm heaven's darkness, but it

223

went too far," he spits. "A divine war was brewing on Earth and God summoned a batch of his strongest warriors to defend his children. I was the commander to a hundred men, but our power was as much as a million trained humans, only we were much, much stronger." He lets a small smile slip, his mind reeling on memories. "We were sent here with one purpose in mind, to find and destroy all that was unholy."

With a shaky breath, I ask, "So God sent you here?"

He shakes his head slowly, "It's hard to explain but there's a lot of higher-ups we have to go through, we were sent by the council, the ones who pay close attention to Earth's divine balance."

I nod my head, trying to retain the information.

"We were ordered to wipe out every unholy entity on the planet and we went gladly, they thought that was a solution to the rebellion that was sweeping across humanity." He gives a look that says 'give me a break' while letting a small chuckle escape his lips. "I ordered my men to annihilate and we began the sweep." His tone is casual and it's not hard to imagine him leading an army, he breathes confidence and his movements are always fluid as if he's a trained killer. This should scare me, but it only makes me feel safer whenever he's near.

He lowers his head. "The problem was, while humanity grew and the evolution of evil became more evident..." He looks at me, trying to rid himself of the memory. "We didn't understand why humans were prone to kill other humans, even when they weren't possessed.

They were just evil in their own right."

"The higher-ups believed it was genetic." He bites his lip as he shakes his head. "We were ordered to kill all family members of the 'dark humans'. Humans like the guy from the club, or the alleyway.... you know with the aura I can see."

I nod in understanding as he continues, "That was the problem, they said it was genetic and we needed to kill off their bloodline." He looks at me pointedly. "ALL of them," he whispers as he bows his head.

The realization hits me and I gasp, "Pierce!" I stutter, "You didn't."

He whirls his head and gives me a look of disgust, "Of course not." he chokes, then he straightens himself out, and looks at me with a sweet intensity. "I couldn't do it. The children, the babies. They were innocent!" His voice booms through the empty beach and I clutch myself.

He steadies himself, "So I deflected. I went against divine orders." He shrugs.

When his eyes gloss over, I take his worried face into my hands for comfort. "So now that I know your past life and what happened..." I frown, thinking of what a difficult decision it was to turn against everything you know. But, it was undoubtedly the right decision. "I'm curious how all of that made you... this." I gesture to his body and he slowly nods.

"When I decided to stop the insanity, I halted my men and ordered them to return. I stayed to defend the children." He shrugs. "I couldn't risk their punishment for my orders." With a long breath, he says, "I knew it was only a matter of time before they came for me. Angels don't die so when someone does something to defy the orders of The Council we go on trial and a life sentence to us is a much different monster," he elaborates.

"When they hauled me away I was placed in a room. Large marble pillars cascaded down from the high ceilings. I had heard stories about angels who had been on trial before but they were normally fallen angels, the bad ones. Not men like me, we were considered the darkness of all that was holy but we protected fiercely and did what was right. They created me for that purpose, so why didn't they see that my actions were for the greater good?" he questions. "I was in a massive marble room, statues adorned the walls in between wide pillars. A man in a hooded cloak walked up beside me, I looked at him for one moment before facing my eyes ahead. To my right was a small woman, tiny in her voice and frame. She approached me with a smile. Protruding from her back were white wings that stretched out so wide they made the statues behind her look insignificant. She reached her hand out to me and I placed mine in hers. The cloaked man firmly grabbed my arm, taking me by surprise as the angel tugged me her way. Her strength didn't match her size, she was incredibly strong. No words were spoken between the two of them as she gently pulled me towards her and he forcefully jerked me back,"

A beat of silence passes between us before he speaks again. "The massive doors opened and a third person stepped in the room. I knew it was my judgment time, they would decide right then if I was going to stay in heaven or be banished to hell. His tone was authoritative but calming as he looked between the three of us. 'Neither of you can have him,' he stated as he walked further towards me. They both released me and tilted their heads to the old man,"

"I looked back and forth between the angel and the cloaked man, but my gaze was stuck on his hooded face as a set of white teeth peeked through the black in his hood. He held a terrifying smile and then just vanished, his cloak falling in a heap on the marble floor. I looked back to the angel and she started to back away slowly until she faded out of sight. I fell to my knees against the hard floor and lifted my hands to my face, I felt a thick fabric fall down my arms and I looked down to see that I now had on the cloak the other man wore." He shivers. "I was stripped of my rank, but they respected what I had done so they didn't want to banish me to an eternity of burning."

I straighten my shoulders, taking a deep breath. "How did you know what you had become? Did he explain?"

He throws his hands up. "The man walked up to me, ethereal light was surrounding him as the cloak laid against my skin. He looked me in the eyes and said, 'You have been given the burden of being the Angel of Death. You will pay for your abandonment by serving the very humans you protected. Since you turned your back on us, you can stay with them.' After he spoke, I can't explain how, but I knew what I was and what I now had to do. My soul purpose now was to bring souls to decide their fate. For so long, I've done this." He gestures to himself. "But then I met you and it all changed."

"Why me?" I ask in astonishment; I still don't understand it myself.

"I think you were meant for me, Scar," he says, and my heart does its usual flutter when he's around. I try to calm the butterflies in my stomach. "Before you, I was a void, a shell doing one duty. I had no one, no friends, no family. But you gave me all of this." He gestures around us. "Love, companionship, family." His voice is low as his eyes bore into mine. I can't help but admire the way he is looking at me, lines of seriousness between his thick brows and his emerald eyes like an amethyst crystal staring back into mine.

I can't hold it in any longer. "But... you spent your life before that trying to make the world a better place and that can't be overlooked. Which if I were in your shoes I would have done the same thing, they were children! Everything else be damned, they were just kids!" I shout. I see the guilt behind his tired eyes. He was an angel, an innocent angel shipped down to earth, caught by the horrors of our race. I see him in a different light now, a man who was once a soldier of God, a soldier of the angels. I wonder what the previous reaper did to hold the spot before Pierce.

"Wait," A light clicks on in my head. "you obviously took the place of the previous Angel of Death, so do you think one day you'll be free?"

He laughs, "No, the hope to be something else, even just nothing, diminished in me long ago." His longing gaze prompts me to deflate. "I won't ever be anything more or else, just always this."

Tears threaten to release, "But you did what was right Pierce! It's unfair." I stand up, pacing in the sand. "You are good." I grab his face and look into his eyes. "You didn't deserve this. Why would they strip you of everything you've done for them? Why would they sentence you to this life?" I spit.

A defeated look on his face is all it takes for me to sit back down, he grabs my hands as he speaks. "It's a loaded question, one that I can't understand nor answer. But from what I can gather, I wasn't good enough for heaven anymore, but I wasn't evil enough for hell."

Twenty-nine

Hi, Kayla!

We've been spending the last day in comfortable silence. More so it's Pierce giving me room to work through what I told him about my father. He thinks the silence is also about him and I can't explain why but he doesn't frighten me. I've never felt more secure or better than when he's beside me.

Kayla will be getting here soon and I'm excited to get to know her. We're all going to dinner tonight at a restaurant on the beach. I'm excited to dance with Pierce, the music is supposed to be amazing from what Mom and Brian said.

After playing checkers for the tenth time with Pierce and failing miserably each round, I hear the distant sound of a front door shutting. "Hey, Kayla!" Mom calls from the kitchen.

I grab Pierce's King that's about to make me lose, again, and chuck it across the patio. He -of course- grabs it with ridiculously fast movements. "Cheater." I stick my tongue out playfully and rush inside, him chasing after me.

Kayla's eyes widen in surprise at our chasing game of cat and mouse as we head into the dining area. "Hey!" She smiles, her short black hair bounces as she carries an impressive amount of school books. She sets them on the kitchen table with a huff. I know she's my age, but mom mentioned she started summer classes at her new college already, I wonder what she's going for?

"Nice to see you not in a hospital," she jokes and I laugh as I greet her with a hug. I know I should feel more awkward since we don't know each other but I miss Liv so much already and sometimes, you just need a hug.

My smile brightens when she pulls me in tight, hugging back. "Thank you for the flowers again, that was so sweet!"

My eyes trail to the stack of titles in front of us. "What are you going to school for?" I nod my head to the table.

"Law," she beams. "You?" I try to imagine Kayla as a lawyer. I don't know her well, but her small frame and soft voice don't scream Lawyer to me. She seems too sweet to deal with such a cut-throat profession, but maybe I shouldn't judge her so quickly.

"I'm undecided," I admit with a shrug. Pierce gives me a confused look from where he sits at the table.

For dinner I opt for wearing a white short sundress, knowing this is an outdoor restaurant at the beach and I don't want to sweat to death.

As we arrive at the beachfront bar/restaurant I note the stylish decor. The entire place is dotted with happy beachgoers. Drinks are flowing and a live band is playing. The music is nowhere near what I would describe as amazing - as my mom and Brian described it - I stifle a chuckle when mom nudges my arm and gestures to the band. "Great, right?" she asks with enthusiasm. I nod my head, lying to the poor woman.

Pierce pulls the seat out for me, he looks perfect in his dark jeans and a black t-shirt. I admire him in the warm light of the restaurant. His demeanor doesn't match mine, he's nervous about being in public like this.

Mom glances over the menu with her reading glasses on. "I think I'll have the fish tacos." She smiles while looking at all of us. I can see the change in her so much, from being sad to happy all because of Brian. I need to let go of my fear of someone replacing my father. She would never let that happen, she just needs someone to share life with, like I need Pierce.

"I think I'll do the same!" I smile at her, not regretting my decision when they come out and I devour them in under five minutes. Delicious.

I reach for Pierce's hand under the table and notice that his fist is clenched. I look at his plate, untouched. He's on edge and it's freaking me out.

I lean against his shoulder. "Relax," I whisper to him, but he shakes his head defiantly.

"Dance with me," he offers, I follow him out to the small dance floor.

The music is awful, but loud enough for us to talk without anyone hearing too much. I lean my head against his shoulder. We sway back and forth as he talks, "This was a mistake."

My body stiffens at his words, does he mean me? Us?

Per usual he knows how I'm feeling, and he lets out a quick laugh. "No, not us. This." He gestures around the busy room and I nod my head in understanding.

"I know you're worried. I am too, but it's just one night." I give him a pleading look, trying to will the universe to give us just a weekend of safety with a dramatic pout.

He relaxes his shoulders, "Fine. But I'm not joking, if I feel something being the slightest bit off I'll make us disappear in front of everyone." I laugh but he doesn't. Oh, he's serious.

I look him in the eyes, trying to keep a calm tone so he doesn't make my mom see us disappear, the thought is almost comical. "We have to live sometimes. It will be okay." I try to assure him and myself, but he shakes his head. Luckily, I don't have to swallow my words as dinner goes by without incident.

After dinner, Mom and Brian head to bed. Pierce, Kayla, and I head out to the balcony in the room I'm staying in. Kayla steals a bottle of wine from her father's

233

cabinet and giggles as she runs to the room.

It's so easy to laugh around her, to have fun with her. Finding friends is hard and I think I got lucky with her.

She braids my hair into a messy but perfect fishtail. "I miss having long hair," she groans, tying a rubber band around my braid.

I look at her sleek black bob in admiration, "I love your cut, I think it's perfect. Do you regret cutting it or something?"

She laughs, "No way! I watched a YouTube tutorial on bleaching your own hair." She takes another swig from the half-empty bottle of wine. Pierce is reading a book in the corner of the room, his expression thoughtful. She makes an explosion motion with her hands.

"You didn't!" I yell. We both fall into a fit of giggles.

That night, Pierce and I lay in bed together. My hands tracing the outlines of his muscles as the warm summer breeze blows through the open doors.

He taps my shoulder, "So what do you think of Kayla?" he asks, and I don't hesitate.

"I like her."

He smiles, "I do too. She reminds me of you." She's so smart and sweet I don't know why he compares us. I shrug, he takes a deep breath. "Why did you say you were undecided?"

I shrug, again. "Don't know. I just don't know what I want to do with my life." I roll on my back, looking at the ceiling in thought. He turns on his side and looks me over.

"That's okay. No need to rush, I was just hoping you weren't holding back out of fear.. of you know. Everything."

"No, it's nothing like that. I've just always been that way. I get interested in one thing and throw myself into it, then I get bored quickly and move on. I just truly don't know what I want to do with my life."

I'm done playing twenty questions about myself, "Where do you normally sleep? Like before you met me and I forced you to stay with me every night," I joke but I have always been curious about this.

"Nice conversation change." He laughs, "I have a place, it's not much but it's mine."

"How do you make money?" I ask.

His brow raises, "You're inquisitive tonight." He lets out a laugh, letting me know it's okay. He tilts his head, giving me a thoughtful look. "When you've been around as long as I have you'll learn that investments are your friend," he says.

"So, what do you want to do tomorrow?" I ask him, wondering if he's having an okay time on an awkward family vacation.

He looks thoughtful, "No more bars." He looks at me pointedly and I roll my eyes. "I'm serious. I'm too paranoid. We need to be careful."

I shrug. "Okay, check. No busy restaurants. What

sounds fun to you?"

He thinks for a moment, then decides. "A beach day with you would be perfect."

Brian and Mom are sitting underneath a flamingo clad pink umbrella, reading books while Kayla tans her pale skin in the scorching Carolina sun.

I want to bring her sunscreen so she doesn't burn but as Pierce exits the glistening ocean, drenched in saltwater, I can do nothing but stare at him. The translucent beads roll down his cheeks from his dripping black hair. Mesmerizing me.

Suddenly, I'm not feeling too confident. After last night's wine charade and a heavy dinner, I feel bloated and uncomfortable. I'm on the edge where the sand meets the tide, covering myself with a towel. Afraid to show myself in a bikini for some reason.

Pierce's long strides guide him to me easily, I blush when he gives me a knowing look. "You're being awfully shy today," he says as he pulls the towel from my clenched hands. I pout, he laughs. "You look perfect. I've seen you like this before... what's so different today?" he asks with a tilted nod. His dimples glisten in the hot sun.

I bite my lip and shrug my shoulders. "You just look so... perfect." I gesture to his statuesque physique. He's the type of man they would carve from rock to place in front of a greek warrior coliseum.

He throws his head back dramatically. "You're impossible!" he shouts over the wind, a mischievous grin adorning his sculpted face. He throws me over his shoulder, I yelp. No point in protesting, I'm going in whether I want too or not, but we all know... I want to.

Under mom's watchful eye, Pierce doesn't use too much PDA. I see her watching us from her chair, smiling. She returns to her book and I plant a big kiss on his dimple. They deepen as his smile goes wider.

I push my fingers through his drenched hair, "You're calm today." I narrow my eyes.

He throws me up and I splash back into the water, I didn't even feel his hands go under me to toss me. "Not crowded." He gestures to the empty beach. "There's nothing to be worried about."

I point my finger to the darker part of the ocean farther out. "Sharks," I remind him and he rolls his eyes.

Squaring his shoulders and deepening his voice he says, "I'm more dangerous than a shark." His confidence is potent. I stand closer to him in hopes that some of his bravado will leak into me.

Even through the heavy warm salt air I still smell his perfect scent. Earthy, minty, divine. He dips farther into the water, only his head sticks out. "I love it, you know," he says, his arrogant tone is palpable.

I roll my eyes playfully. "What?"

He grabs my inner thigh under the water. "The way your body reacts to me." To hide my blush and embarrassment of him feeling everything he does to me, I splash him.

His laughter roars through the waves. "Is that all you got?" he challenges, rushing towards me. I try to swim away but my laughter slows me down. Pierce goes under and I surface out of the water in an instant. I assume I'm about to fly back in but as I look down, I'm sitting on his shoulders.

He's so strikingly tall that I'm way out of the water. The seagulls chirp above as the waves crash against his stomach. "Sailboat!" I point out towards the sea in excitement. He nods, tossing me up once and making me splash into the water.

Once I surface I pull the wet mop of hair from my eyes and huff at him, Ariel style. He grabs my hand under the water, pulling us behind a formation of rocks that were placed there to subdue the tide during hurricane season.

Out of sight from any wandering parental gazes. He cups my face in his warm hands and kisses me deeply as the water laps against our shoulders. His long fingers graze the length of my body under the water.

I'm on fire.

An absolute mess, panting and flushed cheeks. His wandering hands all over me as the birds chirp overhead creating a rhythmic melody of music.

He wraps me tighter in his strong tanned arms, his body towering over me with his massive frame as he plants kisses along my jawline.

I reach farther down his chest and he hesitantly jerks away before it can go anywhere. Leaving me breathless.

I sigh dramatically. "Why do you always stop?" I complain with a pout.

He takes my hands in his, his eyes look behind me for a moment and he shakes his head. "We have plenty of time." I bite my lip and he rubs a thumb across them. They're swollen from the kiss and my entire body is gravitating towards him with every look and touch.

I have to change the subject. "Why did you drag me back here?"

He laughs, "To kiss you, of course." He smiles. "But also, you got really excited about the sailboat. Let's go."

Before I can protest, we're no longer behind the rocky barricade but standing on what I think is called the Bow of the ship, the front.

I turn towards him as I see the shore in a faint distance, our umbrella on the sand looks like a dot from way out here.

I hit him playfully. "What about the captain?" I whisper against the strong winds.

"Passed out drunk, already checked." He shrugs and I admire the boat for a moment.

"Beautiful," I say in awe as my eyes dart to the glossy dark wood that our feet stand on, and the massive sail as it whips in the wind.

Pierce smiles before turning me out to the water, he lifts my arms reminding me of Jack and Rose as he whispers in my ear. "You are the most beautiful."

My heart flutters in my chest at the calm, perfect moment we share on our last day of vacation.

Thirty

Damnit, Zack.

That night after arriving home from Brian's beach house mom excused herself to her room, exhausted from the fun we had.

To my dismay, Pierce had to leave for the night.

He made me promise to stay in, and that he would be back around six in the morning.

I would have kept that promise.

If Zack didn't text me an urgent message needing my help.

Now, I'm in the car rushing to his house. Trying to keep myself calm as I speed down the road. If my body or mind gives even the slightest indication that I'm upset, Pierce will be sitting next to me in no time. I dial Kayla's number on my phone.

"Hey!" she answers, on the first ring. Now that I

know Zack kissed me I don't want to meet up alone with him, but he's still my best friend and whatever is going on sounds urgent. Pierce will be less mad if I drag Kayla in, right?

"Hi, I was wondering if you were busy?" I say, with a hopeful tone.

I can hear her smile through the phone, "Not at all, wanna hang out?"

"Actually, I need your help. My friend from the hospital, Zack... somethings wrong."

I can hear her rummaging through something, "Say no more, I'm at the pier come get me."

Guilt floods me, "Oh no! If you're out with friends I don't want to interrupt your night."

She laughs. "Girl, I'm by myself at an ice cream shop using their wifi to study."

Small world. "Pop's?" I ask.

"That's the one!"

I smile. "Be there in five." I hang up, so thankful she was available.

I'm so nervous about what may be going on with Zack that I feel like I'm going to throw up at any minute. But, I'm keeping my heart rate calm somehow as I weave through traffic.

It's midnight. Whatever is going on, I hope I get back on time before Pierce returns.

I know he hates him, but it's not that Zack is a danger to me. Besides, to keep them both safe I will refuse to go anywhere crowded. My logic is, if it's the three of us in the car or somewhere where no one is; then a demon won't be able to enter anyone's body. Brilliant, I tell you.

My tires squeal as I slide in front of the pier, Kayla hops in with her bookbag. "Thank you so much," I tell her, peeling out once she buckles herself in.

"No, thank you for saving me from studying. I never get to go out, and I don't have anyone to go out with," she admits sheepishly.

"You have me now," I assure her, and Liv too when she gets back. "And sorry this isn't a fun trip, I don't know what's going on."

Arriving at Zack's house I send him a text letting him know I'm in the driveway. The passenger door flies open causing me to jerk back in fear, Kayla almost screams. I instantly put my hand over my heart and breathe deeply.

I need to keep calm.

He closes Kayla's door and jumps in the back, holding a black backpack in between his legs.

"I need your help." His voice is frantic as he rocks back and forth with wide eyes.

I give him a curious look, "What is it?"

"Just drive."

Kayla turns around in her seat, extending her hand to Zack. I watch in the rearview as his eyes widen a little at her cheery tone. "I'm Kayla" she says, in her sweet voice.

His worried demeanor calms slightly, "Zack," he

says, returning her gentle shake.

We pull into an empty small park, secluded enough but fear still eats at me.

"Let's stay in the car," I suggest but Zack shakes his head, we step out and I hesitantly walk behind them, becoming paranoid with every step. Kayla's bubbly attitude tries to cheer up whatever is wrong with Zack, but he's mostly quiet until we reach a clearing.

We sit on the grass and Zack pulls his black backpack into his lap, fear rakes through me as he reaches in. Could Pierce be right? Could he be dangerous?

A mischievous grin crosses his face when he pulls out a bottle of liquor. I sigh in relief. It was all a ruse. Thank God.

"What the actual freak, Zack!" I playfully slap his arm, relief flooding through me.

He laughs. "What? I missed you. I knew the only way to get you alone," he points at me and I give him a sarcastic smile, "and away from your boyfriend was to tell you it was urgent." Kayla laughs at his remark.

"They are the cutest!" she squeals, making Zack do a little eye roll.

"Not cool," I groan, angry he lied but I get it. And now will be the perfect time to tell him that we are just friends, I promised Pierce I would after the bonfire incident. I don't want one drunken mistake of Zack's to cause a wedge between Pierce and I.

We catch up as I try to stay neutral, my body jerking at every crack of limbs or cars that drive by. I don't drink since I'm driving, and Zack only takes a couple of swigs. Kayla becomes a little tipsy after a few gulps, her small frame was not made for hard liquor. She giggles at every word we say, I love her bubbly personality. But my nerves are getting the best of me, it's just so quiet.

An hour later and a few more sips, Kayla walks into the woods to pee. I want to go with her but she hiccups and says it's fine. She sways as she walks to the nearest bush, still in eyesight. I can tell the liquor is having an effect on Zack as he looks at me, admiring me.

He cups my chin to draw my attention to his face. With liquid courage he says, "Scarlett, I am better." He places his hand on mine, rolling his thumb along my skin. I pull back quickly. My heart is racing. Shit.

I need to tell him it won't happen. I love him as a friend. "Zack, listen I love Pier-" I cut myself off as a large figure materializes behind him. Towering over us as we sit.

I crawl backward, about to scream for Zack to run but Pierce's body sharpens and comes into view behind my unsuspecting friend. Thankfully, his back is turned but when Pierce takes a long step to place himself in front of me, Zack gasps from the sudden change in dynamic.

We stand quickly.

Pierce is in front of me, his furious gaze darting between Zack and I. "This is why I don't want you hanging out with him." His tone is venomous. "He's got you out here in the middle of the damn night!"

Zack collects himself and steps around to face us.

"Did you seriously follow her here?" he slurs. Zack's attention turns to me. "Do you see why I'm better for you, Scarlett? This is insane!" He roars.

I don't know what to say, everything is happening so quickly. Zack squares up to him, putting himself in front of me. "Got a problem?" he asks Pierce in a drunken mumble.

A deep laugh rumbles in Pierce's chest, his size next to Zack is intimidating even to look at. "I know," he laughs again. Pierce crosses his arm and waves a solitary finger at Zack. "I just fucking know you didn't step in front of my girl to protect her from *me*."

"Guys!" I yell in defeat, it does nothing.

Kayla stumbles back in a drunken stupor, "Hey Pierce!" she slurs, Pierce's eyes dart to mine, and then they widen.

"You know better," he tells me. I want to explain the situation, but he looks so furious.

Pierce beckons me with one finger. I go to step toward him and Zack pushes me back slightly causing an unearthly growl to resonate low in Pierce's chest.

Zack raises his head to him, "You can't tell her what to do. You don't own her."

Pierce chuckles, throwing his head back. He narrows his eyes at Zack. "Oh... but I do." His voice is dark. He leans down to be eye level with Zack, placing his hands on his knees as if speaking to a child. "She is mine."

Great.

With that, Zack's fist collides with Pierce's jaw. It

doesn't do anything. Pierce just looks at him and laughs, manically.

He places his large hand on Zack's throat, suspending him into the air. "You need to learn your place in her life." He spits on the ground beside Zack, and Kayla cowers behind me.

I don't want to know what happens if Pierce loses control. I jump in between them, catching a glimpse of his clenched jaw and the looks of determination on his face. I shove his arm, but he's too strong, I'm helpless. His skin begins to glisten as if a fog of gray is spreading around his body.

"Pierce! I swear I'll never speak to you again if you don't stop." I threaten, and he cranes his neck to look at me. Haunted jade eyes, flecked with black, swirling smoke stares back at me, no humanity in them at all. He looks terrifying, I whimper and take a step back. Kayla wraps her slender fingers around my arm as we step away from Pierce, who looks like a monster, and we're the helpless girls in a horror movie.

He drops Zack, who crashes onto the ground, choking and gasping for air. Pierce runs to me, but I fall on the ground trying to get away from him. "Scarlett." His voice is soft now, his eyes returning to a shimmering emerald.

"No," I cry out. "You could have killed him!" The gray smoke subsides from his body and I watch him in terror.

I look over at Zack, his wide eyes on us.

He pushes hair behind my ear, "Baby, I would

have known if he was going to die. I wouldn't kill your friend."

"That doesn't matter!" I can't catch my breath. "You looked like you were losing control!"

"I don't lose control," he assures me, but the panic is still deep inside of me.

"The problem now is that they're going to hate you!"

He scoffs, "I don't care if he hates me."

"What about Kayla!" I shout, worried about my new friend.

He throws his hands up, "I've been watching you the entire night. I knew this had something to do with him when your heart rate thumped around midnight." He breathes out, "I was fine until he put his hand on you."

I sigh, getting off the ground with his help. "Why don't you trust me?"

"It's not you that I don't trust, it's him." He sighs, "He kissed you, Scar. How would you feel if someone did that to me?"

"I would be pissed, but it was one drunken mistake. I was going to talk to him tonight. You have to remember he doesn't have any recollection of kissing me and he doesn't recall me turning him down."

He nods, reaching out to cup my face, "I'm sorry I scared you."

I look at him in disbelief, not caring about any of that. I just need them to not remember this night. "Make them forget," I demand.

"I'll make him forget about you. That he likes

you." He rubs his chin in thought and I shake my head. It's pointless.

"No. Just make him forget that you just acted like a caveman. I can make my own decisions. I'll tell him soon." I tap an impatient finger on my wrist.

He holds my face in his hands. "Sweetheart, you need to understand where I'm coming from. You know as well as I do why he brought you here," he growls.

I nod in understanding. "Yes, but I was about to tell him off, Pierce. He's still my friend and you embarrassed him." I sigh, "I brought Kayla so we wouldn't be alone together out of respect for you." Biting my lip. "He told me something was wrong. I was worried something happened," I admit.

His eyes narrow. "Of course he did." He laughs, "And he should be embarrassed. You're taken. He shouldn't be putting you in that position."

I roll my eyes, "What do you expect when you act like this?" I inquire, and he lowers his head.

I gesture to my new friend who is staring at us in shock. Pierce grits his teeth before turning to them and placing his hands on each of their shoulders.

Making them forget the night ever happened.

Thirty-one

How were the fifties?

I wake to an empty bed, my mind races as I open my eyes to pan the empty room. Pierce was pissed when we got back home. He hadn't said a word to me, and he slept on the other end of the bed.

Last night, our little park fiasco went smoothly after Pierce made them forget what they saw. I dropped Zack at home and Kayla back at the pier. They just thought we had a wonderful night.

I'm not happy with him, either, so the feeling is mutual, but this isn't a normal thing for him. Having a girlfriend, dealing with best friends liking said girlfriend. It's a lot for him to take in and if I'm being honest... I should have talked to Zack a long time ago.

I wipe the sleep from my eyes and calm my fears as Pierce appears next to me, a set of keys dangling in his hands. I tilt my head to the side.

He shrugs. "I wanted something to drive myself." He leans down to kiss me.

Seeing his dimpled smile, I can tell he wants to make up and I'm too excited for him to be less obnoxious. "You got a car!" I squeal.

"Something like that," he mutters as he pulls me out of bed and into his arms. With his face wrapped in my hair he says, "I'm sorry about last night."

Regret in my voice, "I'm sorry too. I promise I'll tell Zack."

He pulls me back to face him. "It's not just Zack, Scar, it's everyone and everything. You have to be more careful. You know better than that."

After a beat of silence, he grabs my hand and begins to lead me out of my bedroom while I'm still in pajamas.

"Wait! Let me get dressed. I want you to take me for a drive." I smile while I throw on a pair of jeans and a t-shirt from the pile of clean clothes that have taken residence on the accent chair in my room. Folding laundry is the least of my concerns lately.

I finish getting ready and try to put everything in the back of my mind, to have a *normal* day on a typical date with my out of this world boyfriend.

We head out the front door and my jaw drops. An intimidating black motorcycle shimmers underneath the sun, and my breath catches in my throat. "Umm,

Pierce..."

"Yes?" he questions, but I hear the humor in his voice.

I shake my head. "That's a death trap." I point towards the bike.

He gives me an amused look. "Sweetheart, I'm a death trap. Literally." I stifle a laugh as he continues, "When would I ever let you get hurt?" he asks, crossing his arms against his broad chest.

"You can't control everything," I remind him.

"Tell me one situation where I couldn't keep you from danger." His eyes narrow as I think of different dangerous scenarios.

"What would you do if we crashed in an airplane?" I ask with a smug expression.

"I would grab you and bring us somewhere safe before it hit the ground." he counters back, and I realize he's right. Even though I want to think of something else to wipe the smug expression from his face, nothing is coming to mind. He's the solution for everything, always.

That makes me wonder why he has never brought us to safety during one of the fights with the demon.

"Why don't you do that when Preta comes after us?" I ask curiously. Knowing his name and speaking it, burns like venom on my tongue.

"It would make no difference." He shrugs. "Unfortunately, he's always too close to us for me to decide to take us to safety. If he had touched either one of us while we were walking through the threshold, he would just come with us and the whole situation would be disorienting."

I ponder that for a moment, it makes sense. Hopefully next time – I shiver knowing that with my luck, this calm state I'm in will be flipped upside down soon – we are far enough away that we can make our escape.

His voice brings me out of my daze. "Just trust me," he says as he hands me a matte black helmet, I'm happy it covers my full head, unlike the ones I see where their face is exposed. I look for his helmet but can't find it.

"You're not wearing one?" I plant my feet on the ground, tapping my shoe against the pavement impatiently.

He straddles the bike, throwing his head back dramatically. "Come on Scar. I don't need one. Please just get on."

After some persuading, he gets me on the bike. I'm wearing his riding jacket as well as his helmet. The roads whip past us at a steady pace as we glide towards a more wooded area, flat road, and curves ahead.

I lean my face close to his ear. "Okay... What about if a piano falls from the sky?" I yell over the rustling wind.

He shakes his head back and forth and I see his shoulders bouncing from laughter.

He turns his head sideways. "Do you want to keep underestimating my ability to protect you?" I see his deep dimple on the side of his face, I just know a mischievous grin is underneath it.

"Yes," I respond, jokingly.

He shrugs. "Hold on then." He turns his attention back to the long stretch of road ahead of us. His hand twists the throttle all the way back and the bike stands on one wheel for a moment before it smashes back down onto the pavement. I scream, not out of fear, but out of excitement as we fly down the road. I can't help but hold him a little tighter out of instinct, but he is right. I'm safe with him. We whip down unfamiliar roads at an alarming speed.

I tense up when we reach a sharp curve, it feels like we're flying as we glide in perfect precision past the harsh bend. Nervous laughter booms from my chest as we continue down the tree-lined roads.

Hours have passed and I don't know where we are, nor do I care as I hold him close. The world passes us by in a blur.

I point when I see a diner, he nods as he pulls in. The entire building looks like it's wrapped in aluminum and the bright colored lights add to the fifties style decade theme. He helps me off and I peel off the leather jacket and place the helmet on the seat, hoping my hair doesn't look too wild.

I step into the cold, air-conditioned diner and shiver; Pierce offers me his hoodie and I graciously accept. The restaurant is near empty, minus one man who sits at the bar picking at his fries.

A sign directs us to sit wherever we like, so I head to the farthest booth at the end of the diner so we can have privacy to talk. The seat is the color of a fresh-picked strawberry, and the old leather has a few torn spots. I slide in and glance out the large glass windows that line the room.

Rain begins to patter outside; I stare at the black motorcycle and groan realizing I'm going to be soaking wet on our journey home. Pierce's warm hand wraps over mine from across the table.

A woman in a red poodle skirt walks over to us. Her lipstick is almost a perfect match to her ruby skirt and her brown hair is pulled up into an elegant bouffant to match the theme.

She pulls out a notepad. "Ready to order?" she asks with a wide smile.

I haven't had time to look at the menu, but the man seated at the old school bar top has a plate in front of him that looks delicious.

"I'll have whatever he has." I point to the man who is facing away from us and she glances over.

"Chocolate shake, fries, and a cheeseburger?" she asks, and I nod.

She directs her gaze towards Pierce, and I see her cheeks blush as she looks at him. I can't blame her though; he draws the attention of a room just by being in it. Plus, the fact that he's watching me with a curious expression means he doesn't notice her interest.

"Same," he replies in a neutral tone. "But just one milkshake, two straws." He holds the correct number of fingers up and sends me a wink.

"Right away," she says as she scurries off.

"What are you thinking about?" he asks, tilting his head sideways.

"I'm just imagining you in this era." I gesture around at the old black and white photos that adorn the walls.

"I didn't do much mingling." He shrugs

"Oh?"

"I told you at the beach. Before you, my life was just being the reaper. Not much else piqued my interest." He states with a matter of fact tone.

I know he mentioned that, but I didn't think about it too much. I mean, didn't he have a friend throughout the years? Was he all alone? The thought saddens me, and he runs his fingers on the side of my hand that he's holding.

"Don't be sad, okay?"

"It's just... I hate that you had no one to talk to all this time. No friends to turn to." I say.

"Why would I make friends with people that are just going to die? I outlive everyone on this damned planet." His tone holds hostility.

I play with the silverware in front of me, slowly spinning a fork as I look down at it. "You do know I'm going to die one day and you're close enough with me."

His sweet expression turns into a scowl. "That's different."

"How?"

"I just... I don't want to think about that."

I open my mouth to protest but I see the waitress approaching us with a large milkshake.

"Here you go." She sets down the clear glass, filled to the brim with sweet, chocolate ice cream and topped with whip cream and a single cherry. I thank her with a smile as she walks away to check on the other man.

"I want to know what our plan is. Yes, I'm eighteen now but I'll just keep getting older."

"I don't mind," he tells me.

"I do. I mean, is that what you want? For you to look like that." I gesture at him. "And me to grow older?" He leans back in his seat, sprawling his legs out under the table. I can feel them touching mine. When he doesn't reply, I sigh and point to the milkshake. "Is this safe?"

"Already checked the kitchen, the guy making it was a dull boring man, no poisoning going on here," he jokes, but I don't laugh. We need to talk about what's going on between us.

Finally, he caves. "I just want you; I don't care if you have gray hair and wrinkles."

"I just wish you would tal-"

He cuts me off by holding his hand up. "Okay, so about the era," he changes the subject.

I tilt my head curiously. "I thought you said you didn't mingle."

"Anything to get you off that subject," he jokes and I huff. He knows I'm curious about him, so I wave my hand for him to continue.

He plucks the cherry off the top of the milkshake. "Give me." I playfully demand and he shakes his head.

"Open wide," he grins.

I give him a look but open my mouth, ready to catch this cherry no matter how stupid I look. He throws it with perfect precision of course, and I don't have to move a fraction before the sweet cherry plops onto my tongue.

He laughs as he pats himself on the back. "Should have played baseball," he says with a smug expression.

"Okay you had your fun, now spill," I gently order as I bring the red and white striped straw to my lips.

He sighs. "I didn't do much, but I did enjoy watching films."

I lean forward, a curious expression on my face. "Oh, tell me!"

Our food arrives and over the meal we discuss his life. "I used to sit at the drive-ins or go to the theatre. I just really enjoyed watching stories unfold through the screen." His expression is longing.

"Romance?" I ask, hoping he will say yes. I'm a sucker for romance. He nods hesitantly, and I can tell he's slightly embarrassed which is a new look for him. He's always so confident, I love breaking down these walls he builds.

By the time we exit through the doors of the diner, it's dark. The light rain is gone but it has been replaced with a hazy fog that travels a foot or so off the ground. I hand Pierce his hoodie and pull on the leather jacket before throwing the helmet back on.

I hop onto his bike, finding that it's easier the second time. I rest my head onto his back, feeling comfortable. Before taking off, he leans back to steal a kiss.

We head down the street at a steady pace, the roar of the motor drowning out my busy mind. I'm thankful we're not zooming down the slick roads; I don't think my stomach could handle taking the turns at such a quick rate since I ate so much.

I run my fingers through his hair, worried about him not wearing a helmet. He would be fine of course, but it still terrifies me.

I place my chin on his shoulder and look ahead to the pitch-black road, a streetlight flickers in the distance but it's low light is muffled by the thick fog that surrounds us. Only when we get closer, and the light flutters on can I make out the silhouette of a hooded figure that is standing in the middle of the desolate street.

I scream as the bike screeches to a halt; Pierce jerks the bars violently, sending the bike sideways. The crashing sounds of twisted metal colliding with the pavement rips through the air. My body flies off the leather seat, barreling towards the hooded figure who is now mere feet away.

Thirty-two

Leather & Mint

With a swift calculated movement, almost like he stops time. Pierce reaches his hands out to me, gripping me fiercely. I watch in horror as the road comes closer and closer to us, then suddenly we're floating in mid-air. Just like he promised, he keeps me safe.

I hear the crunch and crash of metal twisting and then perfect silence. I open my eyes, trying to recognize the room we're now in. It's dark and I'm shivering from fear.

The screams won't stop as I sit on the soft floor of the unfamiliar room. Pierce standing in front of me frantically searching me up and down with his eyes as well as his hands, his gaze holds pure fury beneath the deep emerald. He carefully touches my neck, checking to make sure nothing's broken and then he removes the helmet.

"What happened?" I squeal.

"I'll be right back." His eyes soften as he looks into mine, but he can't hide the anger that's in his tone. He vanishes before I can stop him from leaving. Nothing more than a slight breeze that makes my stray hairs fly is left in his wake.

I rest my hands on the dark gray rug that's beneath me as I take in slow steady breaths. That was the demon! Pierce went back for him; the thought terrifies me.

Uncontrollable shivers take over my entire body. Will he come back soon? Will it be a while? I dart my eyes around the dark room, the moonlight shines in through a window and it gives a faint glow of what looks like a desk. I stand to examine it, looking for a light source.

I extend my hand to a lamp and click it on, the heavy black shade numbs the bulb, lighting the room in an ominous shadow. It's dim, but I can make out my surroundings. Red exposed bricks take up most of the space, dotted with old film reels hanging on long nails. One wall is covered from corner to corner in bookshelves filled to the brim with spines that I can't read in this lighting.

The faint hint of leather and mint invades my senses. Making me realize I'm in his room, Pierce's room. The thought warms me as I make my way to the large bed that's positioned opposite the window. I find one lamp on the left side and turn it on, the room brightens with more intensity now. I pull back the heavy gray comforter and rest my head on the single pillow that decorates the bed.

So this is where he sleeps. I look at his room from my horizontal position and my eyes find comfort on his small nightstand. The only other things that reside on the surface next to the lamp is a single photo of me, I lay floating on the soft waves of the Brazilian waters. I never realized he took this, it warms my heart that he got it printed. My hands pick up the small frame as I think of how perfect that day went.

We had an entire day with no one trying to kill me.

Pierce materializes in the middle of the room, startling me with his sudden presence. He takes two long strides and ends at the side of his bed, looking down at me with a thoughtful expression.

"What happened?" I question, jumping up beside him.

He holds my shoulder as he sits down on the bed, comfort takes over me as I follow.

"It wasn't the demon." His voice holds amusement, the hint of a smile creeping up his full lips "But we did scare the shit out of some high school kid." His deep laugh takes over the room as I let out a loud sigh of relief.

I plop back onto his mattress, sinking into the soft material of his pillow.

"Did he see us disappear?" I tense as the question comes out, he had to have seen us vanish into thin air. It was foggy, but that was unmistakable.

"Yes, but I coaxed him into forgetting. I should have been more alert, I should have known he was human. I'm beginning to become paranoid. I think Preta is trying to play mind games with me," he shakes his head. "So much for my bike, huh?"

"Yeah, I'm sorry." I pout.

"I'll just get a new one." He shrugs.

I grab his hand. "Why was he just standing in the street like that?" I ask.

"He was texting." I appreciate the humor in his voice, because I'm shaken by what just happened. I glance around his bedroom once more to direct my attention on something else.

"So... this is where you live?" I gesture around.

He lays down on the bed. "Like it?"

"Very much. Can we stay here tonight?" I ask, hoping he won't mind. I just need to feel safe and he can check on my mom.

"Of course."

I gesture to the floor to ceiling bookshelves. "So you read a lot?"

"Yeah, I love to read."

I nod. "What other things do you enjoy?"

His dimpled smile threatens to melt me. "You," he says, his deep baritone filling the room.

I laugh. "Any hobbies?"

"Same answer." He winks, I playfully swat his arm.

He raises a brow at me. "Why are you so curious?"

"I'm just trying to figure out what you would do if you didn't do... this." I gesture to him and a half-smile creeps up his face.

"If I was human, like you." His eyes hold something I can't put a finger on, longing maybe? "I would find a suitable job and marry you. Start a family and we would live a beautiful life. I don't care what job I had, as long as I had you my life would be perfect." He looks at me pointedly, placing his warm hand on my thigh. "More importantly, what do you want to do? You have your entire life ahead of you. I know you said you were undecided but that surprises me."

I give him an odd look. "Why does it surprise you?"

"You're just so good at so many things." When I don't respond he continues, "You're really good with people. You would make a great nurse or doctor. You're smart, funny, -"

I cut him off before he can continue, embarrassed at all of the compliments. "I think you give me too much credit."

A long silence passes before he lets out a deep breath. "I'm being too careless," he sighs and I give him a curious look. "With Preta, I mean I thought a random kid in the street was him. The bike could have crushed him."

"But it didn't."

He looks at me for a long moment, "I would like for you to come with me somewhere soon."

"Your version of somewhere and mine are different. What does it have to do with him?"

He begins to pace the small room. "I've been trying to find more information on Preta... I've heard of a library of sorts. It's ancient and filled with information for things like this but it's abandoned, I'm not sure what we will find."

I shrug. "Let's just go now." I would like to know more and after what just happened, I'm in no mood to sleep.

We materialize in front of a cathedral style church. Large chunks of broken rock decorate the overgrown lawn, having fallen from the crumbling building.

"Where are we exactly?" I look around at the desolate scenery.

"Venice, well the outskirts anyway."

"Wow." Italy. My eyes gaze in awe at the deteriorating building. Roads that would have led to the church have been taken by nature, nothing around but the quiet patter of wildlife in the dense wooded area around us.

"Yeah." He takes my hand, leading us towards the cathedral.

I admire his tall frame, dominating the landscape even though we're in such a hauntingly beautiful place. "Before you, I've never really been... anywhere," I admit.

He turns to look at me, his gaze traveling my features. "Me either."

I find that hard to believe, obviously, but I catch

onto his sweet word usage.

As we walk further it becomes eerily quiet, the birds have stopped singing as they flee in a hurry above our heads. The only sounds are the crunch of our footsteps on the ground.

Pierce gestures in front of us as we make our way through the tall grass, dodging large pieces of fallen stone. "This is where exorcisms used to take place. It's rumored that the basement holds what we need. Diaries and ancient log books from long ago." He throws up his hands imitating a ghost as he laughs. "For real though, don't let go of my hand. I'll get us out of here if the foundation begins to fall. By the looks of it, no one takes care of this place."

"Why wouldn't they have gotten the books out?" I ask.

He raises a brow, contemplating if he should tell me. "No one will set foot in this place." He stops talking and I nudge his arm.

"Sure you wanna know?" he asks, tilting his head to the side.

When I nod, he stops walking and plants his feet in front of me, his height forcing me to crane my neck up. "A couple hundred years ago there was an exorcism performed here." A funny thought pops into my mind, remembering how comical this would have sounded to me such a short time ago when I thought demons were just things of nightmares.

He continues, "Things went wrong. Three priests died and two were possessed. They went home and slaughtered their families and villages."

A shiver courses through me, "Why are you bringing me here? What if something tries to possess us?"

He grabs my waist. "It may not seem like it because of what's happening with Preta but demons don't normally mess with me. That's why I need to find info on him... but I need you with me, I can't leave you alone and focus on this at the same time."

I raise my brow at him. "Are you sure they won't mess with you?"

"Have you ever noticed how when I walk in a room it gets quiet, or when we walk past animals on the street they cower or whine?" I recall the dog in Brazil as he continues, "Yes, your mom likes me and I haven't figured out why." He laughs. "But for the most part humanity is afraid of me. So are demons."

"Oh." I take a deep breath, thinking of the poor priest. "I thought you said only bad people get possessed?"

He shrugs his shoulder, "That's a gray area. Children, for example, are more vulnerable. The priests, in this instance, were welcoming the spirit into the room with them. When you call upon them, it's a different ballgame."

Got it. No calling on demons.

He rubs his chin in thought. "Every other time I've found a demon sucking someone's soul I would stop them and they would normally just walk away, move on to someone else. There's more to Preta's game."

With my hand in his we head into the broken

building. Darkness overtakes me as the heavy door creaks to a close behind us, stealing the sunlight. "I can't see," I squeal, gripping his hand tighter.

"I can," he jokes. "You're brightening this whole room for me." I feel him gesture around as he pulls my hand up for the movement, but I can't see anything. I stomp my foot on the ground, feeling thick dust and pebbles beneath my shoes.

"Seriously Pierce, I'm scared!" He places something in my hand.

"Flashlight," he tells me, and I flip the switch. The warm light comes into focus and I gasp at the sight of the room. A massive stone arch sits in front of us, a tall cross is nailed to the wall but from years of neglect, it's tilted into an ominous angle and covered with dust and cobwebs. The sight gives me chills.

We walk carefully over the cracked stone and through the congregation room. Wooden pews line the space but they're splintered and cracked from years of abandon.

Down a set of rocky stairs, we guide ourselves through the labyrinth of hallways and rooms, one, in particular, catches my eye.

A pentagram is painted on the stone floor, chains and manacles adorn the walls. I close my eyes to rid myself of the visual, the world was a different place then.

Finally, we reach what we're looking for. Pierce never lets go of my hand as he pulls dust-covered books from ancient shelves, opening them against his chest to peek at the information. Squinting his eyes, he pulls my body closer to get a better view at the words. I keep quiet as he studies them, he hands me a smaller one as he clasps his free hand around the larger one. We ascend the staircase.

Near the exit, turning at a sharp corner, Pierce's hand stiffens closed around mine. His eyes widen before he swiftly pulls us into a dark room.

"What is it?" I ask him with a quiet voice, but he shakes his head. Grabbing the flashlight from me and turning it off. He pulls me close against him, "Don't say a word." He whispers. My breathing becomes heavy and he clamps his hand over my mouth. He places a soft kiss on my temple and I try to relax while clutching the old book in my hands.

"We're safe now," he tells me, the familiar hum of the ocean whirls around us.

I let out a large breath of relief as he guides me to sit down. He pries the book from my hands and places it on his lap, under the large one. We stare at them for a brief moment, wondering what secrets they hide behind their tattered spines.

Thirty-three

A dead one

We sit in silence, perched on the familiar rocks that sit above the ocean. Where he first told me who and what he was. "What happened back there?" I ask, wondering what he saw.

He shrugs. "Nothing," he lies.

A nervous sound escapes my lips and he elaborates. "I saw darkness, it was creeping on the floor. Someone was there, I don't know who. Hiding you in a dark closet doesn't protect you from monsters, you shine too much," he sighs. I tremble and he places a hand on my leg, rubbing his thumb in circular motions to soothe me.

"I'm becoming paranoid. I don't know what to do

to keep you safe." He groans, throwing his face into his large hands. He shakes his head as if trying to rid his moment of weakness. His expression grave.

His fingertip slides across the book cover, about to open it. I place my hand over his, noting the deep-set lines of worry on his face. I long to feel a moment that isn't urgent with him. "I know you want all the answers, but can we just have a moment together, a normal moment?"

His lips, which are pressed into a concentrated line, curve into a small half-smile as he tilts his head to look at me. "What's up?" he asks, setting down the large book on his lap. Not letting it out of his reach.

"I know you said I light things up," I say quietly, wanting to ask another question besides what he saw in the cathedral.

A thoughtful smile plays on his lips, "Yes, you emit a very bright white light around you at all times." He chuckles. "It's really hard to sleep next to you. It's like headlights blaring on a dark road." I playfully swat him realizing that's why he sleeps with his head squished into a pillow.

"Why? I mean, I know you said I'm good or I'm destined to do something great... but what am I going to do?"

He places his hand on his chin in thought. "I couldn't say. Maybe save me?" He winks and I blush.

"Maybe." I smile, imagining a world where Pierce didn't look down on himself, what a world that would be. Sitting up straighter, he looks at me with an odd expression before his features turn serious.

His voice is grim as he looks at me intently. "It was a joke, Scar. There is no saving me."

I shake my head. "You don't know that."

"I do. Let's not talk about this." His voice is harsh, and I look away, upset.

His fingertips on my jawline, he guides my attention back to him. "Well that's not the only thing you do... tell me what you see." He gestures out to the beach.

My brows crinkle. "What I *see*?"

"Yeah... like around us right now."

I take in the area around us. "The children far out over there making sandcastles, the two women tanning on blankets." I smile. "And of course, my favorite... the crystal clear ocean ahead."

"Now tell me the colors."

"Okay?" I think of what colors to point out so my eyes trail back over everything I explained. I gesture back to the children. "Their buckets are blue and the umbrella over them is red." I bring my hand back down on the rock to prop myself up as I lean back. "The girls there," I nod my head towards them, "left is in a banana yellow and the right is in bright white. And my favorite color is right there." I look forward and smile at the water. "Blue, almost teal."

As I look back at him I note that his gaze hasn't followed mine anywhere, his eyes are attached to mine. "Why?" I ask.

He shrugs. "Can't see any of it. It's all black and white."

271

"What?"

A dimpled smile. "Yeah, weird right?" he laughs. "I used to be able to see color before the trial."

"That's crazy."

"Want to know the even weirder part?" he asks and I nod.

"There is one exception." He looks at me pointedly. "You."

I narrow my eyes at him. "What do you mean?"

"Not only do you emit a light that could blind the blind." he laughs and I shake my head. "But, I see the golden tone to your skin." He caresses my arm with his fingertips. "I can see your brown hair as it blows with the wind." He twirls his fingers through my unruly hair. "The colorful dresses you wear are my favorite."

My cheeks redden. "Which one is your favorite?" I need to know so I can wear it more often. He thinks for a moment.

"I like you in any color." He winks and I make a mental note to go shopping for more vibrant dresses.

"Why do you think it's like that?"

"Not sure." He fidgets with his thumbs, becoming impatient. I noticed his eyes darting to the books while I asked him questions.

I grab his forearm and smile as I nod my head towards the book. "Can I read it?" I ask and he laughs.

"You can try, but it isn't in your language."

"Oh, what language is it?"

"A dead one."

"Well, start then." I gesture towards the books

and he opens it, I try to watch the other things around us, but all I can focus on is him. His concentration as he studies the ancient material that I can't decipher.

I wait patiently as we sit on the rocks for hours as Pierce reads the large book and then the smaller one. His brows furrow in frustration as he pours through the material at a fast rate.

When the sun begins to set, I decide we need a break. I lean over and kiss his cheek. "Why don't we take a pause and grab some food and you can tell me what you found?"

"Yeah, yeah." His voice is distant as he looks up from the book for the first time since we sat here. His sharp edges darken his features.

With a straight face and a rigid posture, he grabs my hand leading us to a hidden barricade, we materialize inside my bedroom.

He throws the books on the ground, they hit my hardwoods with a loud thud. The cracked yellowed pages fly out as he puts a hand through his hair.

He looks so upset. "What is it?" I ask.

His eyes wide, he takes me in for a moment then. "Damnit!" He hisses. He lets out a deep breath. "It just doesn't make any sense! None of this does. Something else is going on here."

Thirty-four

Sleepover

A month passes by, nearing the end of summer and the end of spending every day with Pierce. We're still not certain of anything and we're constantly on high guard. I don't know how we will tackle the obstacles while I'm in college, but hopefully we'll be okay. I lay on his chest, trying to forget the things I do not understand.

In one summer, I've fallen in love with a man... who is the Angel of Death. Stopped talking to friends out of fear for their safety. But I've also learned so much about myself, I'm strong and resilient and when faced with trials I find my way through.

My phone rings, I grunt, going to hit ignore but Pierce beats me to it.

Holding the phone in his hands he squints in the darkroom, "Why is Zack calling you?" he asks in an annoyed tone.

I shrug, "Just ignore it."

"Hello?" Great, he didn't listen. Putting the phone on speaker I hear Zack on the other end.
"I need to talk to Scarlett." Zack says.

"Scar is asleep on my chest; she will call you tomorrow." He goes to hang up, but Zack quickly says, "Wait! It's about Liv."

I grab the phone, keeping it on speaker. "What's going on?"

"Hey," he's relieved. "Can we meet up?"

I feel Pierce chuckle beside me, shaking the bed with his laughter. "I'm coming with," he informs me.

"I don't care who comes, I just need to talk to Scarlett," he groans.

"Where?" I ask.

"Wherever."

Pierce speaks up, "Meet us at the park, in thirty."

After changing, Pierce brought us to the park. We waited patiently until Zack pulled up. Pierce is completely invisible as he lurks in the shadows for protection. We couldn't risk anything, and Pierce wanted to have the momentum of surprise by being invisible tonight in case anyone followed us.

Zack looks frantic, he runs his hands through his thick hair. "Look I don't have an easy way to say this, but I really hurt Liv tonight."

I'm confused. "What? How?"

"We were hanging out-"

I cut him off, "Hanging out?" I shake my head. "She's been on vacation."

He shakes his head, "She got in tonight, she was going to surprise you in the morning. Please don't tell her I told you, she was looking forward to it."

She still had two more weeks; I wonder why she came home so early. "What happened?"

He sighs then says, "She told me she was in love with me."

I can't help the laugh that escapes my lips, "Okay, Zack, sure." I would know, she's my best friend.

His straight face tells me he's not playing around. "So, what did you tell her?" I ask.

"I love someone else," he tells me, my stomach sinks. He doesn't remember the last time we were at the park. Pierce wiped his memory, he only thinks Kayla, him, and I had a normal night without his announcement that he loves me.

I feel Pierce put an arm around me protectively and I hope Zack didn't notice the ruffle of my clothing. His eyes seem trained on mine as I open and close my mouth trying to find the right words.

"Listen," I bring my hand to his shoulder, "Zack, I love Pierce-"

He cuts me off, a smile tilting on his face. "I know that Scar, I'm not in love with you." He pauses, worrying his words were too harsh. "I mean I love you, but you're my best friend and yes, for a long time I thought what I felt for you was like love love but I think I was confused. I'm happy for you, and for Pierce." His tone and words are so sincere, I let out a deep breath. I feel Pierce relax against me. I never wanted to lose Zack as a friend.

But if it's not me, "Who?"

His smile lights up the night. "Kayla."

I squeal, upset for Liv but happy for Zack. "How did that happen?"

"We had so much fun that night, I got her number and we've been hanging out so much... I really do love her, Scarlett," he beams.

I catch up with him, excited for his newfound love but sad for Liv. I didn't know she liked him, she never said anything.

I frown thinking of her, "Did she seem mad?" I ask, wishing she would have told me.

He shakes his head, "She was upset, she said she understood. But I don't want to lose her as a friend."

"Zack. You won't," I assure him.

Pierce walks away, invisible still, as we catch up, he materializes from the parking lot and heads our way. I see Zack stiffen a little until Pierce reaches his hand out for a shake.

I knew if they would just have a conversation my two favorite guys would get along. We stay for a few more minutes before heading home.

Laying back in my bed, my head laid comfortably on Pierce's chest. I think about texting Liv. I know I'm not supposed to know she's home but how can I sleep comfortably knowing my best friend is upset? Like the angels answered a prayer, my phone chimes.

'Hey Scar, can you come over?' Liv texts me, I let out a deep breath.

'Of course! What's wrong?' I ask, even though I know.

'Long story.' she adds and I sigh, I feel so bad for her.

"Who's that?" Pierce peeks over my shoulder.

"It's Liv, she wants me to come over. Should I tell her I know about Zack?" I frown. I know I shouldn't go there because I want her to stay safe, but nothing has happened in months. I've missed my best friend so much and she needs me right now.

"I need to go over there, have a girl's night and make her feel better," I plead with him.

"Now isn't a good time," he says as he twirls a strand of my hair.

"Please, Pierce, I haven't seen her in forever!" I pout as I climb on his lap, looking at him with wide eyes. "Plus, we just saw Zack and everything was fine," I add.

"I know but..." he starts but when I bat my lashes, he caves.

"Fine." He sighs as he wraps my arm around his waist.

I squeal. "It's just one night, plus you can be right outside the entire time. I would tell you to just stay the night with us, but I don't want to make her feel awkward

278

around another couple." I reassure him as I kiss his cheek and hop off his lap to pack a bag.

We pull up to Liv's house, I'm so excited I get to see her after all this time.

I lean over and give Pierce a sweet goodbye kiss and rush up the stairs and unlock the door with the key I have. Liv nearly tackles me to the ground as I walk through the door.

"I missed you so much!" I say through her thick blonde hair.

"I missed you too!" she cries, her voice breaking.

I wipe a tear from her cheek. "Liv, I'm so sorry. What happened?" I ask, knowing what happened but not wanting her to be embarrassed that Zack already told me.

"Can we talk about it later?" she asks, and I nod. Poor girl, her eyes are bloodshot.

I gesture to the couch in the living room. "Want to watch a movie?" I suggest.

"Please!" she throws her head back. "No romance though." She feigns a smile.

"Okay, horror it is," I state as I plop onto the couch and grab the remote.

She leans forward to study my face, "You okay? How has life been without me?"

"Miserable," I tell her with a warm smile, "but everything's been fine!" I lie, this night is about making her feel better, not me. It's not like I can confide in her about any of this anyways.

"I'm going to get a snack, want anything?" she asks.

"Popcorn!" I say as I watch the demonic fight on the screen, the similarities to my life in the movie are striking.

Liv comes back in with our signature hot chocolate and a bowl of popcorn. She scoots in next to me and we share a blanket as we laugh at the gross, overly dramatic scenes on the screen.

"He did not just get his arm ripped off by a child!" Liv laughs, her mood elevated. "Eww!" she squeals when the monster rips the head off the main guy.

Her usual cheery face is hidden under dark circles. "I'm exhausted," I yawn, knowing she's the one who needs rest.

"Sleep with me?" she asks.

We crawl into bed, talking until we pass out.

I feel pressure on my ankle and immediately wrench forward, only to be jerked back from my wrist being tied by thick rope to the metal headboard overhead. A shadow looms at the edge of the bed and I frantically look around the dimly lit room.

What if the demon came in and took Liv? The moon casts a faint shadow on the silhouette, relief floods through me when I see Liv standing there.

"Liv! Help me untie myself." I stammer.

She twirls a strand of blonde hair around a manicured nail. "So, don't you want to know why I'm back early?" she asks, her calm tone catches me off-guard. Does she not see me tied up? Pierce appears behind her silently; his expression is deadly.

I try to wiggle from my restraints.

"Shh... It's okay," she coos with a sweet menacing tone.

"Liv seriously, help me!" I beg but she shrugs at my cries.

Her eyes narrow, "I need you out of Zack's life," she deadpans, continuing to twirl her hair around her finger. I look at her other hand and see a shiny object, the moonlight glints against the thin metal, a syringe. I gasp. "Then he will love me."

Thirty-five

Shut up and sit still

Pierce grabs her by the wrist, making her drop the needle. The clinking sound it makes against the hardwood floors makes me cringe. "What are you doing here?" she screams. He pushes her down onto a chair at her desk to the left of me. She screams and thrashes from his grip, but it's useless.

He firmly places his hand on her shoulder. "Shut up and sit still," he demands, and she nods obediently.

He rushes to my side and unties the ropes from my wrists, I rub the soreness from them while he frees my ankles. All the while staring at Liv's angry expression in utter shock.

My entire body shakes. "Pierce, what's happening?" I ask.

"She's covered in black," he spits through his teeth.

My eyes widen in disbelief. "What do you mean?" I peek around him to look at Liv.

Pierce's tone is thick with disgust. "Her aura, Scar it's gone black." I gasp at his words, it doesn't make any sense.

"Is she possessed?" I look into her eyes from too far away in this dimly lit room, but they weren't black earlier?

"No," he looks at her curiously, flicking on the desk light as she stares at us with a hollowed expression.

"Why couldn't you see it before?" I ask him, my eyes brimming with tears.

He runs a hand through his hair. "I haven't seen her." I look at him in confusion. He has, right? How could he not have seen her? "I mean, before she went out of town, I only checked on the house. I never saw her. I just checked to make sure everything was okay." He grunts and shakes his head while he looks down in disbelief. "I guess her feelings about you changed for some reason."

My stomach drops. "Why did you do this?" I cry out to Liv, but she doesn't reply.

"I coaxed her; she won't talk."

"Pierce, please. I need to know why," I plead with him.

He walks over to her. "You're going to tell her everything. Stay in this seat." His tone is venomous as he lets go of her shoulder, she stays put in her chair.

She becomes animated as a sinister smile spreads across her face. "You see, I got the idea from the guys at the club. You know, when we were drugged," she laughs and violent chills rake through my body.

What idea? "What are you talking about?" The words are slurring out of me.

"I just... well frankly you were in the way. You always are. I was gone on my vacation," she scoffs, "And I came home so excited, hoping that since you and Pierce had been together that Zack would finally be over you. So, imagine my surprise when I tell him my feelings and I find out he's in love with Kayla, someone you introduced him to. I mean how many things can you fuck up for me Scar?" she seethes.

Tears soak my face. "I didn't even know Liv!" I cry, "Why?"

"It all started the night you flirted with Zack at his party to piss Pierce off. I knew what I needed to do. I needed to protect him from *you*." She spits as she throws an accusatory finger in my direction. Pierce holds my hand and a low growl rises from his chest. I squeeze my fingers around his to balance myself even though I'm in a sitting position on the edge of her bed.

She looks at me with such hatred, such seething resentment that I can't comprehend how I never noticed her disdain for me. "I tried to get him to love me, but he wouldn't. He couldn't because he loved you too much! He always has!" she screams into the quiet house.

"You could have just told me!" I hiss.

She shakes her head. "No, it's always all about you

Scarlett. Your dad dying, your new boyfriend, it's always you! I don't have any of that. My parents are never at home! They don't love me like your mom loves you. I hate you, Scarlett. I had to be close to you so I could drip more and more into your drinks every day." My heart drops at her confession. "I couldn't stand to be near you, but when I would drop the poison knowing I was slowly killing you, it made me happy. I know I sound crazy, but I don't care! My parents already think I am, that's why they ship me off every summer for my 'mental health'. It just... well it needed to be done," she states flatly, crossing her arms on her chest like I mean nothing to her.

I try to summon up my courage. I need to know everything, but do I want to? Knowing full well she won't touch Kayla I ask, "Why still come after me? If he loves her now?"

She sits up straighter, excited. Her wild eyes darted between me and Pierce. "I had to get you back here and finish what I started. She's just a hiccup, I'll get rid of you and then her. Zack will be all alone, and guess who will be there for him? Me," she grins.

"How did I not know?" Pierce mutters. I look to him, his face guilt stricken.

She continues her maniacal tangent. "You know, the week you were pathetically moping around when he left you?" She nods her head at Pierce, and I hear a growl escape his chest. "I poisoned you. That entire week and you were too stupid to notice. I made sure I only did it to your to-go food. I learned my lesson with the hot chocolate the first time you got sick, I didn't want your death on my hands... well I did but I didn't want people to know I had anything to do with it." She shrugs, her demeanor is so cold, so different than the Liv I have grown to love. I have known her for two years, she never mentioned being in love with Zack. Maybe she did? I can't think straight.

Pierce stands, but I shake my head... I need to know everything and she's happily spilling her secrets. "I only put a little in at a time but it was never enough. Especially when Zack stayed the night. I didn't want him to come over since you were here but of course, he threw a fit on the phone when I told him Pierce left you and you were upset. I figured it would be over that night, but he slept in the bed with you!" she screams. "When he called me to tell me you were sick and he took you to the hospital I was so confused why they said you had the flu. I was thankful no one was on to me, but then you got back with Pierce and you finally left us alone again. I tried to get my parents to not ship me back to the institution, but they forced me! I quit taking my medicine, you know the kind I religiously take? I could see clearer, the answer was your death."

I'm shocked as the words leave her lips, I can't move or speak. *The iron pills.* I look at Pierce's face, but his eyes are burning as he looks at my best friend, or who I thought she was.

She begins to scream, and I can't stand the sight, so I shut my eyes. Pierce covers my ears for a moment before the wailing sounds of sirens cut through the high-pitched screech that seems to seep through every crevice in the room. He gives me one last sad look before he walks back over to her and rests his hand on her shoulder again. His eyes pan to me as he asks, "What do you want me to do?"

I attempt to think, trying to weed through my emotions so I won't have to deal with this any longer. I don't want my mom involved in this and I only have moments to decide. "She needs to go back to the mental institution, permanently." I state and Pierce nods his head in agreement. "Do whatever you need just don't make it about me, I don't want to ever see or deal with her again," I cry as the words come out. I'm not sure how I'm capable of making that kind of decision, but I have no other choice.

I'm thankful when Pierce takes control of the situation and addresses her. "The police are about to come in, I already unlocked your door. They will be here for a confession and you will tell them you have been plotting to kill your family by poisoning them. If they ever try to release you even if it's twenty years from now you will walk back in and readmit yourself. Do you understand?" he instructs, and she nods obediently, I sob behind them. The tears so thick and my heart so broken it's hard to breathe.

"You're a monster," he spits as he continues to hold her shoulder. "You will forget we were here tonight. You will forget what Scarlett and I have said to each other."

When we hear heavy footsteps coming up the long flight of stairs, Pierce pulls me to his side. When he releases me, we're standing in a small field. The grass is damp, I feel it against my skin as I fall to the ground.

My body void of any emotions, I pull strands of grass from the dirt. I peer up to meet Pierce's gaze, and a dimpled grin plays on his face, is he smiling?

"We can finally relax," he sighs, his voice is enthusiastic, and I can't understand why as I stare at him with confusion and anger. He quickly grabs both of my hands in his. "I killed Preta that night in the alley, Scar. No one has attacked you since that night. We thought he had a new edge with the poisoning... but it was her the whole time."

The realization hits me deep. "You're right," I say, wishing I could be happier in the moment but the feeling of betrayal stings heavy in my chest.

"We are safe now, love," he whispers into my neck. "I'm so sorry for what she did to you, I know it's going to be hard to trust anyone again. I'm sorry I didn't notice, I should have been around her more, I should have known the darkness consumed her." His eyes dart around my face. "But her medicine, it must have made her good when she was taking it and when she wasn't... the darkness hugged her."

"I'll be okay, we will be okay." I cry as I lean in to kiss him, rain begins to drizzle overhead but we stay put letting the cool drops cascade over our bodies.

I know it might make me weak, but I need to feel better. "Pierce, I know this sounds weird but... can you make me feel better? With the thing you do, don't make me forget but make my heart understand. I can't handle this," I sob.

"Not weird at all. You deserve a moment of peace." He places his hand on my shoulder, whispering sweet words into my ear. I melt into his arms, lying on him as I investigate the stars. My heart is shattered, even Pierce can't help that, but I will figure this out later, right now I just want to feel okay.

I could let what Liv did to me change me, but I refuse to let that happen. There is still good in the world, and she wasn't well.

Thirty-six

Mostly swimsuits

A couple of uneventful weeks have passed. Uneventfulness is completely welcomed by open arms in my life. Pierce and I have grown so much closer and our relationship is stronger because of the hardships we've faced together.

I finally talked him into breaking the bond, and he agreed considering the looming threat of Preta is no more. I'm also more comfortable that Pierce can no longer sense how nervous he makes me through the bond, that was the only part that I loathed.

Mom is still in shock from the news of Liv, but thankfully she's under the impression that I have been safe from her wrath this entire time.

I stretch my arms wide over my head as I see Pierce leaning against my doorframe, arms folded loosely against his chest. A wide smile plays his face and I can tell he's up to something. "What are you planning?" I ask.

He nods to my window. "Want to get out of here? Maybe go on vacation. We can have fun now that I won't be looking over my shoulder at every turn."

The heartbreak is fresh, the betrayal from Liv is haunting me in my dreams but I really want to give myself a break. After everything, I deserve an escape, especially knowing now that Pierce ended the demon that horrific night in the dark alley. An unfamiliar sense of calm has washed over me, through all the bullshit. It's finally over.

"Yes!" I squeal, jumping up to greet him. "I need to call mom though."

He snaps his fingers. "Already done."

I lean into his embrace. "You're everything to me, you know that right?" I ask, peering up into his emerald gaze.

The room transitions before my eyes, slivers of sun peek through the floor to ceiling windows, illuminating his sharp features. "You're more to me." His smooth voice hugs me as he plants a soft kiss on my forehead.

I jump from his arms and begin to examine our new room. "How long?" I squeal, walking around the large bed.

"A week," he tells me.

I see my suitcase leaned against the wall. "I hope you packed appropriate clothes." I give him a knowing look.

He shrugs. "Mostly swimsuits, that's all you need."

He winks at me and then gestures out behind him to the floor to ceiling windows. All I can see is water through the tall glass.

I slide open the heavy doors and hear him chuckling under his breath as I dash outside and onto the beautiful dock. We're in a cabana over the open ocean. Warm saltwater air invades my nostrils. The sun beats down, warming my skin. There's a long stretch of what I'm assuming is a pier and we are neatly tucked at the very end. To my left are four other cabanas but with a huge distance in between, to my right there's crystal clear waters.

Snorkeling, swimming, cuddling, kissing, more cuddling. Our vacation is just what I needed to heal.

On the sixth day of our getaway, I walk into the kitchen for breakfast. The walls are all glass and they give a beautiful view to the morning sun rising steadily above the shimmering waters. When I reach the counter, I find a note in Pierce's handwriting.

Love,

I'm heading to grab ice cream. I thought that I stocked everything, how could I forget your favorite! I'll be back home soon.

Yours forever,

Pierce

Normally I would be scared to stay alone but with everything behind us, I'm happy to have a moment to reflect on my life and enjoy the scenery. Through all of the awful things that have happened, so much good has come out of it. Mom and Brian being together, finding a true friend in Kayla, then Zack meeting Kayla and the three of us talking in group chats daily... and most importantly, falling in love with Pierce. This is exactly what I needed, a quiet getaway with the man I love.

I head towards the fridge and open it to find an array of treats. I reach for the orange juice and a colorful tray of fresh fruit. I bring my breakfast outside and sit at the same circular glass table that me and Pierce have enjoyed dinner at every night since we got here. I watch as the water gently rolls underneath the dock.

I look out to my left to see a tall man walking towards me with a smile coming out of the cabana next door. I go stiff and immediately laugh at myself for the unnecessary fear. He waves a hand at me and I return the gesture.

"Hello! I'm so sorry to bother you." His voice is kind. "My wife and I got in yesterday and she forgot to pack... feminine products." His cheeks redden and I stifle a laugh. I can tell how uncomfortable he is as he balances on his heels waiting for a response.

I've been in that situation before. "Hey! It's no problem, I'll be right back." I stand from my chair.

"Thank you so much, miss. I'm so embarrassed to ask this of you. She's in the bathroom and she wouldn't let me run to the store." His blush deepens and I want to put him out of his misery, how thoughtful of him to do this for her.

I head inside the open door and retreat to the bathroom to grab my bag, I pull a few tampons out and shove them into my pocket. I hear footsteps coming from behind me, thankful Pierce is back so we can spend the day together.

A loud voice echoes through the small bathroom. "Wow, your light is so bright, I missed it."

I stumble but quickly gain my footing and slowly, I turn around. I'm met with the man from outside, but his eyes that were as blue as the ocean have transformed into a familiar obsidian as he glares at me. I cringe away when he reaches his hand towards me, a sinister smile spreads on his lips.

"Run," he sings in a haunting tone. I don't think twice before I rush past him in a hurry. I try not to trip over the rug as I jump through the French doors that go out to the deck. My two options flash through my mind. To my left is the long dock, everything else is open ocean.

My heart races with the impossible decision. I tremble in fear realizing my chances are slim to none. The man lunges out of the doors at me and I tiptoe dangerously close to the edge of the dock. I jumped off of it yesterday and it's not a far drop, but who am I to say he won't pull me under and drown both of us in his fury?

Pierce appears beside us; his eyes frantic with worry as he reaches his hand to me, but Preta's quicker. He grabs me by the neck, pulling my body into the air.

My feet dangle off the ground as I choke. The scenery around us changes instantly.

Through a cloud of thick dust, my eyes pan around the new space, taking in my surroundings as he throws me on the ground. I slam against the concrete with a painful thud. The hard floor is dirty with what looks like years' worth of dust settling from the disturbance of us being here. Cracked marble pillars rise to an impressive marble carved ceiling. I squint through the darkness to see how massive this room is.

I can't see the demon, but I hear him. How did he bring us somewhere else like Pierce? How does he know how to do that?

"How did you bring us here?" I demand to know.

"Simple, I just had to leave the human body." His voice is different, it's more of an echo laced with venom as he makes his way in front of me. A small shimmer of light makes me gasp in horror as I take in his true appearance.

He towers over my shaking body, his obsidian eyes graze over me and his razor-sharp teeth smile down. A deep laugh echoes through the vast room like a wave as he speaks in tongues. This is his true form; I recognize it from the books Pierce was studying.

He continues to chant in tongues in a low voice. "I don't know wh- what you're saying." I whimper, my confidence gone as he strides to my cowering body.

His slimy lips turn to a frown. "I'm sorry I've been gone so long, I did miss you. I tried to keep you calm so he wouldn't recognize your fear." He sneers, "It's tricky you know. I've never had an Angel of Death attached to anyone I've almost taken a soul from. I usually finish my business before he even knows what happened. But with you, it made it so much more fun that he wanted to protect you." His laugh is a mixture of high and low pitches at the same time and it makes me tremble at his feet.

"He… he will protect me! He'll find me any moment now." I stutter.

He scowls as swirling black smoke pours from his eyes and ears enveloping his entire body, when the thick fog lightens, I cringe in horror. He brings his hand to my chin making me look into his eyes. "I'm counting on it!" he screams. Broken glass shatters to my right from the pitch of his unearthly tone.

"He can't protect you, dear. Well, he can try but I'm stronger here." His maniacal laugh bellows through the room. "See this place was built long ago, eons before Pierce even became the reaper. It's where demonic souls like me can walk around in our true form."

Dust swirls to my left, my heart sinks when I see Pierce materialize. "It's a trap!" I yell, but he ignores my warnings, his eyes trained on Preta.

Pierce is so close to me, but not close enough. Preta's slimy hands wrap through my hair, causing me to gag. "No, no. Take one more step and I snap her neck," he threatens, and Pierce stops in his tracks. His eyes glance around the dark room, looking for something.

Preta looks into my eyes and I feel myself waning. With all my might I take one last look at Pierce; his expression is pure torture. His longing gaze meets mine and I can tell he's thinking of a million possible scenarios in his brilliant mind, but I don't see any way of this going differently. 'It's okay, I love you.' I mouth at him and his hard edges soften momentarily.

"Take mine!" Pierce shouts into the empty room, his voice bouncing off the ancient marble walls. Preta's obsidian eyes flicker towards him, a sinister smile rising on his face at the offer. He drops me on the hard marble flooring, and I lift myself up on my elbows to see him heading with purpose towards Pierce.

"Take what?" I scream at Pierce. He looks at me once and turns his head towards the demon. "My soul, take it, and leave hers alone," he states and my stomach drops. I know he has one, but he said it's dark. What would Preta want with it?

Pierce takes in my features as if it's the last time. His eyes roam my face, my body, my hands. "I love you more than I love myself," he declares. My heart sinks, this seems like a goodbye and I can't handle it.

He doesn't put up a fight, he doesn't try to take Preta down... it would harm me.

"Don't try anything," Preta warns with a hiss.

Pierce looks to me, then back at the snarling demon. "I'm not, my soul is yours to take. I won't fight, not if you give the oath to leave her be for eternity."

Preta's long body looks back to me once, he nods. "I will obey," he agrees, bringing one of his razor-sharp nails to cut into his skin, blood draws and I wince. The two supernatural beings make their oaths while my heart shatters into pieces.

"Don't do this Pierce, fight back!" I scream at him.

"You're worth backing down for, Scar. I'm so sorry." He looks proudly ahead, raising his arms, his shirt shreds and floats around him. As the dust settles, I see his black and tattered wings in all their tragic glory. They take up a vast majority of the massive room as he submits to Preta.

A thick, black substance escapes Pierce's body as Preta drinks in his soul. I try to run towards them but then I realize why his wings are out. He moves them and the gush of wind throws me back, one hundred-year-old dust invades my lungs making me choke.

The wind subsides and Pierce collapses to the dirty marble flooring with a thud.

There's no blood, no gore, no gruesome red showing his demise. I sit next to him, laying on his black feathered wings as I touch his cheeks gently. He is so still as he lays on the cold ground. I'm broken, and at a loss of what to do. Normally he would wake up, right? But his soul... it's gone. I lay my head onto his chest, praying for a miracle. Praying for a second chance for a man who deserves one.

My eyes trail along the cracked marble floors and up a tall pillar. A brilliant gleaming light that I hadn't noticed before trails from a broken stained window. My eyes follow across the golden stream of light to a platform raised high above. I gasp when I see a beautiful woman, dressed in pure white.

Her white hair cascades down her tiny frame. She looks down at us with a smile and with one quick movement she throws her arms up. Glorious, pearl-white feathered wings escape from behind her back. Her small frame with the massive wingspan makes me completely silent and still. I take in her angelic figure and when her eyes meet mine relief washes over me.

"Help us, please! He won't heal!" I scream through my dry throat. "He normally heals by now, but he took-" I cut myself off when she lifts from the platform, floating midair as she graciously descends to the dust-covered floor. The contrast of her pure beauty in such a dark and tattered place makes me shiver.

When she lands beside us her wings gracefully collapse until I can no longer see them. She kneels on the other side of Pierce, her small body resting on his other wing as she touches the center of his chest.

"He gave up his soul, yes?" she inquires with an angelic tone; it's laced with a faint accent that I have never heard before. I nod, trying to hide my shaking voice, unable to speak.

"For you?" she sings and her melodic voice is so tranquil I can't help that it calms me, but why isn't she helping him.

"Ye... yes. Please help him. I can't lose him," I stutter through my heavy sobs. My fingertip trails along his jawline, while my other hand strokes his tattered wings.

"You love him?" she questions, no judgment in

her tone. It's like she's humming a melody as she talks.

I nod frantically. "I do! More than my own life. I will trade my soul if you let him stay. Take it, please take it! I don't want it without him." I cry and she brings her small hand to my shoulder.

"I can't give him his soul back, darling," she frowns but the notion looks odd on her face. I look at her with tear-filled eyes. She looks around, a small smile taking over her perfect features. "But you are connected to him, yes?"

I nod. He broke the bond but since he arrived at this horrific scene it means we were tethered once more.

"That changes things. If you are okay with it may I try something?"

When I nod, she places her small hands onto Pierce's broad chest and closes her eyes. The heavy dust begins to rise from the ground and swirl in circular motions. Each tiny particle doesn't falter from the other as it dances in twisted circles around the three of us. I watch in wonder as she brings her hand to the same spot on my chest. Bright light takes over the room, and my chest warms.

The light fades slowly, and Pierce gasps for air. His body jolting forward.

Thirty-seven

Tethered

I throw myself on to him. "You're okay!" I sob into his chest as he rubs my hair.

I lift my head to see his face, and confusion takes over him. He looks over at the angel. "Why do I feel like this?" he asks with a curious tone.

He reaches for his wings, touching them with wonder.

She grabs both of our hands and places them on top of Pierce's chest. She covers hers atop of ours. His heavy breathing makes them move up and down slowly. "Why did you give the demon your soul?" she asks.

"I didn't think he would want mine, but it was all I had to offer him."

"Oh, dear boy." She moves her hand to place it

on his cheek. "The demon wanted your soul more than hers."

He shakes his head. "Why? It's dark and worthless, hers is full of light." He gestures to me.

"Not anymore, well it wasn't..." she says with a slight frown.

"I don't understand," he says flatly.

"The demon wanted yours because it's a much more powerful soul to take. He can't ask for it but if you offer..." she trails off, standing up and dusting her pearl white dress which hasn't retained a trace of dust. "The Angel of Death willingly offering such a powerful soul, the only human piece of you that you had, is an offer that can't be refused."

His brows furrow. "How am I not in hell? I died."

"You were, but that soul doesn't belong to you anymore." A smile plays on her face, lighting up the room.

He shakes his head. "Why?"

"Scarlett and you have been connected for quite some time. She is your soulmate, even without that bond. Her lifeforce is attached to you. You now share one, together. She gave you half of hers."

He looks at me with tears brimming his eyes. "What does this mean for her?" he asks the angel, but his eyes are still focused on me.

"No change, she's a human." She looks over at Pierce, "And you are too." She sings, clapping her small hands together. I gasp at the same time Pierce does.

He sits up as he grunts in pain from his bruised

body, his expression turning dark. "How will I protect her now!?" he screams at the angel; she backs away slowly.

She holds her hands in front of her. "Now, calm down. There's no need for hostilities. Your soulmate is perfectly safe. Preta is no longer a threat and we will do our part to make sure this doesn't happen to her again." Her voice is calm and reassuring and I feel Pierce's body relax against my side.

"Th... Thank you," he beams, his voice full of gratitude.

She looks back and forth between us, a bright smile showing on her face. She lifts her arms and her wings expand from behind her, the white is so bright I have to squint to be able to see her better. "Oh, and Scarlett, your father can't wait to see you again in heaven. He loves you dearly." Tears soak my vision as she flies away through a small window overhead.

A long moment of hushed silence blankets the room. "What just happened?" I ask stunned, my heart pounding.

"What just happened is..." He stands, reaching his hand out for me. We both look down at his black and tattered wings as they lay on the floor, not attached to his body anymore... not weighing him down. He picks me up, grunting in pain but when I try to stop him, he grips me tighter. "It's over Scarlett. This is it. We can be together."

A happiness that I've never experienced before cascades over me, I bask in it. It's over, now our life can begin.

Pierce places his hand under my chin, tilting my

303

head to meet his striking gaze. "We share a soul now, Scar. We're tethered together for eternity. When you inevitably go to heaven, we will never have to be apart as I will arrive there with you."

"Heaven," I whisper, leaning in closer to him.

"Life on earth, an eternity in heaven," he repeats, crashing his lips to mine. He pulls away, leaving me breathless. "Our story will never end, my love."

One year later

I diverted from my original college plans, opting for adventure. Pierce and I decided to take a year to travel, and after everything with Liv, Mom didn't totally hate the idea.

Life is short, and after the trials we've both experienced, it just made sense to take a breather.

During our gap year, Pierce quickly discovered that life as a human was a learning process. Mostly he struggled to travel without his wings. There's been so many times where he grabs me to take us somewhere. He never complains though. His emerald eyes gleam with joy every time he realizes he doesn't carry that burden anymore.

We've strolled the streets of Paris on a blossoming spring afternoon, joining in on the tourist traps and loving every minute. Zip lined over the Hawaiian jungles. Rode horseback through the Grand Canyon, in awe of the beauty nature has to offer.

It's been the best, most extraordinary year of my life.

But now, Mom and Brian are sending us off to college.

My car is packed full of our belongings, and I'm dancing on my toes with excitement for the future. Pierce stuffs Ferris into the backseat before returning to my side.

Mom dabs a tissue against her cheek after I peel myself from her iron grip. "Be careful!" she gently orders as she grabs Kayla, who receives the same tight squeeze as I did.

Her and Brian moved in with us shortly after everything happened and whenever we're free, we're together. I can't count the nights we've spent buried in laughter, rolling on the floor. The sting of Liv's betrayal will always weigh like a ton of bricks on my shoulders, but with Kayla, she bares part of that heavy load.

Kayla hugs her dad before heading to Zack's jeep. She climbs into the passenger side and kisses him on the cheek. They've been going strong since that summer, and I love them together.

"Come on!" Zack cheers, a smile stretching his face as he honks his horn.

I can't believe we're all going to school together. Kayla's junior year, Zack's sophomore, mine and Pierce's freshman.

I turn my attention forward when mom tugs on my shirt. "Please visit soon," she pleads.

My fingertip traces her ring. "Duh! We have a wedding to plan!" I grin, wrapping her into one more hug that was more for me than her.

I slip into the passenger seat and a few happy

tears escape me. "Take care of her!" she tells Pierce.

"Always," he replies, looking at me.

Pierce is going to study film, as it's his passion.

As for me, I haven't quite figured out what I want to do yet, but that's okay. I've thought of getting a degree in Psychology, to help people like Liv, but we'll see. All I know is, my freshman year will consist of what every nineteen-year-old should experience. Spending time with friends, core classes, and ripping my hair out over finals.

Normal.

And I love it.

When Pierce places his hand on my leg I look to him, admiring his sharp edges and the deep-set dimples that rest on his cheeks, even when he's not smiling.

The crisp fall air floats in from the open windows, bringing in a comforting sense of home with me as we drive towards our future. I wonder if Pierce feels that way too, like I'm home for him. "Do you miss heaven?" I ask quietly, not sure if he heard me over the rustling winds.

He doesn't respond immediately, and my heart races from the beat of silence that passes through the car. Finally, he brushes his hand against my cheek, and when he looks at me, his dimples deepen. "I'm already there."

THANK YOU

It takes a village to publish a book, and this wouldn't be possible without the help, support, and talent of these amazing women.

To my incredible editor, Erica. I couldn't have done this withot... withut... WITHOUT you! Thank you for your talent, time, & hard work. Bzzzzz.

To Jessica Scott at Uniquely Tailored, my cover designer, who floors me with her work every single time!

To Kristen Jay, for ALWAYS being there, without fail to lift me up when I fall.

To my Wattpad family, thank you.
To my family family, I love you.

And last, but not least, the motivation behind publishing GBD. The girls who've been by my side since the beginning.

Heidi
Kristen
Kristine
Meera
Melissa A
Melissa G
Phoebe
Sabrina
Mia
Ray
Kawaiola
Autumn
Adiah
Allie
Kayla
Marie
Sapna

ALSO BY H.L. SWAN

Aiden
Emilia
Emilia's Sweet Treats

Made in the USA
Las Vegas, NV
24 September 2022